ANARCHY

Preserve, Protect and Defend, Book 2

D. S. WALL

Russet Leaf Press

ANARCHY

GUIDE TO THE ANARCHY
CAST OF CHARACTERS

Jace West – Clairvoyant. Part of the Special Investigations Unit with Charlotte (his wife) and Special Agent Grace Madson.

Charlotte West - Assistant U.S. Attorney. Part of the Special Investigations Unit with Jace (her husband) and Special Agent Grace Madson.

Special Agent Grace Madson - FBI agent in the Norfolk, Virginia field office. Part of the Special Investigations Unit with Jace and Charlotte.

Joe Harkness - Owner of the '51 Chevy and crystal meth cooker.

Chairman, aka Kelena (Kel) Zakis - Leader of the drug gang, the Corporation.

Tiny - Large armed guard at the meth lab.

Bubba - Armed guard at the meth lab who was booted from the Marines.

Virginia (Gin) Vandermire - Manipulative billionaire conspirator.

Viktor Vandermire - Gin's father.

Jaana Karjalainian - Leader of Antifa in Portland, Oregon.

Piper - Jaana's second in charge and best friend.

Christian Waingate - Journalist, unrest organizer, and Jaana's boyfriend.

Andrea O'Shea - Speaker of the U.S. House of Representatives.

Marvin Thompson - Man shot dead by police in Detroit.

Chen - Gin's trusted director of security.

Michael Zakis - Kelena's father.

Trace Zakis - Kelena's mother.

Supply, aka Kaitlin Murphy - Kelena's best friend, and the first Head of Supply for the Corporation.

Distro, aka Missy - Kelena's and Noah's friend, and Head of Distribution for the Corporation.

Sherley Johansson - Owner of Sherl's Coffeehouse in Portland.

Security, aka Noah Vann - Kelena's old boyfriend and Head of Security for the Corporation.

Detective Boatwright - Virginia Beach PD Special Investigations unit and interrogator of Joe Harkness.

Caroni - Joe Harkness' boss and later promoted to Supply.

James - Lead cooker and Joe Harkness' partner.

John – Security's rear guard at the meth lab.

Bill - Chesapeake PD investigator at the old Ford Plant.

Ephron Huffman - Founder and CEO of the dominant online news and social networking site.

Dr. Ike Allo - Parapsychologist and Jace's mentor.

Millicent (Mil) Jackson - College student, friend and mentee of Charlotte and Jace.

Octavia Jackson - Millicent's mom.

Zo (Daniel Alonzo) - The organizer of the DC street captains.

Mohammad al-Qahtani – Islamic extremist terror cell leader.

Hu - The Chinese agent who contracted with Mohammad.

Fahad - Mohammad's trusted second in command.

Jeffry - One of Mohammad's men, and van driver.

Isabella (Bella) – The girl who accompanied Zo to Norfolk.

Ice - Zo's acquaintance, and assassin.

Janco - Chen's trusted operator leading the assassination team.

Congresswoman Youngblood - Outspoken freshman representative disliked by Speaker O'Shea.

Deputy Special Agent in Charge (DSAC) Smyk - Second in command of the FBI DC field office

Vlad Miller - CEO of the dominant internet search engine.

Darcy - FBI analyst assigned to the terrorism unit.

Special Agent Barnes - FBI agent in New Jersey.

Trooper Transue - New Jersey state trooper.

Ali - One of Mohammad's shooters.

Tomas - One of Mohammad's shooters.

Special Agent Angie Shackleford - Fresh out of Quantico, FBI agent in the DC field office.

Lode - On-site leader of the hit team.

Rob - Uniformed Secret Service agent in front of the White House.

President Hargraves - Current President of the United States.

Bess Williams - National News Network reporter.

Megan Marche - National News Network anchor.

Sam Perry - National News Network reporter.

Tamryn - Witness interviewed by Sam.

FBI Director Raymond - Director of the FBI

Chapter 1

The two men in the pickup truck led him into the backwoods of southern Virginia Beach. Jace wasn't supposed to follow them. His job was to determine where the cookers' lab was and then call his colleagues in the FBI's Special Investigations Unit. They made it clear he was never to engage suspects —just sense what the bad guys were up to and report back to them. But he didn't have enough time to get a read on the location of where they brew their crystal meth. He knew they were leaving the coffee shop to go there, so he tailed them. When he called his teammates, he wanted to have something to tell them. It was his first time working alone and he didn't want it to be a bust.

***

It was less than a year ago that lightning jumped from the tree Jace was under and bolted across his body. He recovered from the ill effects, but his neurologist speculated he suffered a traumatic injury, or at least the massive electrical current caused a flood of neurotransmitters in his brain. In either case, the supercharged jolt changed the way he received information. His mind opened to new channels of communication that most people don't perceive. Those channels are always there, like radio and TV signals, but the human mind doesn't normally tune them in.

Parapsychologists believe everyone is born open to receive these channels, but those abilities dull quickly. They linger in the subconscious, and many experience this sixth sense without recognizing it as the shadow of clairvoyance. Scientists speculate the sensation of déjà vu is a person remembering a vision of the future they had in a dream. A gut feeling may be a flicker of foreknowledge, and the sudden sense of misgiving a precognitive event.

With the help of his mentor, Dr. Ike Allo, Jace developed his abilities to read thoughts, sense feelings, and see near-future events in a very short time. He experienced emotions of other people as though they were his own, and saw visions of what was to come, usually in his dreams.

He stumbled into his role as a consultant to the FBI. His wife, Assistant U.S. Attorney Charlotte West, and her partner, Special Agent Grace Madson, were members of the Joint Terrorism Task Force in eastern Virginia. They knew they had terrorists in their midst but didn't know who they were and why they were in Norfolk. Jace's chance meeting with the leader of the covert terror cell, and his sense the man had evil intentions, led Charlotte and Grace to uncover the terrorist's plot to kill Americans on their own soil. If not for Jace, they would not have tracked down the jihadis bent on a holy war. And the unusual circumstances thrust the three into a special unit aimed at taking advantage of Jace's unique investigative skills.

***

The dominant illegal drug distributor in the region called itself the Corporation, and their leader went only by Chairman. Chairman found an ideal location for their meth lab in the remoteness of southern Virginia Beach. It was a three-room wooden structure at the end of a long dirt driveway, off a gravel lane that connected to the paved Blackwater Road. The owner inherited the house from his father who died years earlier. The son lived in another state and couldn't believe his luck finding a buyer for his dad's hunting cabin that had been on the market for years. It suited Chairman's needs to a tee. There was little law enforcement presence, no neighbors, and it still had electric service. The seller had renovated the well and pump for water and the septic system for waste hoping that the place would be more attractive to those looking for a quiet getaway. But the condition and the location made it desirable only to someone who wanted to hide.

The pickup truck was a 1951 Chevy, the prized possession of one of the meth cookers. He found it stashed in a barn, abandoned and forgotten. Joe was a gearhead and loved working on cars. He was a mechanic by trade but cooking meth for Chairman was more lucrative. He couldn't resist his hidden gem, though, and restored it to street-legal, running condition. Joe wasn't into bodywork, so exposure to the coastal humidity covered his baby in orange-red surface rust except for small splotches of the original sky-blue paint that peeked through the oxidation.

Joe and his partner led Jace into the rural southern part of the city. Jace stayed well behind the rusty old jewel, shadowing it deeper into the wooded lowlands. As dusk approached, it was harder to keep sight of his quarry, and he thought he should turn back. Soon, he'd have to turn on his headlights for fear of slipping off what was little more than a dirt path with drainage ditches on both sides. That would alert the men in the truck. But the two amateur chemists arrived at their lab. Down the driveway, through the trees and scrub, he saw the Chevy pull off the trail and stop. Wary of driving closer, Jace stopped his car and considered what to do. He could barely see the orange rust of the truck through the thicket of trees and underbrush. Had they arrived at the lab or was this just a stop on the way? Did they head down another path through the woods? Too enthralled with the hunt, he forgot his mandate not to engage. The thrill of discovering what lay beyond the trees pulled him into the forest. He continued on foot, carefully and quietly picking his way through the woods, drawn to the rusty pickup.

Chapter 2

A ssistant U.S. Attorney Charlotte West's post was to the Criminal Division of the Eastern District of Virginia. She developed the reputation for being a thorough, persistent, and hard-nosed federal prosecutor of those engaged in organized crime. Unlike the early days depicted in the movies, she and the G-men were not fighting the mob. Their mission was to put gangbangers behind bars. Street gangs had become the scourge of urban and suburban America, distributing illicit drugs, dealing firearms, and trafficking humans. They imported their wares from all over the world. This transnational criminal activity fell to the feds to prosecute, and she relished the opportunity to take the amoral traffickers responsible for untold tragedy in American society off the streets. Selling weapons and dangerously addictive drugs like heroin and fentanyl was horrible. But in her mind, stealing young children and women to sell into slavery was the worst — the mark of purely evil, soulless demons.

Charlotte was extraordinarily good at her job. Her conscience would not let her fail. She worked with the FBI, ATF, and other federal law enforcement agencies to investigate those dregs and put them away. She didn't go to trial until there was enough evidence to prove beyond doubt the suspect was guilty. If Charlotte West took you to court, you knew, or at least your defense council knew, that you'd be going to prison for an extended stay. Lawyers who didn't know her had trouble taking her seriously. She was the kind of attractive woman where men couldn't help themselves from turning their heads to prolong the view as she walked past them. She pulled her long blond hair into a ponytail, her eyes were bright turquoise, and her tailored suits showed her feminine figure. But for counselors who already had the unfortunate experience of facing her in the courtroom, it was common for them to offer plea deals that resulted in a decade or two of incarceration for their clients.

A few times throughout her career, her reputation caused her and her family significant concern. Arrogant and bold criminals facing serious time in the Big House thought it a good idea to threaten her life if she didn't back off. Twice they followed through with their threats and tried to kill her.

The feds caught wind of the first plan to murder her and arrested the bangers before they got close to her. Only serendipity saved her from the second attempt. As she did most days she was in court, she left the federal building in downtown Norfolk to grab lunch and walked to the deli a few blocks down Granby Street. The leader of the South Town Boys, the gang that controlled the southern section of the City of Newport News, was about to go to trial. Charlotte had refused his plea deal, so two of the Boys parked their car near the eatery and waited. As she approached the storefront, they sauntered across the road, replete in their gang's colors, and obviously interested in her. Unfortunately for them, it was the closest and favorite place to eat for many who work in the courts, including law enforcement officers. An FBI special agent exited the shop and held the door for her. The bangers looked out of place and headed straight her way. He reached for his service weapon, and when they brandished their guns and pointed them at their target, he unholstered his Glock and fired. The sudden violence stunned Charlotte, but the agent yelled for her to, "get down," and that's what she did. A couple of Norfolk Police Department cops behind the shooters engaged the would-be assassins with gunfire too. Except for a scrapped knee, she was unhurt, and the only casualties of the gunfight were the South Town Boys.

This was the reason she and Jace bought handguns. After that incident, friends and family urged her to carry a sidearm for self-defense. She dragged her husband on a date night to Patriot Shooting, and they spent hours choosing their favorite pistols. She fell for the Smith & Wesson Shield nine-millimeter. It was small, lightweight, and felt good in her hand, and concealed well in a handbag holster. He chose the Walther PPK. It was easy to handle and shoot, and it was the gun 007 used, so it was too cool not to buy. At least every month they practiced at the range and enjoyed competing to decide which of them was the better shot. The winner got to choose the restaurant they'd eat at that evening.

Because of the threats on her life, Charlotte carried her Smith & Wesson with her everywhere the law allowed. The gun was easy to tuck into her bag using a holster made for that purpose and was no bother. Jace didn't like the bulky feel of the PPK tucked into his belt or strapped to his torso, so his handgun stayed locked in its biometric safe in his study until it was time to try to win the date night competition with his wife.

But that would change.

Chapter 3

T he terrorist attack three months prior brought Jace and Charlotte even closer together and gave them a renewed appreciation for how fragile life could be. Before the attack, they were content with their lives. She loved being a federal prosecutor, and he was passionate about running his company, West Clean Energy. Their two college-aged kids rounded out their happy existence.

But circumstance and fate colluded to string unrelated and uncommon events together. They culminated in Jace, Charlotte, and Special Agent Madson facing off with a terror cell bent on killing hundreds of people. As civilians, Jace and Charlotte were to stay clear of the point of attack, but she found herself on the nasty end of an AK-47 automatic rifle. A terrorist dropped the police officer standing between her and danger with three rounds to his vest. Fortunately for her, the Norfolk cop landed a bullet from his service weapon to the chest of the Yemeni. That gave her the seconds needed to pick up the officer's nine-millimeter and empty its magazine into the thug before he leveled the AK at her. She saved untold lives that day.

Almost losing his soulmate in an unthinkable act of violence caused him to reevaluate his purpose. Her death would have created a massive hole in the kids' lives, and his. Running West Clean Energy would feel irrelevant to him, and losing their mother would irreparably damage his daughter and son. So, Jace and Charlotte no longer took life for granted — not theirs and not those of the people around them. Two months after the attack, he turned over the day-to-day operation of his company to his leadership team and vowed to use his skill to help others.

The FBI recognized he was an asset, as did the U.S. Attorney in Norfolk. They collaborated to hire him as an investigative consultant and teamed him with his cohorts responsible for taking down an active terror cell, Grace Madson and Charlotte West.

Charlotte's shootout with a terrorist prompted her and Jace to elevate their personal protection to a more earnest level. They spent more time firing down-range at paper men, but it felt inadequate. One advantage of living in Virginia Beach was the tens of thousands of active-duty and retired military in the region. Folks loved to shoot and took defending themselves seriously. There were a dozen tactical ranges within an hour's drive from their home. They trained to move, take cover, stand and fire at different kinds of targets. A favorite was the shoot-house where they entered a building, distinguished the bad guys from the good guys, shot the bad ones, and safely moved through the structure. This not only prepared them to defend themselves in sudden changes in environment, but it was fun. Whoever made it through the drill the quickest without shooting friendlies, but killing the hostiles, won the date night challenge.

More confident in his ability to carry and use a firearm, and mindful of unknown threats to his wife and kids, Jace no longer kept his PPK locked in his study.

Chapter 4

The Corporation called a low-level male employee, a 'jack' and a female, a 'jill.' Two jacks were guarding the meth lab that evening. The Head of Security for the 'company' assigned overnight guard duty to junior status members. It made them feel important and valued by Chairman. Besides, they felt cool. It was the only time they got to carry automatic rifles.

Each jack and jill worked for a supervisor who had the responsibility to assign nicknames to their charges. Tiny was one guy outside the meth lab that night. His nickname was not from his diminutive stature but from his bulk. He was six feet four inches tall and carried 250 pounds of muscle. An imposing figure, he relied on his size to intimidate people and was more than willing to take a job that required that skill. Bubba, his partner, was from Boston. The name his mother gave him was Robert, but his boss had a strange local accent. When he said Bob, it came out Bub, so his name became Bubba. Bubba was a gung-ho guy who wanted to be a marine, but his indiscretions in boot camp got him drummed out of the Corp.

When Jace reached the opening in the woods where the men parked, his common sense slapped his face as a scorned woman would. He realized he strayed far from his swim lane. Once he saw the shack on the other side of the clearing, he decided it was time to get the hell out of there.

The sun sunk below the horizon, making the forest pitch black and too dangerous to return the way he had come. There was enough light in the open for him to make it to the trail and back to his car, but the shack hid in long shadows cast by trees in the light of a low-risen moon. He crept toward the path, staying as close as he could to the tree line when he saw the flash of a lighter, followed by the orange glow of a cigarette. Someone was outside in the cabin's darkness. Jace froze, exposed without the cover of the trees. His heart thumped in his ears, and he tried to calm himself, drawing slow, deep breaths of the chilly April air.

"Did you see that?" Tiny asked as Bubba lit up a smoke.

"Yeah, I think I saw something move over by the trees."

Their eyes grew wide, and the cigarette fell from Bubba's mouth as his lips parted. They exchanged glances of unsettled looks, and each fumbled with his rifle to find the charging handle and pull it backward. Pointing their guns at the shadows, they eyed each other as if to ask, 'are you going to shoot?'

Jace estimated he was 15 yards from the shack and about the same from the trail to his right. Having been a football player in high school, he always thought of distances in yards. When Jace heard the distinctive, metallic click-clacks of charging handles forcing rounds into firing chambers, the hair on the back of his neck stood on end. It was past time to leave but sprinting 15 yards to the trail and running for his car was out of the question. He was a good athlete, even at 44 years old, but he couldn't outrun bullets. So, he dove to the ground and took cover behind the closest thing to him — Joe's pride and joy, the '51 Chevy.

Jace kneeled behind its rear right fender and held his breath, listening and wondering if they noticed his dive in the murk of night. What sounded like jackhammers on concrete provided the answer. Automatic weapons fire ripped through the cargo bed. He crouched next to the wheel, trying to make himself as tiny as possible. He wasn't a big man, but at five feet eleven inches, he wasn't small either, and using a rim with an inflated rubber tube as cover was not a comfortable feeling. The bullets tore through both sides of the truck, leaving exit holes that looked like barnacles on a boat's hull. He watched as the punctures danced across the sheet metal searching him out, and he dove for the ground. The pop of the tire where he was just hiding let him know that if he had waited a second longer, he would be dead. Wide-eyed and unable to breathe except for rapid shallow pants, he army-crawled through the grass to the front end of the pickup. There he found respite. The thick engine block stopped the projectiles from punching through the fender that was now his protection. He stared at the trail of shredded steel after him, relieved he was alive and his first thought was, *Charlotte's going to kill me.*

He had little time to admonish himself for getting into such a mess. *Fool. What was I thinking?* His right hand reached under his jacket for his Walther holstered under his left arm. *Are you crazy? You really think you'll blast your way out of this?* He decided the best thing to do was to surrender, but he couldn't decide how to do that without dying. As he pondered that dilemma, the shooting stopped.

Security didn't expect any trouble at the lab but staged the guards there to look dangerous and deter any rivals who may stumble onto the property. Until they completed their training, he allowed them each to have only the one 30-round magazine loaded into their weapons. Professional shooters fire for effect while conserving ammunition, but Tiny and Bubba were not yet pros. On full auto, it's easy to blow through that in just a few seconds, and that's what they did.

At the thunder of automatic gunfire, Joe and his partner rushed out the door. The pungent smell of propellant from the spent rounds hung in the air, and he tried not to breathe as he looked out into the clearing to see what caused the young jacks to un-load their ammo. The scene was not pretty. Joe's jaw dropped as he surveyed his baby. He was speechless for several seconds, his mind stuck between sorrow and rage.

Jace took shallow breaths, wondering if it was his chance to rise with his hands held high. *Maybe they calmed down and won't shoot.* As he rose from his haunches to stand, he peeked above the hood of the truck and glimpsed the four men standing on the ramshackle porch of the shack. All eyes were on the cooker who drove the pickup.

"We thought we saw something in the shadows," Tiny said as if he were a child caught with his hand in the cookie jar. He realized that was the wrong thing to say as soon as it came out of his mouth.

If anyone on the porch looked his way, they might have seen Jace spying on them from behind the truck, but all eyes were on Joe who ranted at the young guards with their now empty rifles. The impulse to leave replaced Jace's decision to give himself up. He crept as fast as he could to the woods, keeping the bullet-riddled Chevy between him and the gang-sters. Once in the cover of the shadows, he rose to a crouch and painstakingly stepped through the trees and underbrush as stealthily as he could. He picked up his pace as the voices grew farther away. No one noticed the noise he made stumbling through the forest in the dark. All they could hear was the pro-fanity-laced ass-chewing courtesy of Joe.

The last thing Jace heard before backing his whisper-quiet Audi Q4 e-tron up the trail to the gravel road was the angry cooker yelling, using three times more words than he needed — mostly beginning with 'F' — that what they saw was just a coyote.

Chapter 5

G in married for money. She didn't want his sur-
name. Her family signature was one of respect
and influence built by her father's financial acumen
and her mother's social graces.

Viktor Vandermire started his business with
his earnings as a carpenter. Working on the construction crew was a steppingstone as he saved his
pay to buy a house in need of repair. He renovated
it in his spare time and made enough profit to start
the process again. Soon, he owned his first company,
renovating several houses at once. The profits in the
San Francisco area were high and the opportunities
to make money in the 1980s real estate market were
endless. And that's what Viktor did, expanding his
businesses, investing his income in budding tech
companies, and becoming an extremely wealthy
man. Together with his wife's penchant for social-
izing with California's rich and famous, the Vandermire name became synonymous with power and
affluence.

Growing up, Gin knew only wealth and comfort but was very astute. Her father demanded per-

fect grades in the exclusive private school reserved for the children of the monied and powerful. She realized at an early age that she easily outperformed the arrogant boys being groomed to take their places in business and politics. The other girls, no matter how bright, preferred the ease and luxury afforded to them through their parents' hard work and presented no challenge to Gin's dominance in academics. Harvard was her father's idea of the most prestigious university in the country, so that's where she went to college. She yearned to attend Stanford, though, and persuaded Dad to let her earn her MBA there.

Armed with her degrees from two of the country's most prominent schools, Dad's work ethic, and Mom's ability to influence influencers, Gin set out to conquer all she encountered.

Her first conquest was the older man who accumulated his fortune through his family's vineyards and wineries. He built the family brand into one of the biggest and most recognizable in the industry, and best of all, he had no children. Happy to marry the much younger woman with the auburn hair and the beautiful sandy complexion, he understood her wish to keep the important Vandermire name.

With two fortunes at her disposal, the first step of her plan was complete. Someday in the relatively near future her husband and father would pass. As the only heir to both men, she would become one of the richest women in the world.

That fortune, though, was just the beginning.

Chapter 6

M ost Americans agree, unless they weren't paying attention during the preceding 10 years,
that there was a growing fracture in American
society. Nowhere did it play out more obviously
than in national politics. By the time 2020 arrived,
the schism between liberals and conservatives had
grown wide and deep while politicians acted like
vindictive middle-schoolers who could only focus
on punishing and canceling the other side. Meanwhile, their 'leadership' plunged the country they
had sworn to preserve and protect deeper into crisis.

Political leaders didn't recognize the under-
lying causes of the divide, or more likely, used
them to gain more influence and power. Whatever
the reason, aggrieved citizens felt the overwhelming
need to fight back — against the other side or against
the system. Many on both sides thought they were
one and the same.

The righteous civil rights movement in the
1950s and 1960s led to federal legislation that
spurred sweeping reforms in America, but racism didn't disappear. As decades passed, animos-

ity, prejudice, and inequalities subsided but didn't die. The change for good was most evident in the middle-class — around 50% of the population. But the roots of hatred and unrest festered, and seedlings sprouted where people still felt wronged and angry.

One of those places was Portland, Oregon. It has been called the whitest and most racist big city in America. In 2020, only five percent of its population was black. Its racism had deep roots. When Oregon joined the union in 1859, it was the only state in the nation that banned black people from entering and living there. The bias among police and elected officials was still so egregious in the 1980s and 90s that progressives became more vocal with protests and actions against the Government. That indignation spread to other victims of discrimination, including indigenous peoples, other ethnicities, and the gay and trans communities. This explained why the nightly riots in Portland that Americans witnessed in 2020 were almost exclusively white.

Folks noticed the rioters wore black and covered their faces. They had helmets, respirators, and goggles; carried shields, umbrellas, clubs, fireworks, and Molotov cocktails; had their own medics, makeshift ambulances, and food trucks. They were angry and violent — and organized. These were a newer breed of protesters who were not interested in protesting. They learned tactics and adopted doctrine from antifascist groups in Germany and communist propaganda. In their minds, white supremacists controlled the Government and the economy where the rich became richer, and the poor got nothing. That was their problem with America. They believed direct action against those in power was the only solution to the injustice. The antifascists considered that their mission — to abolish police, prisons, and capitalism and to spread the wealth of the nation to all.

Factions of this so-called 'social justice' movement sprung up in large cities across the country. They were mostly young, white people. They communicated with encrypted apps and message boards on the internet, enabling them to coordinate their actions.

Their stated goal, in some form or another, depending on which group spoke, was to abolish the United States. That, of course, didn't sit well with most Americans. Some thought they had to respond in kind and take up arms to fight the antifascists. But most people believed in America and hoped it would sort things out as it always has. And the divide between liberals on the left of the political spectrum and the conservatives on the right widened, while the average citizen waited for their elected representatives to lead them out of the calamity.

And the abolitionists — the soldiers taking their action to the streets — did not know of their rich and powerful orchestrators.

Chapter 7

VIRGINIA BEACH — APRIL, THE CAFE

E ven though the temperature had dropped into the 40s, beads of sweat formed in Jace's hairline and meandered down his face. That was a close call — too close, he told himself as he steered his Q4 back the way he had come. His overconfidence could have blown the entire investigation and gotten him killed.

That was his first assignment after he helped Charlotte and Grace foil the jihadis. Then, he was a civilian who was in the right place at the right time, with the right skills. Now, he was a hired consultant to the FBI investigating organized crime. The Special Agent in Charge of the field office intended this case to be less intense than the terror attack and thought the team could explore ways to use Jace's clairvoyance. Charlotte's expertise was prosecuting gangs, so she could guide the investigation and decide how to best use his skills.

***

As they had done several months ago in the Near East Café with the terrorists, the idea was for

Grace and Jace to follow the cookers into the shop, order coffee, and place themselves as close to their targets as possible to eavesdrop on their conversation. Jace could listen to their unspoken thoughts and learn more than he could from their casual small talk. Days earlier, she received a tip from one of her confidential informants and learned of the meeting, so they set their familiar plan in motion.

Charlotte speaks to other federal prosecutors, giving them tips on how to secure ironclad indictments of gang leaders. She was in DC doing that the day of the coffee meet. Her teammates didn't need her for the surveillance, so they told her to go ahead with the trip. Unexpectedly, Grace's Special Agent in Charge summoned her to his office to brief visiting SACs on the terror investigation. Two hours before the rendezvous, she called Jace.

"We need to call it off. I can't make it."

"Why?"

"I have to talk with some VIPs for my boss. Can't get out of it."

"Okay, but this may be our only chance. Should I do it alone?"

"No, I'm not comfortable with that…" her voice faded. She didn't want to lose the opportunity, and he was right; it might be a onetime shot.

"I can do it. We did it before. It's not hard." Grace considered that and wanted to let him go ahead with the plan. Her role in the surveillance was to make sure he was safe, but there was no reason to think he wouldn't be. She pondered the idea before she agreed.

"Okay. It will be a benign situation. There should be no trouble. Just get close and listen. That's it."

"That's it," he said, sure he would sit in the shop, learn the location of the lab, and he'd be done.

***

Jace followed the cooks into the cafe, ordered his favorite, sat at the table next to them, and pretended to read. Nothing he sensed indicated to him where they were home-cooking their methamphetamine. The bad guys' minds just were not there. When they finished their coffee, they stood to leave.

"Well, we better get to it. They'll be waiting for us," one said.

"Yeah, I never look forward to this."

As they walked out of the shop, Jace felt their apprehension. They didn't want to go to, but they had to, so they stopped for a caffeine fix before the nighttime shift. Neither hinted where they were going, but he knew it was the lab.

He followed them outside and watched them climb into the rusty pickup that brought them there. No one noticed him and there was a lot of traffic, so he thought it wouldn't hurt to know what direction they headed. The truck pulled out of the shopping center and went south on General Booth Boulevard. He did too. He was going that way, anyway. Soon, they turned left onto Princess Anne Road. Jace and Charlotte lived a minute or two away, and he was at ease driving on his home turf, so he turned left, too. From a distance, and blending with dozens of other vehicles, he saw his target veer right and continue south.

Princess Anne led deep into the undeveloped southern part of Virginia Beach. *I'm so far away from them I can follow for a while. I'll turn around before they see me.*

***

"You what?" was the only thing Charlotte said in an unemotional, seemingly uninterested voice. Jace knew the tone. She was not pleased. He called her when he returned from his unintended adventure as she cruised south on Interstate 95 on her way home from DC. He started with the positive news that he found the location of the meth lab. But like a good prosecutor, she probed for details. As the story unfolded, it took only a minute for her to learn why he sounded so sheepish on the phone.

"Are you okay?" she asked calmly, not betraying her urge to cry with relief that her husband survived being shot at with automatic weapons. It was a weird moment. This was a business call, and a personal one, and it was hard to know what to say on the phone. If she were home, she'd wrap her arms around him and squeeze, thankful he was alive.

"Yes."

"No bullet holes?"

"No."

"And you are certain they didn't see you?"

"I'm sure. Everyone was preoccupied screaming at each other, and the last thing I heard was they concluded it was a coyote." Charlotte's pause was much longer than needed to make Jace uncomfortable. She wasn't angry, but he expected her disappointment with his escapade. She sensed his embarrassment over the phone and felt it with him.

"Have you called Grace?"

"No."

"Well, better get it over with. She must be wondering what happened by now." Charlotte had no thought to admonish him for his mistake. He knew he had screwed up and didn't need to hear it.

"Yeah." Jace was not looking forward to that call.

Chapter 8

"Jaana!" Piper called for her comrade, but she didn't hear over the amplified speech coming from the historic bandstand in Portland's Peninsula Park. She weaved through the crowd loosely gathered around the speaker to get closer.

"Jaana!" she said louder, catching her friend's attention. "There's a guy over there who wants to interview us," pointing to a man, maybe in his 30s, standing near a booth selling herbal tea. "We've been looking for you."

"What does he want?" Jaana was careful who she talked to and who she allowed in her direct-action group. Founded by young women, they called themselves ADA, one of several factions of antifascists who loosely aligned themselves under the banner of Antifa. They formed to counter white supremacist events in Portland. 'Direct action' was a euphemism for physical confrontation with the right-wing radicals. ADA's aim was to prevent or break up their opponent's rallies, and if they couldn't do that, then they'd dox the racists responsible. Posting their names and addresses on social media for all to see, and perhaps prompting personal visits from unfriendly protestors, was fair game.

"He's writing an article about the movement for a magazine. He's been asking people what the purpose is and why, and if we have upcoming protests planned."

"Why does he want to talk to *us*?"

"He just randomly asked me, and I told him we organized ADA a few years back and we were a big part of the change here in Portland."

"Did you tell him who we are?"

"No. I know better than that." Jaana thought for a moment. The crusade against the right-wingers was becoming powerful across the nation, and she reasoned more exposure would help.

"Okay. Let's go, but use fake names."

As she approached, Jaana sized up the man claiming to be a writer. He wore a lightweight hoodie, jeans, and a camera slung around his neck — pretty much how everyone else at the Antifa rally looked.

"I'm Christian Waingate," he introduced himself. "Thanks for talking with me."

"Call me Maria," Jaana told him, "but that's not my real name. We don't want the cops to know our identities."

"I understand. Tell me about your group."

"Who do you write for?"

"The Main. We have quite a wide distribution. Have you heard of us?"

"Yeah," she said dismissively. "We named our organization ADA, or Antifa Direct Action. 'Katie' and I founded it a few years ago to counter the white supremacists who were rallying downtown. They were spewing their hate and the city just let them, so we had to do something. We started by doxing their leaders, and the cops and politicians. When we got bigger, we took away their platform by confronting them at their rallies with other Antifa factions."

"Took away their platform?"

"Yeah. These right-wing fascists metastasize if they go unchecked. We have to fight them in the streets and everywhere else so they can't organize. We need to snuff out their voices and not allow them to spread their message. If we don't, the white nationalists will grow stronger."

"'Snuff out their voices' sounds like you use tactics typically associated with fascism. How do you respond to that?"

"Well…," she considered her answer and thought it to be honorable, "you have to fight fire with fire."

***

Jaana grew up in the Portland middle-class suburb of Cedar Mill, known for its big homes, manicured lawns, and excellent schools. Most residents were college-educated and held well-paying jobs. Her father was a defense lawyer and her mother a social worker in the city. Life was comfortable for her.

She was a smart kid, and after high school studied at Portland State University, just seven miles from home. It would have been a short drive to classes but she wanted to live on campus to immerse herself in the entire university experience. Mom and Dad understood. They wished for her to enjoy the same freedom they had when they went to college, and they could afford it.

Throughout her time in school, she volunteered with several organizations and had a penchant for helping people. That led to her degree in Community Development. Not wanting to leave Portland after graduation, she moved back home to Cedar Mill with her parents and spent her time volunteering for social justice groups in the city.

Piper and Jaana became fast friends at PSU. The college assigned them to be roommates as freshmen, and they had been together ever since then. Piper worked at a coffeehouse in Portland — one that had become a favorite hangout for a klatch of allies active in social justice advocacy. It was at that coffeehouse where she introduced her best friend to those new acquaintances who believed in direct action against authorities. Police and the politicians who controlled them were fascists, they said, who oppressed people of color and everyone else they didn't like.

It wasn't long before Jaana joined Piper and the coffee klatch in a protest decrying the treatment of a black man arrested for suspicion of robbery. The activists insisted the arrest was a travesty, and the righteous indignation imbued by their new friends was breathtaking — and addictive. Most of the group were men, some older, but mostly not, who thrived on conflict in the streets. The young women found the cause and the fray thrilling, but tired of what they considered testosterone-driven aggression, they formed Antifa Direct Action. They still aligned with their male colleagues, but ADA was more inclusive of women and the queer community.

As the years passed, the number of direct actions Jaana organized grew, and so did physical confrontations with the law. Every time she witnessed cops defending themselves with fists and batons against swarms of violent protesters, her anger swelled. Each non-lethal bullet and pepper ball that struck her; each time she choked on tear gas, and mace burned her eyes, she hardened.

Jaana's reputation as a woke, passionate leader swelled, and it drew followers to her. ADA grew in numbers, and its focus became clearer. The oppression of women, people of color, and the queer was the work of corrupt white men who controlled the power and wealth in America. It was up to the anti-fascist movement to force a fundamental change in the system.

Chapter 9

G in Vandermire didn't earn her fortune, she in-herited it. She didn't produce steel or manu-facture cars or build infrastructure. Her compan-ies didn't make goods needed by consumers. They didn't create jobs for Americans in the lower and middle classes. Her hands were not dirty from hard work. She was not a wealth creator. She was a wealth appropriator, as are most modern-day billionaires. And they wield seductive influence wherever they need to, especially in government.

"Hi, Andrea. Thank you for getting back to me so quickly."

"Hello, Gin. It's good to hear from you."

"How are we doing on the tax bill?"

"We're close, but we don't have the votes. The problem children from West Virginia and Georgia don't want to vote for the corporate tax increase."

"Still worried about jobs?"

"They have higher unemployment rates in their districts and worry about bad optics to their constituents."

"Did you earmark social programs for them as we discussed?"

"Yes, but they're stuck on the loss of jobs."

"Should I call them? Sounds as though I can alleviate their concerns with contributions and media campaigns."

"I'm sure that will do it, Gin. Please do."

Gin and the extraordinarily wealthy have long sheltered their riches from the Government. They hide their money in tax loopholes, offshore accounts, and businesses licensed in foreign countries where tax rates are much lower. High corporate taxes and high minimum wages in the U.S. protect the Gins, making it more difficult for the small and mid-sized business owners to get ahead. The little guys must work longer and harder and produce more to capture their share of the American dream. And people like Gin profit from their productivity, and fortunes grow.

The Gins own the too-big-to-fail banks that loan the money everyone else needs. They own the stocks and bonds that fund business and governments alike, enjoying the growth in value and monthly deposits to their investment accounts — all on the backs of the producers. And they own the monstrous technology companies — the ones that control what people see on TV, read in their newspapers, and what they consume on social media and the internet.

The Gins need everyone else to stay right where

they are. Jobs and opportunities for Americans are bad things. Government handouts and keeping people dependent on the dole are good things. The more welfare programs there are, the more money the Government sucks from ordinary citizens, and the less likely the super-elite would have to share the wealth and power of the nation with others.

And sharing is not in their nature.

Chapter 10

"Well, I guess you won't do that again, right?" Grace didn't admonish him. A younger peer may have gotten an earful for being reckless, but not him. He was too good a friend and deserved more respect than that. We all make mistakes, she told herself. Jace appreciated the discretion and just wanted to move on.

They met in Charlotte's office in the World Trade Center in Norfolk to review the case and decide what to do next.

"Thanks to Jace, we've got trained eyes on the meth lab. There's not much doubt what it is. The telltale signs are obvious." Grace produced eight by ten photos of the property, taken from above.

"Drone?" Jace asked. Charlotte didn't need to. She'd seen plenty of aerial surveillance images from past investigations.

"Yes. See those brown spots on the ground outside the shack? They dump the waste chemicals there and it kills the vegetation. They're pretty safety conscious too."

"How can you tell?"

"The ventilation fans on the roof. Making meth is extremely dangerous. The process creates toxic and explosive fumes. The original construction of this type of cabin wouldn't include such a large vent system. Notice we took those photos during the day."

"There are no vehicles in the clearing like I saw that evening. They must not cook in the daytime."

"That's probably true. We flew over the cabin on five different occasions during the daytime. No sign of activity. Check these out." Grace showed her team more photographs taken at night.

"Infrared," Charlotte said. "Something is going on in there," pointing out the red hotspots inside the house.

"Those look like guards." Jace pointed to two smaller orange spots on the edge of the structure. It looked as though they were on the porch he knew too well.

"We thought about sending in a ground team at night, but the place is so remote, the lookouts might notice us coming. The odor from the building would put a 100% stamp of assurance on it, but we really don't need to, so we decided not to chance it."

"I smelled nothing unusual," Jace offered.

"That doesn't surprise me. You were there when the crew first arrived, and they weren't cooking. If they were, you would have sniffed a pungent, urine-like odor. You couldn't miss it."

"So…," Charlotte said to redirect the conversation to the purpose of the meeting, "we know these guys are cookers, but they are small potatoes. We need to work our way through the network to get to the guy in charge."

***

Two weeks earlier the U.S. Attorney of the eastern district, Charlotte's boss, called her into his office to give her the assignment.

"It appears there's a big player in the region that hasn't been on our radar screen. Virginia Beach, Norfolk, Portsmouth — all the locals report the familiar signs. Their sources say it's harder to find pills and marijuana, a new crystal is abundant, and the gangs buying coke and pot for resale can't get it from their normal suppliers."

"What about heroin and fentanyl?"

"No changes that we know."

"That tells me a few things," Charlotte confirmed what her boss was thinking. "There's a new operation selling a lot of pills and weed, sucking up supplies and making it harder, at least temporarily, for the street thugs to get their stuff. The newcomers have an alternative source of meth, thus the availability of the crystal. They're moving large amounts of coke and pot to other distributors, squeezing out the street gangs. And with the politicians and cops focusing on opioid overdoses, they're not messing with heroin and fentanyl. Smart."

"The Special Agent in Charge is assigning Grace and Jace to the investigation, so you take it on our end."

Chapter 11

T he Detroit race riots in July 1967 ended with 43 people dead, hundreds injured, and more than 1,400 burned-out buildings. The rebellion, as they called it, left 5,000 individuals, mostly black, homeless. Decades of institutional racism and deep-rooted segregation came to a head that day when law enforcement raided an unlicensed after-hours bar on the corner of 12th and Clairmount streets in the city's West Side. Violence erupted and five days of massive unrest followed.

The decline of the American auto industry in the 1980s struck hard, leaving modern-day Detroit with 20% unemployment and billions of dollars of budget shortfalls and debt. Middle-class flight to its suburbs left the city with a population that was 80% black.

So, when a white police officer shot dead Marvin Thompson, an unarmed black man, the tinderbox that was Detroit erupted in flames and ignited civil unrest in large urban areas across the country. African Americans, angry from living their lives under the specter of racism, and their paradigm that cops were murdering blacks at will, took to protesting in the streets.

When the sun set, the protesters went home, and the rioters came out. Once again, black neighborhoods and businesses burned.

***

Gin Vandermire watched the 24-hour cable news for two days. Angry protests in Detroit spread to other big cities — Portland, Seattle, San Francisco, LA, Minneapolis, St. Louis, New York, Washington, DC — and the internet exploded with organizers vowing to continue until politicians abolished or reformed their police departments. Indecision paralyzed officials. Afraid to offend the protesters and their supporters, city and state leaders did nothing — and Gin noticed.

The private landline on her desk high above San Francisco atop the Transamerica Pyramid rang with its distinctive, low-tone bing. She knew who it was without looking. It was time. She could feel it in her bones.

"This is Gin," she answered with a knowing voice.

"I think the time has come."

"Yes. I do too. How long will it take?"

"We have resources in most cities. We can start tonight."

"Good. Execute Torrent."

"Yes, ma'am."

The line clicked as the caller hung up. She strolled to her office window and immersed herself in the panoramic view of San Francisco Bay and the Golden Gate Bridge. Lifting her arms, beholding the beauty, she inhaled deeply and filled her lungs with the rarified air of power. A minute of satisfaction and excitement passed before she sauntered back to her desk to watch more news reports of the unrest.

Chapter 12

VIRGINIA BEACH — THE OCEAN LAKES YEARS

M ichael Zakis loved his work as a quartermaster on the guided-missile destroyer USS Ruffian. Standing watch with the officer of the deck and the navigator was important, ensuring the officers got the ship where it needed to be when it needed to be there. He married his high school sweetheart, Trace, in Pittsburgh and enlisted in the U.S. Navy soon afterward. The couple settled wherever the Service posted him. And after his first deployment, she gave birth to their daughter, Kelena.

It was difficult being a military spouse, especially for a young woman just a few short years out of high school. Life got lonely living away from home, alone while her husband deployed for six, or even nine months at a time. A baby to care for made it doubly hard. There was no one to give her a break or to share in her baby's many milestones when she was the only parent twenty-four hours a day, seven days a week.

By the time Kelena reached high school at Ocean Lakes, the strain of being a lonely single mother most of her young adult life had worn on

Trace. Following his calling, Michael had worked his way up through the enlisted ranks of the Navy. But she felt left behind now that her daughter was away from home much of the day and wanted independence from her mom. Alone in Virginia Beach, she had no career, no job, no college degree, and no purpose. Drinking provided solace. At first wine did the trick, but the liquor store was right next to the grocery market, so tequila, vodka, and gin rotated through her menu each week. The doctor wasn't aware of her growing use of alcohol, and he prescribed Xanax to help with the anxiety and Vicodin to treat the headaches.

Michael and Trace had lost their youthful love, and it felt more like a burden than a blessing for him to go home after work. He preferred deployment, and when on shore duty looked for reasons to stay late and spend as little time with his wife as he could.

Kelena found herself with no parents. The Zakis family lived in the same house, but Dad stayed away, and Mom was sleeping it off when school let out each day. She had to fend for herself, including earning income for clothes and the other necessities of being a teenage girl. Her mother wasn't there to shop for her, and her father couldn't help. When she asked him for money to buy what she needed, it reminded him of the state of his wife and marriage, and he became depressed and angry.

Although she dreamed of a career in corporate America and joined the business club and leadership workshop, Kelena understood her future did not include college. Some lucky military kids got free tuition to in-state schools, but not her. Not in Virginia. The hurt she endured when the other students talked about the colleges they applied to and what they planned to study drove her to escape her miserable situation.

In her junior year, she took Xanax from her mother's purse and sold it to classmates. The demand was high, and the cash kids gave her for a pill shocked her. When she offered them Vicodin, a bidding war ensued, and the green flowed freely. Trace, too under the influence of alcohol to realize that she had not taken the drugs, refilled the prescriptions on time. She told her primary care physician that the Xanax didn't help, so he increased her dose, enabling Kelena to split the tablets in two and make twice the money.

But demand outpaced her supply, especially for the Vicodin, which was more difficult for her mother to convince the doctor to refill. She found Xanax was the popular happy pill for stressed-out parents and convinced her classmates to pinch a few from their mothers' bottles. They obliged, content to sell to her for half-price while she took the risk of distributing the drugs to customers. The clientele grew, spreading to nearby schools, and by necessity, so did the number of her suppliers. By the end of her senior year, Kelena spent more time buying and selling pills than she did in school. The business was lucrative, and logic compelled her to keep and grow the operation after graduation.

The volume of daily phone calls from strangers wanting to buy all sorts of meds, not just Xanax and Vicodin, worried her. She didn't know those people or how they came to have her number. Sooner rather than later the wrong person would call. Whether it be the police, or the local thug dealer angry that she had cut into his market share, it wouldn't end well. She needed to get more organized, hire help, and add security to her business model.

She didn't like buyers knowing her name and calling her personal cell, so she blocked unknown callers. Prepaid phones from Walmart were the new way to communicate, and she distributed them to her trusted suppliers. Kelena thought of herself as the executive in charge of a company, so she called her enterprise the Corporation to add a layer of anonymity. She needed help and appointed her best friend and cohort to be the Head of Supply, and she assigned another good friend to be the Head of Distribution. No longer were they to use their names while engaging in the drug trade. For their protection, and Kelena's, they were to be known only as Supply and Distro.

And fitting of her position, Kelena became Chairman.

Chapter 13

S he felt like an oddity in Portland. Sherley Johansson was one of the few African Americans in the city. The crooked looks flashed her way were something she learned to live with, especially when she told people her full name. Sherl defaulted to explaining she married a man with Swedish ancestry before the person with the puzzled look on their face asked. What did you expect, 'Washington?' she always thought, but never said it out loud.

Sherley owned Sherl's Coffeehouse. She and her daughter ran the café by themselves except for their one employee — the cute girl named Piper. Piper was good for the shop. Her friends loved coffee and flocked there, often filling the entire store with paying customers. Sherl noticed the bunch gathered before and after the protests downtown, and it soon became obvious they were part of the group that called themselves Antifa. She overheard the conversations. Young white kids discussed social justice and confronting the police. *Let ME tell you about racism,* she wanted to say, but never did. She didn't want any trouble.

***

It was the evening of the third day of protests after the Marvin Thompson shooting in Detroit. Like the last two nights, people packed into Sherl's, getting their caffeine fix and a sandwich to fuel their nighttime activities.

"Right there," Piper said, pointing across the room crowded with full tables and black-clad bodies, making it almost impossible to move. Christian Waingate waved to Jaana from his cramped corner, coffee in hand.

"What's he doing here?"

"He told me he wants to join us to experience the protests up close."

"I don't know." Jaana barely knew the writer she met last summer. He and she talked for two hours on that pleasant September day in Peninsula Park, but that was just talk. She wasn't keen on letting him tag along on a direct action, especially now. Things had gotten nasty, and she expected worse in the ensuing days.

"He's coming over here. Be nice," Piper said as the journalist made his way towards them. "See you in a bit. I've got customers."

Jaana watched as he politely pushed through the crowd. Wearing light blue jeans and a white shirt, he stood out in the black sea. Obviously, he didn't want to be mistaken for a protester by cops. She spoke first when he reached her.

"Piper said you wanted to go with us," realizing too late she used Piper's real name. Christian must have seen the expression on her face.

"Don't worry, I won't use your names, and I never reveal sources if they need to remain anonymous." Jaana liked him. A handsome guy with a quick smile, he was easy to talk to, but she tried not to lower her guard.

"That's not a good idea. It will get hairy tonight…" She let her words hang.

"That's why I want in. I need to see you in action and understand what you're up against."

"You're not really dressed for it."

"I have safety gear and my press credential. I'm going in either way and was hoping for a little protection."

"Why do you think I can protect you?"

"Because you're Jaana Karjalainian, the leader of this crowd, and they do what you say. Don't be too surprised. I knew your name about a minute after we talked in the park. All I had to do was point you out and ask. Everybody knows who Jaana is."

Chapter 14

C hairman ran the Corporation as a CEO would, and it thrived. The growth was almost too much to handle, but she continued to hire managers, and they hired their workers. She believed in the corporate mantra of take care of your people and they'll take care of your business, so she adopted policies to ensure they employed the right individuals. She insisted her team treat employees with fairness and respect and made sure the company met their financial needs with bonuses and incentives. And her folks rewarded her with their loyalty.

Unlike Chairman, gang leaders ruled with fear and violence. Beatings, murder, and death were part of the gangbangers' brief existence. The average life expectancy of a member was only 20 years and 5 months. Sooner rather than later, their violent chiefs met the same fate, or wasted away their youth in prison. Local bangers came and went and knew nothing more than battling their rivals in turf wars, peddling drugs on street corners, and supplying other two-bit distributors.

Chairman understood the most lucrative markets for her products were in middle and upper-class environments. She recruited students, office workers, and shipyard and factory laborers who made decent wages. These were not people who grew up in the projects and relied on government aid and crime to survive — the underprivileged attracted to gang life. Her customers preferred not to buy their drugs in back alleys from scary goons, but without her, that's what they had to do. The Corporation sold its pills where its clientele lived and worked, cutting off the steady stream of buyers to the gangs' points-of-sale. They left the addicts living under bridges and in crack houses for the thugs. Both her employees and their patrons were more than happy to not interact with the criminal element — at least most of them.

By necessity, Supply and Distro had to deal with unsavory characters. Pills prescribed by doctors had become a small part of their inventory. Supply had a knack for cultivating reliable suppliers who were physicians, or who got their meds from them, but she depended on black market drugs to meet the need. And of course, due to the demand from their customers, their product offerings expanded to a variety of stimulants and depressants, including marijuana, cocaine, and methamphetamine. Distro moved into the wholesale markets, supplying larger amounts of drugs to other distributors. Chairman, though, was not keen on becoming entangled with large drug smuggling operations and cartels, so she insulated the Corporation by only working through middlemen. And her newest endeavor was to be as independent as possible, making and growing her own.

The company and its dealings had grown so large that Chairman had to create a security unit. She was wary of buying from and selling to criminal organizations. And the local gangbangers finally realized they had a powerful competitor that had sucked away a major portion of their customer base. Big business led to huge amounts of money — more than Kelena ever imagined or intended. So, for Security, she called an old boyfriend who left for the military after high school. A couple of tours in combat zones later, he figured that was enough for him. He came back home to a job with his former girl that paid a lot more than being a Marine. He enlisted friends with skills like his, and the core of his team was more than a match for any adversary. For their safety, he made sure the department heads and their managers carried weapons and knew how to use them. And when Chairman added the lab and fields, he recruited promising young jacks and jills and trained them as sentries. Ex-soldiers willing to bend or break the law were hard to find, but he needed the resources to deter or repel any challenges. The market, though, was flush with unemployed but capable people eager for work.

Chairman had become the leader of the dominant illicit drug distribution operation in the eastern region of Virginia. When she started fresh out of high school, her intent was to make a good living and pay for college as a small-time pill peddler. Her ambition to be a corporate executive drove her to grow the business and evolve into the kingpin she never intended to be. She hated the idea of selling heroin and fentanyl — opioids that kill people every day — so she didn't. And trafficking in humans and guns was abhorrent. She couldn't think of herself as an organized crime boss. In her mind, she was just providing recreational drugs to normal people.

Chapter 15

"**W**ho's he?" one of the faction leaders asked.
"He's a journalist writing about our struggle," Jaana answered. "He's coming tonight."
"Noooo…" her colleague drew out the word for emphasis. "That's not a good idea." Like most Antifa, he didn't want reporters recording them, especially with video. That was how people got arrested.
"He's with me." Her voice was firm and a decibel or two higher, settling the issue. The others sitting with her knew not to question her.

As dusk fell on Portland, the faction chiefs gathered at Jaana's table for one final review of their plans. The commanders would gather their people at Pioneer Square in front of the historic courthouse in the southwest section of the city. It was several blocks away, but an easy walk from the café. They confirmed their assignments, notified their troops with group texts, and relaxed. Those in the coffeehouse followed their bosses' lead, enjoying their last few sips of coffee and bites of sandwich. The atmosphere in the shop buzzed as the activists' anticipation for the night's events peaked.

Thirty minutes after dusk changed to dark, Jaana looked at her watch and decided it was time. She rose from her chair at the leaders' table and, with a stoic face, surveyed the room full of black. In a second or two it fell silent, and all turned towards her. She clenched her left hand into a fist and raised it above her head. With a steely look, she said one word clearly and loudly.

"Go." Sherl's filled with the sounds of wooden chairs sliding on the floor and bumping into things. Jaana watched as the shop emptied. In 30 seconds, only Sherl, her daughter, Piper, the journalist, and she remained. Christian waited as the four women worked as a team to clear, straighten and wipe tables. When they finished, Jaana and Piper thanked Sherl and hurried out the door. He trailed behind them, marveling at what he just witnessed. The leaders of Portland's social justice movement took the time to help a coffeehouse owner clean up before they ran off to lead their protest.

***

In stark contrast to everyone else in Pioneer Square, Christian wore white — a ballistic vest with 'PRESS' emblazoned on the front and back, what looked like a bicycle helmet, and wrap-around safety glasses. He found his way to the police line and made himself obvious, hoping to signal them the guy in white was just a journalist doing his job. After making himself visible to law enforcement, he wandered to where he left Jaana. It was not a pleasant walk.

While his press credential may or may not have protected him from police action, it attracted aggressive vitriol from the antifascists. Many had as much disdain for journalists as they did cops and were not shy telling him that.

Both Jaana and Piper wore black bloc riot gear — clothes, sneakers, body armor, helmets, face covering, and backpacks. Perhaps not noticeable to the casual observer, the leaders bore markings that let the troops know who was giving the orders. Jaana's was an inch-thick, vertical white stripe that stretched from the top of her head, down the middle of her back to her waist. Piper had one chevron on her helmet and again on her pack.

"What's in the knapsack?" Christian was curious. Almost everyone had some sort of pack slung over their shoulders.

"Oh, mostly safety stuff. Facemask, goggles, first aid kit. I have a couple of bottles of baking soda water for eyewash. I have sports drinks and snacks. It gets intense, and it's exhausting." Jaana explained while she kept a close watch on her people and the police in front of them.

"What else?"

"Um…" she avoided eye contact. "Some other things we may need."

"Come on. What else?"

"I have a Taser, a couple of bottles of 151, rags… and a lighter."

Christian realized what that was for and didn't ask. She was referring to 151 proof rum with 75.5

percent alcohol, and he imagined it made an effective fiery cocktail.

"That's normal stuff." Jaana was nonchalant, hoping to downplay the implication.

As she said that, she shifted her gaze south, down SW 6th Ave. A block away, sirens and screaming caught her attention. Clouds of tear gas floated through the crowd, and she saw protesters running in retreat. Christian turned in time to catch the melee.

"Piper, BLM needs help over there. Send two teams," she directed her second in command as she pointed to the chaos approaching them from the south.

"On it." Piper's thumbs flew across her smartphone's keyboard, and she then looked west on SW Yamhill Street. She craned to see her team leaders, but once she found them and they glanced back her way, she used hand signals to rally them southward to reinforce the BLM protesters who were being dispersed.

The group's command and control impressed Christian as the people she had signaled ran along their line, gathered their forces, and hurried south to back up their comrades on 6th Ave. He saw them don their face masks and goggles, then take something from their backpacks and light them. Molotov cocktails rained on the police. Emboldened by the antifascists, those fleeing turned around and charged the police line that had temporarily broken, breaking windows, painting slogans, and firebombing whatever was in front of them. The escalation in violence resulted in a barrage of rubber bullets, tear gas, and pepper balls from all directions as police advanced on the rioters. The field general with the stripe down her back blew a whistle three times to get her troops' attention and beckoned to them to disperse. They understood that they'd do it again the next night, and scattered.

***

Christian had parked near Sherl's a few blocks from Pioneer Courthouse. In his white press garb, he slipped past the approaching police line, walked to his car, and drove to the suburb where he had rented a house. He stripped off his clothes and jumped in the shower, washing away the CS gas and pepper spray.

After he poured himself a shot of Johnny Walker from the bar, he picked up his phone and pressed his boss's number.

"Christian. How are you doing?"

"Man, I got gassed, but I'm okay."

"I saw it online. Was she there?"

"She was there and in charge. I'm impressed."

"So, she's our girl?"

"She is most definitely our girl."

"Did you offer her the money?"

"Not yet, but I'll see her tomorrow. I'll have time alone with her. I'm sure she'll put her first payment to good use."

Chapter 16

"So, do you think you can do it?" Charlotte asked her husband. It felt weird to work with Jace professionally, to consider him a peer in the investigation. Before, in the race to track down Bilal and his terror cell, it was on the fly with no authorization. She and Grace were doing whatever it took to prevent the slaughter of hundreds of innocent people. Back then, Jace was more a resource than a partner.

In their first official case together, he was quiet and let his two teammates do the analyzing and strategizing. Charlotte wondered if it was because of his natural introversion, or deference to their expertise. Was he feeling out of place and not speaking up, or just overwhelmed? Maybe he's getting his bearings and will get more comfortable with time. He built West Clean Energy from nothing, making the difficult and important decisions. Now, not only does he have a boss, but he answers to his partners too. It had to be uncharted waters for him.

"Let's give it a shot. If I find something, then it'll be worth it. Is there a downside if I don't?"

"If the cooker realizes we're on to him, that probably means the organization would too."

"I want to do it," Grace said. "It could shave months off the investigation. If we don't do it, we'll do a lot of traditional legwork and beating the bushes. If we do it and tip off the gang, we'll still have to do the grunt work. I don't think we have much to lose."

"Okay, it's a go. Have VBPD pick him up for questioning. Make it sound like it's for something other than drugs. We'll wait at the precinct to observe."

***

"This is Detective Boatwright. He'll be the interrogator." Grace introduced the police officer from the Virginia Beach PD's Special Investigations — the unit that coordinates with federal law enforcement, including criminal intelligence and narcotics. After brief introductions, she reviewed the purpose of the exercise.

"This guy is a member of an organization that is pushing a significant amount of drugs. We want to get as much information from him as we can without letting on that we're aware of his gang."

"That's cool. We pulled him in for illegal gambling, and he insists he doesn't know what we're talking about," the detective added.

"Good. Start with the standard questions — who he works for, how long, what he does, etc. And when you think it'll catch him off guard, ask him if he's into drugs. Jace is a special observer and will be with you during the interview. He'll scrutinize the suspect for clues but does not intend to take part in the questioning."

"I'm ready," the detective said as he got up to go to the interrogation room. He opened the door and looked back at the trio to invite any last instructions. Hearing none, he walked next door to question their person of interest, and Jace followed.

"State your name, please?" officer Boatwright started.

"Joe Harkness. Why am I here?"

"I'll ask the questions. What do you do for a living, Joe?"

"I'm an auto mechanic."

"That's a good job. Where do you work?"

"I'm in between jobs right now."

"What do you do for cash? A man has to eat."

"I get by. I got money."

The special agent and the prosecutor watched the video stream of the interview and saw Jace taking notes.

"It's working," Grace looked at Charlotte with a curl on her lips and a knowing glint in her eyes.

"I see that." Her partner mirrored the look, and they reverted their attention to the 20-inch monitor.

After 30 minutes, Boatwright glanced at Jace who gave him a slight rise of the chin toward the door, and the detective understood it meant to take a break. They left Joe alone while they returned to the observers next door.

"What do you have, Jace?" Charlotte urged as soon as he entered.

"A lot. Let's review it before you let him go."

As they sat at the table in the center of the small room, she took the lead.

"Tell."

"Detective Boatwright did a great job touching on everything we needed, and Joe was easy to read. When we asked him what he did for a living, I got a flash of a makeshift lab. But we already knew he's a cooker. I heard 'the corporation,' when the detective quizzed him about where he worked. And he thought of 'Caroni' and someone or something he called 'Supply.'"

"Caroni? I know a Caroni," Charlotte said. "NPD busted him for possession with intent to distribute awhile back, but it didn't stick."

"Yeah, he's on our board, too," Boatwright said, with narrowed eyes and jaw ajar. Confused, he shot a querying eye to Grace for an explanation.

"I'm sure Joe's immediate boss is Caroni. And I think he reports to Supply," Jace continued.

"What else?"

"He's comfortable. I sensed satisfaction during the money discussion, so he's not lacking cash. He's confident. Gambling is not his thing, so he thinks he's in the clear. He has to work tonight, and he's hoping to get out of here soon. His partner in the lab is James, and he's the lead chemist, still teaching Joe the ropes. I could see the coffee shop and I think they meet there before every cook."

"Coffee shop?" Boatwright was puzzled.

"Yep. The one at Strawbridge. I heard the term, 'the corporation' more than once and felt a mixture of loyalty and apprehension. When the officer mentioned drugs, there was a tinge of panic, and his mind went right to the corporation. That must be the name of the organization he works for."

"Anything more?"

"No, but I know he didn't recognize me. That confirms no one saw me that night."

At that, the VB detective squinted and looked at Jace in bewilderment. Grace noticed the expression. "I'll explain all this some other time."

Chapter 17

C hristian called Jaana when he hung up with his boss and told her he had something important to discuss. They agreed to meet at Peninsula Park at noon the next day.

"You impressed me when we talked last summer. I kept an eye on you."

"What does that mean? Sounds creepy."

"No, not *that* way. You'd be a perfect fit for a position in the organization I work for. I told my boss about you and he wants to hire you."

"Doing what? I'm no journalist."

"No, not as a writer or photographer or anything like that. We'll pay you for doing what you're doing right now with ADA."

"Huh?"

"We call people like you 'street captains.' We're sympathetic to your cause and want to help. It takes resources and coordination to plan and carry out an aggressive protest. My employer will fund you and your direct actions."

"Fund us?" Jaana looked at Christian sideways, not trusting or believing him. "How? Why would a magazine do that?"

"Don't get stuck on me writing for The Main. We want to give you money to help you fight for fairness and equity. You're doing your part. Let us do ours."

"What's the catch?" she said, still wary of an offer like that coming from a journalist.

"No catch. Just do what you do, but the cash will provide the resources to do it better." Christian handed her an envelope to set the hook. When Jaana looked inside, her mouth opened, and her eyes widened.

"What the hell is this!?" she said with an incredulous tone.

"Five thousand dollars. Do you think it's enough to get started?"

"Get started? I'm not sure what to do with this!"

"Do what you've been doing but do it bigger. Make sure you have the supplies needed for all the Antifa factions, not just ADA. Buy water, food, medical kits, shields, gas masks," Christian paused, and then added, "151, mortars, clubs, bricks, rocks — whatever you want. I can help. I have quite a bit of that stuff already stockpiled for you."

"Ahh…"

"And I'll give you a weekly stipend of a thousand dollars. If you need more for a big purchase, tell me."

"This… this is incredible."

"Come on, I have a car. Let's go to my place and load up for tonight."

***

"Piper, I need help. Where are you?"

"Hanging at Sherl's."

"We'll pick you up in five minutes."

"Who's we?"

"You'll find out. We're in a white van."

Piper saw Jaana through the passenger window when the van pulled in front of the café and opened the sliding door behind her. Only half surprised to see Christian driving, she hopped into the second-row seat. She noticed the chemistry between them and figured it was only a matter of time. She looked at him, then at her, and pursed her lips together with a crooked smile.

Piper let out a knowing, "Uh-huh."

"Uh-huh, what?" Jaana tried to keep a straight face, but the corners of her mouth curled into a grin — the telltale sign that her best friend was on to something.

"Look behind you," Jaana said after they exchanged playful looks.

"What's all this?"

"Stuff for tonight. It's mostly food and water. We're going to stage it for the protest. There are med supplies, too." Piper forgot about teasing her for sparking a romance with the handsome journalist. They hooked up all right, but not the way she expected.

"Where'd you get these goodies?" her attention

turned to their cargo.

"Christian got it for us, but you should see what he has at his house. After we unload, we're going back for more. We'll hand out those things tonight."

When night fell over Portland, Jaana briefed her faction leaders of the newfound wealth of resources. She and Piper had staged the food and drink and told them where to find it. As their troops gathered at the site of the next protest, she would arrive in a white van, and instructed each leader to send at least two people to retrieve the supplies required for a powerful direct action.

***

A block from the federal courthouse, the leader of the antifascist movement in Portland prepared for the night's protest.

"Piper, have some of our guys deliver bats and hammers to the BLMers. Take them twenty cans of spray paint and a box of cocktails too."

"Got it."

"After that, we'll grab these packages of mortars and give one to each faction. We need to make sure everyone understands to hurl them only at cops."

Chapter 18

"To say I'm pleased is an understatement. All is going so nicely," Gin started the meeting with Chen, her trusted director of security.

"Everything was very well-planned and is working perfectly. We had assets in the expected hotspots for months and were ready for you to initiate Torrent."

"How did you recruit captains so quickly?"

"Our people on the ground did the legwork ahead of time. While waiting for the 'go' order, they did an outstanding job evaluating candidates at their own rallies and hangouts. Not one captain turned down the offer."

"What are we hearing from the leaders? What is the momentum in the streets?"

"Stronger than ever. The Marvin Thompson shooting in Detroit was the perfect setup. We could not have done it better ourselves."

"It was exactly what we were waiting for. Do our operatives need anything?"

"No, they stockpiled from the time they arrived

in their cities and still have plenty of supplies."

"Give me a quick rundown."

"Rioters turned the opportunity zones in Detroit to ash. Authorities estimate the number of people left homeless is up to 7500. Low-income districts in Minneapolis are in much the same condition. They burned, looted, or trashed most buildings. Protesters ruined entire depressed areas in LA, St. Louis, Atlanta, Baltimore, Boston, and Washington, DC. High-income families are fleeing New York City in droves. Manhattan looks as though it's from a post-apocalyptic movie."

"My God, it's better than I expected. When do we expand to our primary targets?"

"Already started. Rioters are now turning on the business districts, police precincts, and federal properties in all cities. The protesters in Portland and Seattle are more progressive and experienced, and they began with downtown businesses and government buildings. Some governors called in the National Guard for help, but most are refraining."

"Playing right into our hands. And they'll need to quash the riots eventually, causing more unrest and backlash. That's doubly good for us. Idiots. I'll never understand why they don't move hard and fast to stop the protests and save their cities. Now they've got much more troublesome problems to deal with."

"They should have nipped it in the bud. Instead, they have an uncontrollable Kraken on their hands."

"I'll make the calls for phase two soon. Are you readying phase three?"

"We've started planting the seeds with the street captains, and in a week, preparations will shift into full swing."

"And phase four?"

"I have a unit of five operators. One is the team leader. They are on standby and are ready to go."

"Don't brief them until I pull the trigger."

Chapter 19

VIRGINIA BEACH — JUNE, THE METH LAB

T hey were in the wrong place at the wrong time. Chairman believed she had to earn loyalty from her employees, and that meant showing she cared about them. One leadership book she read said that a good leader gains respect through 'management by walking around.' She needed to visit her people and talk to them; show them she's in the trenches with them. Security was not fond of the idea. It exposed her identity and her person to unnecessary risks, but he knew Kelena from way back and realized she was going to do what she wanted.

The field trip to the meth lab posed little risk in his mind. It was secret, isolated, and secure. To get the most benefit from her visit, Chairman asked Supply to go with her. To be extra safe, Security brought his core shooters with him. He would not trust the young jacks to protect key leaders of the organization, no matter where they were.

The lab's manager told his two guards and two cookers to be there an hour early and expect a visit before they started cooking the night's batch of crystal. Caroni had been part of the drug scene in Norfolk well before he went to work for the Corporation and still hung out in the same bars with the same people from his past. After pounding back six beers, his lips became loose, and details of his new position leaked out. And word of the meth lab in the back-woods of Virginia Beach reached the wrong ears.

The leader of the street gang that did business in the northern part of Chesapeake called South Nor-folk couldn't believe his luck. Not only did he have clues to who had been stealing customers from the local gangs, he knew where they'd be and when. After he sent a trusted scout to follow the loud-mouth from the bar, he found exactly where the meth lab was. He had to admit; it was a sweet setup. No one would find it in the woods unless some dumbass told them where to look. The banger gathered his soldiers. Eight of them piled into a couple of early-model luxury sedans and set out for rural Virginia Beach.

Profits were phenomenal, and Chairman was not shy about sharing with her team, so they rolled up to the lab in two new Suburbans with their win-dows tinted dark. Joe's '51 Chevy, which he had fixed and patched but still not painted, the guards' cars, and the SUVs crowded the clearing at the shack.

"Stay in the truck until I say," Security directed his boss. She understood. She had to let him do his job. He was first out of the VIP vehicle and immedi-ately focused on their surroundings and his team as they exited theirs.

"Two there," he pointed to the right, "and two

there," pointing to the left. "Spread out and lie low." He concentrated his detail on the trail since it was the only way in, but he understood he had to protect their backside as well. "John, cover our six." When the rear guard was in place, Security opened the door for Chairman. As she climbed out and walked to her four employees who had gathered on the porch, Supply and Caroni followed her.

"Who's that?" Tiny whispered to his three lab mates.

"That must be the big dog. That's Chairman," Joe whispered back.

"Hi guys!" she was truly glad to be there, shaking hands with each of them, as the rest of the VIP contingent approached through the grassy clearing. Chairman introduced herself and Supply. They already knew their manager, but she thought it right to acknowledge him too.

"I'm here to tell you what an outstanding job you're doing for us. People love your product, and we can't sell enough." As she thanked them, she reached into her bag and pulled out four thin stacks of 50-dollar bills. Smiles, laughter, and chatter broke out as they admired their $500 bonuses. At first, the group at the porch didn't notice the noise approaching, but Security did.

He was 20 feet from Chairman and scanning the perimeter when he heard the thumping of loud music coming from up the trail.

"Are you expecting anyone else?" he shouted in haste at his leader.

She glanced at Supply and Caroni with a questioning look. Seeing bewilderment on their faces, she replied, "No!" just as the intruders pulled next to the shack and began shooting.

The drivers and the passengers on the left side of each car fired from their windows, still sitting in their seats. The other four gangbangers opened their doors, got out, and shot their weapons from behind the cars. For a moment, Chairman and her group froze by the porch from the surprise of the attack. When they realized bullets were flying in their direction, they dove to the ground.

The untrained street thugs were no match for Security's combat-hardened shooters. Each of them trained their M4A1 assault rifles, favored by U.S. Special Forces, on one of the attackers inside the cars, and took them out with rounds to the head. They killed four assailants as soon as the shooting began. Foolishly, the bangers did not know the capabilities of their adversaries.

Half of the gangsters used semiautomatic handguns, while the others used MAC-10, fully automatic machine pistols. Short and boxy with stubby muzzles, they were wildly inaccurate weapons and emptied their 30-round magazines in three blinks of the eye. Gangs loved MAC-10s. The guns were easy to carry and scary in a close-up drive-by when no one was shooting back. But in a gunfight with professional soldiers, they were almost useless. In seconds, the gunfire stopped. Seven of the eight gang memebers were dead.

Security closed on Chairman to make sure she was all right. John stayed in place to watch for a rear assault, and the others converged on the attackers.

"Kel..." Kelena heard the faint whisper of her name. It was her best friend Kaitlin, who she had dubbed Supply. Only her old friends called her Kel. Still in the grass, she looked at her friend lying next to her and saw fear in her eyes.

"It's okay. I think it stopped." As Kel turned to comfort her, blood gurgled from the corner of Kaitlin's mouth.

"Kel..." The terror on her face told Kelena she was dying. A bullet had found its way into her chest.

"Kaitlin!" Kel screamed in horror. Sobbing, she called for Noah, their old friend in charge of security. "Noaaaah," she repeated in agony. He saw the gunshot wound and ran to the Suburban where he kept a medical kit. With tears rolling down his cheeks, he tried to save his high school buddy, applying Quik-Clot Combat Gauze to the hole near her heart.

"Kel, don't tell Mom and Dad..." Kaitlin barely muttered her last words. Kel understood what she meant. Her parents were wonderful people. They comforted Kelena when life got to be too much and opened their home to her whenever she needed a break. They thought their daughter was an import/export agent for a trading company she and Kel started and were proud of her success. Knowing the real story would crush them.

Kel sobbed, cradling her soulmate in her lap. "What have I done?" It was her fault. She killed her beloved confidant as if she had pulled the trigger herself. No one at the lab knew what to do. They stood by, watching their leader grieve in pain while the man tasked with protecting them tried to console her.

"Boss." At first, Security didn't hear his teammate call for him. "Boss!" His shooter ran up to the group, momentarily distracted by the scene of despair. Then he placed his hand on his leader's shoulder, "One of them is still alive."

"What do we do with him?" The remaining gang member, no older than 16 years, was kneeling with his hands behind his head. Three of the team stood around him as their fourth walked up with Security in tow.

"Is he hurt?"

"Not a scratch. He probably dove for cover when his pals opened fire."

"We can't kill him."

"He's seen too much. He knows where the lab is."

"Send him back to his gang with a warning. You don't screw with the Corporation."

"That may..." Chairman interrupted Security's words. She walked to the group, looked at the captive kneeling in front of her, and raised her .45 caliber handgun to his head. No one spoke, except the kid.

"Wait, I..." The bullet in his brain cut him short.

"Clean this mess up, please. Noah, will you help me with Kaitlin?" Tears were still streaming from her reddened eyes.

In those few minutes, Chairman and her crew became fully initiated gangbangers.

***

The black Suburban with the dark tinted windows waited until no one was in sight. It rolled up to the emergency room entrance to Chesapeake General Hospital. Two people, their faces covered, quickly and gently placed the body of a woman on the concrete in front of the door and drove away.

Chapter 20

N o plan would be complete without a media campaign. And when you have influence over or control the nation's largest technology companies, that means absolute manipulation of any or all information the country sees and hears. Using Antifa to usurp mostly peaceful protests into violent riots was surprisingly easy. Gin smiled at her stroke of genius. Her planning and preparation for the right moment to ignite anti-government unrest throughout the nation was perfect. Now it was time for phase two of her grand scheme.

When she devised her plot, she assumed controlling public opinion would be the easiest part. The multibillionaire boy-wonders who played with computers in their mommies' basements and built their innovations into gigantic monopolies already did it at will. Some were naïve idealists who believed they could change the world with their own ideas of right versus wrong. Some sought only the money and power. All were shrewd and cutthroat business-men willing to do what it took to make their visions reality. And bickering politicians not only let them, but helped them.

To allow the internet to flourish, but protect Americans from its proliferation of pornography, Congress passed the Communications Decency Act. Section 230 of the law protected companies from liability in their efforts to scrub objectionable material from their platforms. That gave the ultra-elite the freedom to remove any content from the internet that they wanted without the government or anyone else keeping them in check.

The present-day result is a tiny group of social justice-minded multibillionaires censoring from their media, news, and internet search platforms people and viewpoints with which they disagree. And Section 230 protects them.

"Ephron, I need a favor," Gin started her conversion with the founder and CEO of the dominant online news and social networking site. "These protests we're seeing all over the country are heartbreaking."

"I agree, of course."

"But it was inevitable, I think. Don't you?"

"Yes, I do. People have finally had enough. They're done with the racism and incivility in society today."

"I'm so tired of hearing the bigmouth politicians spout lies and half-truths about the protesters. They're all over social media."

"I know, it's very frustrating."

"Are you doing something about it?"

"I can put together a team in my fact-check section to weed that stuff out."

"Oh, thank you so much. I'll owe you one."

"No need, Gin. This has to be done. Are there individuals you want to focus on?"

"Yes. Thanks for asking. I'll send you a list."

It was that easy for her. Two more similar phone calls and she could manipulate the opinions of most Americans by controlling what they see — and don't see — in their news feeds.

Chapter 21

"What do we do with them?" one of Security's soldiers asked.

"I guess we should bury them," another answered.

"That would take forever, and what are we going to do with the cars?"

"Hell if I know."

Security left with Chairman to take care of Kaitlin's body. Caroni stayed behind to help his cookers and jacks regain their wits. The gun battle was an unfamiliar experience for them, and he could tell they needed direction. He thought it best to get them back to work. He didn't want them to leave with the deadly scene weighing on them, so they went about their routine under his watchful eye.

It was new to the security team too. They had experience winning firefights in combat, but not at home and having to dispose of their opponent's bodies. Caroni helped them too.

"The safest thing to do is to load them back into their cars, drive them somewhere where there are no witnesses, and torch them and the vehicles. That will destroy any evidence that could lead back to us."

"Where would we do that?"

"There's a place in South Norfolk, and we'd be taking them home."

"You know these guys?"

"I don't know them, but I recognize them. See those black bandanas? They're all wearing them. That's the mark of the gang that calls themselves the Heirs. They control that part of the city."

"Are there more of them?"

He shrugged his shoulders. "Probably. And that's a good reason to dump them there. It would be a powerful warning. Don't you dare mess with us. Otherwise, they may come looking for their buddies." Caroni especially didn't want that. He knew he had talked too much that night in the bar, and this was the result.

***

"The Special Agent in Charge wants us to check something out at the old Ford plant in South Norfolk." Grace briefed the team.

"Why?" Charlotte asked.

"Chesapeake PD is dealing with a gruesome crime scene out there. They have eight charred DBs in two burned-out vehicles."

"DBs?" Jace was still too new to recognize all the terminology law enforcement uses.

"Dead bodies," Grace explained.

"Is it related to our case?"

"We don't know anything yet, but eight dead people sound like the work of a gang, and we haven't seen this level of violence around here in a very long time — forever, maybe."

"Could be the new players in town," Charlotte surmised.

"The Corporation," Jace said. He understood the implication.

***

Grace approached the police officer at the yellow tape of the crime scene and flashed her credentials. The cop allowed the team to pass. She crossed paths with many cops across the region and had worked other cases with the investigator on-site.

"Hey, Bill. What do you have so far?"

"Not much, Grace. Forensics has a lot of work to do, but it looks like each vic has two bullet holes in the skull."

"Double-tap to the head. Any signs of other damage?"

"None."

"The shooters were pros."

"Had to be." Bill agreed. Grace shot a look at her teammates.

"We have a bigger problem than we thought."

When she looked at Jace, she saw the intense, faraway gaze that had become familiar to her and Charlotte. He clenched his arms across his chest as though he was fighting away the chill.

"What is it, Jace?"

"I'm not sure…" he let his voice fade. "I have to call Ike."

Chapter 22

PORTLAND — JUNE

Money is power. No matter who you are or what you do or where you live, the person with the wealth calls the shots. That's true in the most unexpected places, even in the world of social justice activists who rebel against the capitalist system they think keeps them down. The antifascists hate the rich and want their fortune redistributed to the oppressed lower class — them.

So, it was no surprise that Jaana was the unquestioned leader of all Antifa in the Portland area. Already well-respected, she wielded influence, and it's the reason Christian picked her to be Torrent's captain. Her use of the virtually unlimited cash flow from him was clever and efficient. The other faction leaders received weekly stipends from her, not for supplies, but for themselves. Most had low-paying, entry-level jobs, or no means of income at all. By putting much-needed money in their pockets, she had them in hers. They did what they were told and were happy doing it. The provision of gear like gas masks, shields, medical kits, food and water, and weapons endeared her to the street warriors, too.

They would follow her even if their leaders did not. Jaana had power and could get done whatever Christian suggested.

"You are impressive. You're a natural leader," he told her. "Can you keep the pressure up?"

"Indefinitely. We have more troops than they have cops, and we protest in shifts. Folks will take a day off to rest or deal with personal business, and others cover for them. The faction leaders coordinate, so there are enough people each night."

"What about the daytime?"

"Most of them are BLM protesters who go home when it gets dark. There's no need to bother with them. They can do what they want. The meaningful protests are the direct actions at night."

"But it's essential to take up BLM's cause."

"Oh yeah. That's important, but we have to demand more than just racial justice."

"Has anyone from the city responded to you?"

"No. We read in the news that the politicians promise to defund the police, but they won't talk to us — yet."

"Listen, there's something big brewing. Really big, and it will have national consequences. We could use your leadership."

"Like what?"

"We need you to travel to meet with other captains and recruit talent, and then fly back here to assemble your best leaders and crew for another plane ride."

"Where to?"

"DC."

Christian knew he shouldn't but couldn't help himself. Jaana was his dream girl, and he felt it five minutes into their first conversation at Peninsula Park. He had a potent attraction to intelligent and confident women, and she oozed those qualities leading her many followers into battle. That excited him. He'd be attracted to her even if she weren't the perfect image of his fantasy, but she was. Her strawberry blond hair, more blond than red, and deep ocean blue eyes bewitched him, and her shapely, fit figure was more than he could resist.

"And I'm coming with you."

Chapter 23

"So, what is it? Am I sensing things from the dead now?" Like several times before, the sudden revelation of a different channel of clairvoyance agitated Jace. As an engineer and problem solver, logic and stability were in his nature, and extrasensory perception didn't fit into that tidy psyche.

"No, I don't believe that." Ike tried to calm Jace's edginess. As a respected parapsychologist and scientist, Dr. Ike Allo had a distaste for so-called mediums who claimed to talk to the dead. Most of those charlatans gave parapsychology a reputation of trickery and scam-artistry. But the renowned clairvoyant, Edgar Cayce, provided many 'retrocognition' readings — the ability to witness past events. He suggested that clairvoyance is part of everyone's soul, and most people experience it through intuition and gut feelings. Jace's psychic abilities developed far beyond that. "I think you experienced a form of retrocognition. Your spirit perceived the lack of energy around those poor souls."

"What?"

"Spirituality envelops us and flows through our soul. You sensed the fading vitality of those eight people."

"I felt a disturbance in The Force?" Jace used humor in many situations to lighten his mood. As a Star Wars fan, his quip curled a smirk on his lips.

"Ah, yeah, you could say that. Seriously, that we're all connected spiritually is a concept that stretches across millennia. That is essentially The Force."

"So, I'm a Jedi!" The expressionless look on his mentor's face told Jace that he went one joke too far.

"Let's go over it moment by moment. When you first arrived at the old Ford plant, you felt a chill. Was it the same as when you met Bilal?"

"No. He put off a cold foreboding. When we shook hands, a sense of evil coursed through me. At the crime scene, it seemed as though I was in a gray fog, and it was chilly, like the temperature suddenly dropped."

"It sounds to me you were experiencing the absence of their life energy. There was a void. You said you had no emotion at that point."

"Right. Nobody knew they were dead. There was no grieving. There was no happiness. They were just gone, and no one realized — or cared."

"Then what?"

"I had a painful sadness for another — a ninth victim somehow connected to the eight. Someone must have been mourning her. It was strong. I wanted to cry."

"And you saw her?" Jace's light-heartedness about The Force left him as quickly as it came.

"There was the body of a woman lying on the concrete. She was pretty. Dark hair. Nicely dressed. Blood all over her chest. It relieved me she was at rest. She was at a hospital."

"And then what?"

"I saw woods."

"Like in a forest?"

"Yes. It happened there. All of them died in the woods."

***

"That was quick." Charlotte and Jace were with Grace in her office. It only took a few minutes to find the dead woman he had seen in his mind's eye.

"Kaitlin Murphy of Virginia Beach. Twenty-five years old. Shot in the chest. Someone had tried to save her. There was QuikClot on her wound. They left her outside the emergency room at Chesapeake General."

"No one saw anything?"

"No. Surveillance cameras show a black Suburban dropped the body off, but they had covered the plates and they hid their faces."

"We need to check a map to be sure, but I think Chesapeake General is a lot easier drive from the meth lab than is Princess Anne Hospital."

"That would explain the woods in Jace's vision."

Chapter 24

"Mil! How nice to hear from you!" It warmed Charlotte's heart to have Millicent on the other end of the phone line. The two had become close friends over the last year. Mil was an engineering student at the university, and Jace hired her as an intern at West Clean Energy. A chance meeting in the MacArthur Center Mall brought them together. And it made her boyfriend the center of a terror investigation.

She was an alluring young woman. Her long, flowing dark hair and emerald eyes framed by smooth, almond skin attracted the attention of Bilal, the leader of a jihadi cell in Norfolk. They were a couple the entire summer leading up to the attack that fall. When their paths crossed with Charlotte and Jace in the mall, Jace sensed Bilal's darkness, making him a person of interest to Grace and Charlotte.

"It's been a while since we talked, and I want to give you an update." The thought of being used by Bilal to perpetrate a jihadist attack in her hometown deflated Mil's effervescent and driven personality.

She quit work and college to recover.

"Octavia told me you were back in school."

"Yeah, she and Dad convinced me to get to it. It was better than moping around. My professors allowed me to finish the fall semester's material online, so I didn't lose all that time and effort."

"Good. I was a little worried about that." Charlotte had become a mentor to Mil.

"I changed majors, though. I'm in pre-law now!" Charlotte's position as a federal prosecutor inspired Mil, and her mother, Octavia, was a successful attorney and inspiration in her own right.

"Nice! So, you decided on law school. No need to keep your options open?"

"Nope. I'm going to be a lawyer. Tell Jace I'm sorry. I guess I won't be working at West Clean Energy anymore. "

"Ha! I'm sure he'd have you no matter what your major."

"Mom says he's partnered with you and Grace full time." It was more a question than a statement.

"Yes. Jace kind of semi-retired in January, and the FBI and my office hired him as a consultant."

"Are you guys doing anything interesting you can tell me about?"

"There's a new drug gang we're investigating. Seems to be a big player in the area and we didn't know it."

"Hm."

"Hm, what?"

"Oh, nothing. Just a coincidence."

"*What?*" This time Charlotte said it emphatically.

"I've noticed more drug activity on campus than usual. I assumed it was because I wasn't paying attention before. And there's one girl."

"What about her?"

"I hadn't seen her before the spring semester, and now I see her a lot. And every time I do, it seems like she's conducting shady business. She's always looking over her shoulder, and then there's a discrete exchange. I'm not saying she's a drug dealer, but that's weird to me. You reminded me of it when you mentioned your new case."

"When it looks shady, it usually is. She's still around in the summer session?"

"Yes. I was thinking I should go to the campus police."

"Yeah, do that. It may be nothing, but probably is something." That nagged at Charlotte as soon as she said that. "On second thought…" She considered what she was about to say. "Hold off on that."

"Why?"

"I'm not sure yet."

Chapter 25

"This case exploded on us. There are eight families in South Norfolk missing their sons. The community is about to combust, and it looks as though the region is on the verge of a gang war," Grace briefed the team. South Norfolk borders the southern bank of the Elizabeth River, Norfolk is on the north side, and long-time rival street gangs live just across the water from each other.

"We need to focus on the leader of the Corporation. As soon as we identify Chairman, we can start building a case to disassemble his entire organization." Charlotte understood it would be a mistake to shut down the lab and arrest the few low-level players they had identified. That would be a temporary and meaningless victory.

"Have the police determined the names of the victims?" Jace asked.

"Not officially, but eight moms reported their sons haven't come home. Chesapeake PD collected DNA from the remains and the families. Eventually, they'll make positive IDs. CPD says the missing eight are from a gang called the Heirs."

"Looks like they figured out who was flooding the market with crystal meth and went after them."

"What do we do now?" Jace was too new to investigative work, so he followed the lead of his two teammates.

"Let's review what we know." As an extrovert, Charlotte liked to think out loud and engage others in her logic. It was a highly effective tool she used in the courtroom, laying out evidence in an understandable way so the jurors tracked what she presented.

Grace started. She worked with her enough to realize Charlotte wanted to hear the facts. "Joe Harkness and James are the cookers, and their boss is Caroni — a known felon. The organization they work for calls itself the Corporation, and we think Caroni works for someone called Supply."

"They have a meth lab in Virginia Beach," Jace added, "and they only cook at night."

"From Jace's vision at the Ford plant, they probably killed the eight at the lab, and the girl died there too. That ties them all to the Corporation, so it's logical to assume the killers worked for them."

Charlotte finished the summary. "The dead girl's name is Kaitlin Murphy, 25 years old, from Virginia Beach, and she was part of, or friends with, the Corporation. Otherwise, they would not have tried to save her, and would've burned her with the rest of them."

"One thread we need to pull is Kaitlin's connection," Grace started. "If she was higher in the organization, then she may lead us to Chairman. Or maybe she was his girlfriend."

"We need to find Caroni and figure out his part in this, too," Charlotte said. "There's also a third string to follow. It's a longshot, but it's worth a tug."

Chapter 26

"I'm a bit confused," the social media mogul called Gin. There were antagonists on the list she asked him not to censor and it seemed counter to what they aimed to achieve.

"I thought you might be, Ephron, and I expected your call. You need to know why I want to amplify some voices rather than silence them."

"Several of those people are bewildering to me."

"I have no more patience for the old-school, mainstream conservatives and their law-and-order whining. Americans deserve better than that."

"I get that." Ephron understood censoring those on the right — the powerful opinions that play to the Republican base.

"And we must spread the messages of our Democrat leaders. Make sure the entire country hears their commonsense approach to taking care of the less fortunate and giving everyone a fair chance in life. And they need to know about climate change, too." Gin added the part about the environment for Ephron's sake. He was an outspoken advocate for environmental issues, and she knew that would resonate with him. Saving the Earth was not on her list of concerns and caring for the lower class didn't make it either. The last thing she wanted was a fair economic system. But more laws and regulations, environmental or otherwise, were good for her. Those things always meant someone else was being held back, regulated, and burdened. Small and mid-sized businesses, the middle class, had to endure them, not the ultra-rich. Not her.

"Of course. We need to separate and lift our candidates and policies above the crowd, but you want me to let those asshole right-wing, white supremacists get away with their crap?"

"Absolutely. Just until the election. Most Americans don't think as they do. Conservatives don't like what they say and are as sick of it as we are."

"I still don't understand."

"Bleed those disgusting people all over the internet and connect them to the President any way you can. The media are already playing that narrative every day. When the election comes, independent voters will be so tired of it they'll vote for change."

"Ah, okay. Let them hang themselves and take him with them."

"That's what will happen. I guarantee it. Let's expose middle-class America to the egregious personality of the President. They need to see him for what he is — a racist who cares only to stroke his own ego and line his pockets at the expense of those at the bottom. It'll incite more rage and protests. When the election rolls around, most people, except for hard-core Republicans, will want him out of office." An important part of her plan was to take away any leverage the Republican may have had in getting re-elected. A victory for the Democrats was paramount. It was the ultimate endgame of her grand scheme. An incredible bonus would be a liberal-leaning Congress, and she was confident she could achieve that too.

Gin didn't really think, or care, that the President was a racist. That didn't matter. His cutting of red tape and tax reductions had the economy booming. Companies big and small were creating jobs for the lower and middle classes and wealth for themselves. His policies provided a ladder for others to gain influence and power. She had to stop him.

The Democrats and their executive orders, regulations, and taxes will keep her and a tiny number of elites on a level above all others. She can control, or at the least manipulate, her elite brethren and be the most powerful among them. Her wealth would rocket to unmatched heights, giving her even more power. And the cycle would continue. But she had to have liberal tax and spend policies to hold the upper and middle classes in their place, grinding and producing, trying to gain ground, but never getting there — and creating wealth on which she could prey.

Chapter 27

It was easy enough for Grace to develop the background story for Kaitlin. She graduated from Ocean Lakes High School and was an above-average student. Not wanting to go to college, she and her best friend, Kelena Zakis, started an import/export company. Kait had friends but spent most of her time focused on the business. As far as Mr. and Mrs. Murphy knew, she had no boyfriend, and they had no contact information for Kelena. Kel had moved out of her parents' home after graduation, and they didn't keep up.

The next step following the Kaitlin lead was to talk to her best friend, but Grace had no way to get in touch with her. The logical thing to do was to catch her at the funeral. She didn't like to do that, but funerals were a great place to gather intelligence. Many times, the perpetrator of the crime that led to the death, or someone connected to them, attended the burial. The trained investigator could observe the gathering and search for anomalies in appearance or behavior that might develop another string to pull.

She also had a secret weapon. She'd still look for oddities, but she had Jace. He likely would sense a thought or a vibe from someone who may unknowingly divulge a clue or a person of interest. She waited until the end of the service to speak to Kelena but sent him to join the crowd of mourners during the observance. He made his way back to Grace, who stood in the shade of a nearby tree, away from those paying their respects.

"Almost done. All I felt was grief. It overwhelmed some and in others it was more casual, but I sensed nothing unusual," Jace reported.

"Okay. Did you find her?"

"Yes. She's sitting up front with the family. She has a long, brown ponytail and an olive complexion, and she's with a guy who seems equally upset. There was a great deal of grief from all of those seated."

"The crowd's dispersing now. Looks like she and her escort are hanging back with the parents." After a few moments, the couple left the graveside. Grace was thankful for that. She preferred to avoid Mom and Dad on the day they lay their daughter to rest.

"Pardon me." Grace spoke to Kelena. She and Jace had intercepted her and Noah before they reached their cars. "I'm sorry for your loss. Are you Kelena Zakis?"

"Yes."

"I apologize for speaking to you here, but I had no other means to contact you." Kel's cheeks were still wet with tears, and she had a cloudy gaze in her eyes, not quite understanding.

"I'm Special Agent Madson with the FBI, and this is Jace West. We're investigating Kaitlin's death and would appreciate you answering a few questions." Both Kel and Noah stood silent, not knowing what to say. They figured the police would eventually want to talk with them, but the last thing they expected was federal agents confronting them at Kait's funeral. Grace could see the confusion on their faces and may have detected a flicker of panic in Kelena's eyes as she stole a peek at the young man with her. Sometimes she just hands her card to potential witnesses and asks them to call when they're up to talking, but she was glad she didn't. Questioning people while they are at an emotional low point could reveal more than they desired.

"FBI?" Noah spoke first.

"Yes. Who are you, sir?"

"My name is Noah Vann. Kel and I are old friends of Kaitlin's. Why are you guys involved?"

"The folks at Chesapeake General found Kaitlin the same night the police discovered eight bodies at the Ford plant in South Norfolk."

"Ford plant?"

"Yes. It appears to be a gangland-type slaying. It's probably a coincidence, but we need to investigate to eliminate any connection."

"What do you want from us?" Chairman spoke for the first time with a hint of defiance replacing the grief that had consumed her a few seconds earlier. She and Security had practiced their stories for when the questioning came, and that moment had arrived. They assumed it would be for the police, but it didn't matter now.

Jace felt the change. Kel's mind transitioned from deep sorrow to hardened confidence in a flash, and then she did something that stunned him. With a slackened jaw, she turned her head and searched his eyes. *What are you doing?* He heard her question as though she spoke it out loud. She continued to peer at him in astonishment.

Startled, Jace's gut reaction was *what the hell?* When he regained his composure, he returned her stare. They stayed connected for a time that neither grasped.

What the heeeell? You got that right. Chairman directed her thoughts at him. *Am I hearing you in my head?* She was still in awe.

Yes, yes you are. Jace then broke the trance. He feared exposing himself and the investigation to Kelena. "I'll see you at the car," he said to his partner and hurried away.

Chairman retreated to her vehicle as well, leaving Grace and Noah alone.

"What was that?"

"I have no clue," Noah replied. "Maybe we should do this another time."

"Alright, Mr. Vann, please call me." Grace handed him her card.

***

"Are you okay?" Noah asked when he got into

the car.

"Um..." Kel's mind was still processing what just occurred. "Yeah, I'm fine."

"What happened?"

"I'm not sure." He sat patiently, hoping she would gather her thoughts and explain.

"He knows I'm Chairman."

"What? How could he possibly know that?"

"I'm certain of it."

"How? What went on back there?"

"There was a link between us. I heard what he was thinking, and he could hear me."

Noah involuntarily crinkled his nose in confusion. He saw the glimpse of wonderment in her eyes. "I don't understand. Nobody knows who Chairman is except you, me, Kait, and Missy. That's it."

"I told him. I must have, somehow, when I reacted to that FBI agent."

***

"What did you get?" It was obvious Jace and Kelena connected.

"She's Chairman," he said, surprising Grace. She wasn't expecting that.

"What happened? You and she kind of went offline for about ten seconds. We just stood there wondering what was going on."

"I've never experienced that."

"You had an 'I've got to see Ike' moment."

"That's for sure. She and I coupled telepathically — two-way telepathic communication."

"Tell me more."

"She was in deep mourning before you introduced us. When she realized we were investigating Kaitlin's death, she flipped a switch. She was ready to talk. They had rehearsed what they would say. Chairman rang in my head like an alarm."

"What do you mean?"

"It was just an awareness. She didn't consciously think it. But the impression, Chairman, screamed at me. It was her."

"What was that long gaze?"

"She talked to me first. I don't know what she sensed from me, but she suddenly looked at me and said, 'What are you doing?' Caught me by surprise. I thought to myself, 'What the hell?' and she repeated it back to me. Then she asked if she was hearing me in her head. I told her yes, she was, and that's when I took off. I didn't want her to read anything else from me."

"It surprised her as much as it did you."

"Yes, it did. There's no doubt in my mind she had no idea she has the gift."

Chapter 28

"**T**hat has me freaked out, Noah. I don't understand what that was." Kelena, Noah, and the last of the friends from the Ocean Lakes foursome, Missy, also known as Distro, met after the funeral to plot their next moves. She had been told the details of the gunfight and cleanup, and the confrontation with the FBI. The three of them were the remaining senior leadership of the Corporation, and they had decisions to make.

"Kel, I don't know how to say this, so I'll be straight," Missy said, "are you sure you didn't imagine it? I mean, with everything that happened, and you were at the funeral in a weird frame of mind..."

"No, Missy, I didn't imagine it. I can't explain it, but Noah saw it. There was a connection and then the guy broke it off and ran away."

"It was real," he confirmed.

"So, what do we do?" Distro asked with the intent to make a point. "The *first* thing we do, immediately, is shut down the lab. If those bangers found it, the FBI will — or more guys wanting to kill us. Shut it down and find somewhere else."

Security agreed, "Absolutely. I have an idea for a new lab that could be up and running in a day or two. Distro wouldn't miss a beat."

"And we have to get someone to replace Supply," Distro said. She and Security glanced at Chairman, expecting her to take control and make decisions as she normally would. Kel always had answers ready by the time her team looked to her. But she was quiet, with a distant, disengaged look on her face. Her cohorts waited.

"I shot a kid in the head. His brains splattered on the ground at my feet. Kaitlin's dead. I didn't imagine *that* either," Kel said, emphasizing 'that' as a dig at Missy. Her friends couldn't find the words to respond, so they didn't. She was still Kel and hadn't transitioned to Chairman.

After an uncomfortable silence, Security ended the meeting. "I'll dismantle the lab and do it tonight. We'll grab what we need to set up somewhere else and we'll meet again tomorrow."

"I can't talk to him, Noah. If I talk to him, he'll find out everything."

"Let's discuss it later. The FBI expects us to call them back."

"We have to close the business. The whole thing," Kel said. "They're on to us."

Chapter 29

J aana traveled to DC at the request of Christian and was thrilled he was with her. She didn't bother to ask who or what provided the money. It delighted her someone was finally listening to her movement's message and had joined the fight. The organization arranged for the street captains from most of the major metropolitan areas to converge on Washington to meet face-to-face. They planned a march on the White House in October to sway the November election to the progressive candidates. The plan included rallying support from Antifa factions from across the country. The hope was thousands of supporters would gather in the streets of the nation's capital. The captains were to recruit rioters from not only their hometowns but from cities within easy traveling distance to DC.

Chen's intermediaries provided him with several layers of protection from the law and any other backlash. That protected Gin too. To maintain that security, his middlemen didn't know each other, and they weren't supposed to. But Christian didn't know Chen and was unaware he was his middleman. While he was in town, he thought it would be professional of him to check in with his Washington counterpart. He took direction from a man on the board of directors of the magazine he wrote for and wondered if the DC guy worked for the same person. He stepped into the street captain meeting and asked a leader to point to their boss. She led him to a sturdy-looking dude wearing black jeans and a black t-shirt with its sleeves cut out, baring arms that were sculpted by hours in the weight room. The muscleman had wildly unkempt hair and just as messy a beard. Christian introduced himself as the organizer from Portland.

"Portland? You tap that pretty thing yet? She grabbed my eye right away. Not like those other homely weirdos."

"Ah, we're together, yes." That caught Christian off-guard. He was unsure what to make of Mr. Macho and wasn't used to talking about women that way.

"Okay. I'll leave her alone then, but I was looking forward to it. She's fine, brother." Christian was at a loss for words, wondering how he should respond when Macho continued to talk. "What's your story?"

"My story? I'm a writer for a magazine. How about you?"

"I'm supposed to be a biker fed up with it all. That's why the hair and beard. Can't wait to get a shave and a haircut."

Supposed to be? Christian eyes squinted and his forehead wrinkled in confusion. He wanted to look at the guy and ask him an insistent, 'what?' but forced himself to turn the other way. Making small talk, he asked, "So, do they give you a budget?"

"Oh, yeah. I give it to the captains, and they buy whatever they want. I pocket drinking money, of course."

"Yep," Christian said casually, trying not to appear as out of place as he felt. "Is everything on track for October 1st?"

"Definitely. My people are ready *now*. I'll have those Antifa assholes hyped on speed and at max crazy right at 9:00 like they told me."

Assholes? Crazy? 9:00? Christian realized his employer had something else planned, and he was not in the loop. The entire conversation was not what he expected. Macho kept talking.

"That must be when it'll happen."

"Nine o'clock?" Christian longed to ask him 'what will happen?' but sensed that would be the wrong thing to say.

"Yeah. They want a massive distraction right at 9:00. I don't know what they're going to do, but they need all cops focused on the White House. We'll get their attention." Macho said with a broad, knowing smile.

"Well, if you need us to do anything, just ask," Christian attempted to make an exit from the uncomfortable and cryptic conversation.

"As long as you mention it, I hear there's a cheap source of high-quality ice in Norfolk and plenty of it. Do you mind asking around while you're there and make a buy for me? We need to feed it to the crazies."

"Sure. Okay." Christian felt trapped. He couldn't say no at that point. "How do I get in touch with you?"

Christian's mood did not match Jaana's brio when they got back to their hotel room. The significance of what the street captains had planned the previous 12 hours consumed her, and she found it difficult to contain her excitement. That roused Christian, but his conversation with Mr. Macho left him unsettled. There was more going on than he and Jaana understood, and it bothered him.

It was the end of a long day, and both were famished. She didn't want to stray far from the hotel, so they ate a quick dinner in the casual restaurant downstairs. Jaana waited impatiently for Christian to pay the check and then took his hand and almost dragged him back to their room.

He needed to tell her the confusing things Macho said, but she felt too good for him to spoil it. It could wait. Maybe he'd save it for the flight home. He'd explain the request for meth before they left for Richmond the next day.

***

Jaana swelled with self-importance and pride that they had called her to help lead the revolution for which she and her friends ached. The riot organizers assigned her to stoke the antifascist passion in Richmond, just two hours south of DC, and then head to Norfolk. They needed as many bodies in the capital as they could muster. The organization had not identified a street captain, but it was easy to find who to contact. She noticed Richmond Antifa's calls to action online and it was a matter of getting in touch with the originators of the events. She met with three of Antifa Richmond's leaders in a private corner of the loft of their favorite coffee shop. Christian strolled the streets of downtown, letting her do her thing. He didn't want to appear to usurp her responsibilities. She wouldn't appreciate that.

"Jaana, first let me say that we've watched what you're doing in Portland and we're envious. It's very cool to meet you." The Richmond faction leader and his friends were excited to see her in their city and curious why she was there.

"You're doing a fantastic job here, too. But I can offer you help if you want it."

"What kind of help?"

"Direct action is expensive to stage. We struggled at first, but I found a source of funding in Portland that helps me focus on our protests and buy what we need to keep us going. Are you interested in something like that?"

"Absolutely. Tell us more."

"I provide food and water to our protesters every night, supply the troops with medical aid and protective gear, and other essentials."

"Such as?"

"Cocktails, batons, bats, hammers, mortars,

you name it."

"Guns?"

"I can get them, but I won't. We will not win a shooting war with the cops, and we'll lose support from the public if we kill people. It's best not to bring them to a protest." The faction leader looked at his cohorts. They were trying not to react, but the corners of the mouths gave away their grins.

"So, what's the catch?"

"We have an incredible opportunity to take control of this country from the capitalist white nationalists." Jaana lowered her voice even though there was no one in earshot, grabbing her hosts' attention if she didn't have it already. "The history books will mark October 1st as the date we transformed America. The people see our unrest on TV every night and want change. We are organizing an aggressive, game-changing march on the White House. We'll send the message to the entire nation that we're done with the good ole boys in the swamp. It'll be a month before the election, and the Republicans won't be able to recover from the momentum we create for the Democrats. The Dems will win the Presidency and Congress too, and we'll have made it happen."

"But Jaana, Democrats are just as bad. They had the House, the Senate, *and* the Presidency before, and did nothing for our cause. They're swamp people too."

"Most of them are, but there are finally enough antifascist progressives in the House to influence national policy. It'll be the change we've been fighting for." Jaana's passion effused hope and confidence and inspired the three boys in front of her.

"No need to convince us to march on Washington. We're in."

"Good. I have cash for you to start organizing. Call me if you need more and I'll wire it to you. We need all the protesters you can get. I'll pay for busses, food, water. You use the money I give you to buy what you want to support the effort. And I ask for two more favors."

"Whatever you want."

"I need help to rally support from the Norfolk area."

"There's no organization and aren't many anti-fascists there, but we'll make a call. And?"

"We need a good supply of methamphetamine to keep our people going throughout the day and night. Know where we can get it?"

"Actually, you're headed to the right place."

Chapter 30

"Caroni is not one of us." Security reported to Kel, even though she had mentally checked out of running the Corporation. He and Distro worked together and had things well enough in hand, but wanted to keep her updated, hoping she'd snap out of her malaise.

"There was no other choice. We weren't pre-pared for what happened. I *had* to put him in charge of supply."

"He doesn't know our names, does he?" The killings, losing Kait, the FBI and the guy who read her thoughts, and now letting Caroni into the inner circle left Kelena feeling especially vulnerable.

"No. We keep him at arm's length, and I oversee everything he does."

"I told you we should shut down the entire op-eration before it's too late." She wanted to go some-where far away and try to forget the deaths she caused — Kaitlin, the kid, those gangbangers. And she stopped lying to herself. Dope ruins lives.

"That would be dangerous. People depend on us. We need to support them until we figure something out. Besides, I can't do anything else. The only skill I have is soldiering. Missy is in the same boat. This is all she's ever done, and she has no idea what to do if we suddenly stopped."

Kel didn't respond. She was lost in her mind and couldn't find her way. Security had planned to give her the latest news on the meth lab, but he could tell she didn't want to talk, or even care, about it.

He was proud of his brainchild and thought it was much more secure than the shack in the woods. It surprised him they didn't think of it earlier. The idea struck him when he was at Joe the Cooker's house. Joe no longer earned his living as an auto mechanic, but he still loved to tinker with cars. Security took an interest in the lab's employees after what happened. Chairman would have if she weren't fighting depression. Joe invited him to his property to check out his latest project. He found a ten-year-old motor coach that needed a lot of attention. He made it safe to drive, but the interior was in rough shape, so he tore it all out for a complete renovation. As soon as Security saw the empty inside, that TV show about a meth supplier who cooked in an RV hit him in the face. He bought the rig and had Joe outfit it as a lab.

Now the cookers could drive to any abandoned or remote place in the region and make the night's batch of crystal. The next night they might be 30 miles away cooking another order. It was a perfect setup. *Chairman will love it when she comes around.*

***

"How long are we going to let them stiff-arm us?" Grace was eager to question Kelena Zakis. What happened with Kelena and Jace intrigued her, and she wanted to get the two in the same room.

"We found where she lives and we're monitoring the house. If they don't call soon, we'll knock on the door. She hasn't left home since the funeral," Charlotte reminded her.

"Why give her time to regain her composure?"

"Jace said she was ready with a story, anyway. And I'm thinking he'll get a better read once her head clears."

Chapter 31

T he Richmond connection to the Corporation's supply of methamphetamine was a tenuous one, as those kinds of illicit relationships are. The guy who sells on Richmond campuses knew the dealer who does the same on those in Norfolk, and he bought his cache of the inexpensive crystal from her. His Antifa contacts promised they would make it worth his while if he introduced their friend from Portland to his provider, so he drove the pretty girl 90 minutes southeast to coastal Virginia. On a warm and cloudy July day, they met his source on campus, and after first-name introductions, Jaana got straight to the point.

"I'm going to need a large amount of meth coming up in October."

"How much do you want?"

"I'm not sure," Jaana wasn't into drugs and didn't know what a dose was and how many to buy. "How much can you sell me?"

"That is an excellent question. I'll have to find out. The boss gives me a certain stash to sell every week and it goes quick, even during the summer when there are fewer students around. But they always give me more when I need it, so I'm guessing they'll be able to help you."

"How do we find out?"

"Let me call right now. Can you wait? He may want to talk with you."

"Sure. I have nowhere to be." Jaana was enjoying the warmth of July in Virginia and the lazy afternoon in the shade. "I have a flight out tomorrow, so we just need to be in Richmond tonight." *And Christian is waiting for me.*

For security, the dealer only knew her manager, and he only dealt with the head of distribution. So, when Distro called Caroni, he avoided the call chain and handled the inquiry himself. After 30 minutes, he located the girl and her guests on the campus mall. He was a short drive away, but they had to identify themselves using code words provided by Distro. Once they found each other, he introduced himself as Supply, and Jaana explained her needs.

"I'm glad you asked early. We can cook extra batches and have it for you in a week, but getting the raw material is a problem. Since you're asking in advance, we'll get what we need and make enough for you."

Methamphetamine is so easy to produce that thousands of do-it-yourself cookers followed the simple recipe developed by an amateur chemist in the early 1990s. The number of clandestine labs boomed, and the abuse of the drug became an epidemic. In its War on Drugs, the U.S. Government passed a law that made it much more difficult to get the key ingredient needed by a cooker — cold medicines containing the decongestant pseudoephedrine. With the primary component effectively banned, making large quantities of homemade meth was almost impossible, and suppliers turned to illegal imports from Mexico to satiate their customers' appetites. But the smart, young leaders of the Corporation found a way around the ban. With a little research on the internet, they discovered the compound comes from the Ephedra plant, also called Ma Huang, used in Chinese medicine for centuries. The Corporation's production process included extracting the pseudoephedrine from its raw source — a plant that grows in dry, hot climates, including the southwestern United States, and secretly shipped to Virginia Beach.

If Supply could obtain the Ephedra he needed, making as much crystal as he wanted was not a problem.

"How do we complete the transaction?" Jaana asked.

"Tell me the date you expect to pick the stuff up and my guys will have it ready. Come back to Norfolk, call me when you arrive, and we'll meet. You give me the cash, and I deliver the meth. It'll weigh a pound and be about 2,000 doses for $50,000. That's a bargain, especially individually packaged."

"That sounds like a plan. See you in September." Jaana held out her hand to seal the deal, and Caroni gladly accepted. *This will impress Security,* he thought to himself with satisfaction. *Maybe he'll trust me now.*

Jaana left Christian in Richmond and was eager to get back to him. As soon as they shook hands, she turned to her ride, and with a gleam in her eye urged, "Let's hit the road." She had one more night with him and wanted to make the most of it.

***

"What do you suppose that was?" Grace casually asked Millicent without turning towards her. The two sat on opposite ends of a bench, well outside earshot of Supply's meeting with Jaana. Charlotte had a hunch that they should follow up on Mil's suspicion of someone selling drugs on campus. Grace wore a tee and shorts, exposing her honey skin to the warmth of summer, and a university ball cap over her dark, shoulder-length hair. She topped off her student look with her favorite Ray-Bans and carried her service weapon in her bag. She met Mil on the mall, and they were hanging out in the shade near where the suspicious exchanges happen. As they watched, a couple approached the suspected dealer-girl, and they all fist-bumped. Dealer-Girl soon had a phone to her ear, and then they waited. An older man arrived, greeted the three, and after a brief conversation, he shook hands with the young woman and left.

"I didn't see her give anyone anything," Mil offered.

"It looked as though it was an introduction to me. Like the start of a bigger arrangement."

"Definitely seemed fishy to me, too."

"I think you're on to something, Mil."

Chapter 32

G race and Millicent stayed on the bench and watched the meeting end. The older man departed, and a few seconds later, the young couple left, leaving Dealer-Girl alone to enjoy the lazy July afternoon. As they talked about what they witnessed, Grace reached in her bag and removed her phone, touching Charlotte's name on her favorites list. Neither expected anything significant to come from the casual surveillance, so when her smartphone beeped, it surprised Charlotte to see Grace calling.

"Hey," she answered with curiosity rather than a greeting. "What's up?"

"Mil is on to something here."

"Did you watch a buy go down?"

"There was no exchange. We didn't observe a simple, little deal. But it was suspicious, as though a bigger, handshake arrangement took place."

"Hm. That's more than we expected, but what we were hoping."

"We were watching the person Mil identified as the suspected seller — Dealer-Girl. A young couple approached her. The woman was attractive and appeared more mature than the raggedy college boy she was with. It seemed to me they were not together. He was just introducing her to his supplier. Dealer-Girl made a phone call and an older guy arrived. He talked with the pretty woman, they shook hands, and then they all hurried away, leaving our original target to herself. Looked to be an intro and an agreement — definitely suspicious."

"What's the next move?"

"My bet is the payoff is between Pretty Woman and Slick."

"Haha," Charlotte chuckled. "Slick?"

"Yeah, he just looks like a 'Slick' to me. Anyway, if we can identify Pretty Woman and Slick, and surveil them, that should lead to bigger things. We'll hold off on the dealer, but Mil should keep an eye on her, and if she sees either one of our new suspects, she calls us right away."

"We went into this hoping to get a break in the new drug gang investigation, so we need to figure out if there are ties between what you found today and the Corporation.

Chapter 33

C hristian hoped to find an opportunity to tell Jaana about his conversation with Mr. Macho. That night at the hotel was not a good time. Her eyes were bright, and she barely contained her excitement for her role in the planned DC action. She thought of herself as a leader in a much-needed revolution, and he couldn't bring himself to spoil her mood. The plane ride back home from Richmond seemed to be the best option. It was a long trip to Portland. There would be plenty of time for the conversation, and after a couple of days, she had come down from her high. When they boarded their connecting flight in Charlotte, North Carolina, he scoped the situation in the cabin. Their seats were next to each other and few people sat close by. With the muffled jet noise, they would have the privacy to talk. After thirty minutes in the air, she surprised him.

"What did you and Zo chat about?"

"Zo?"

"The organizer for the DC street captains." Jaana was a perceptive person. It was a quality that helped her become an excellent leader, and she knew something had been on Christian's mind since that day.

"So, that's his name. He didn't introduce himself, and I labeled him Mr. Macho."

"Ha, he certainly acted that way. So, what did Machoman say to you, besides using us to get him meth?"

"I've wanted to tell you but didn't want to bother you with it."

"What do you mean?"

"He said some strange things that made it obvious to me there is more going on than we know."

"What?"

"He was very… rough around the edges." Christian tried to be civil. "First, he told me he intended to have you that night and called the rest of the women 'homely weirdos.'"

"Oh, really?" Jaana raised her eyebrows in annoyance with a hint of amusement.

"I told him we were together, and he backed off, but to me it was strange he referred to the others as weirdos. And later all of you were 'Antifa assholes.'"

"What the…?"

"Then he asked me what my story was. At first, I figured it was just an unusual way to ask me what I do for a living, so I mentioned I was a journalist. He told me he was *supposed* to be a biker, and he couldn't wait for a haircut and a shave." Jaana's face went from confused to a chilly stare into Christian's eyes.

"That sounds as though he's posing. Like he doesn't support the cause and doesn't take us seriously. He's playing a role, and we're his fools."

"I agree. And he must have thought I was a poser too, just hired to do a job. The peculiar and worrisome thing is he said *they* ordered him to have you all in a frenzy outside the White House at 9:00 p.m. They are planning something for 9:00 and they need a big distraction, so the cops focus on the protest. That's why he wants the meth. He's going feed it to the rioters to hype them up."

"What does all that mean?" Jaana squinted her eyes and stared into space, considering the question she just asked. "Maybe it'll be a good thing. Maybe it's for the cause and they need to keep it a secret to pull it off."

Christian said nothing. His intuition told him something different.

Chapter 34

G in Vandermire smiled as she sat at her over-sized desk made of African Blackwood with Purple Heartwood inlay. Artisans handcrafted the piece with the rich black and purple tones to suit her position in society. Gazing across San Francisco Bay from the Transamerica Pyramid, she had reached the zenith that no matter what happened in the world, her fortune would grow. She could do no wrong.

But why stop? She was too young to do nothing but admire the view from her office. History was there, too easy for the taking. The most influential person on the planet would not be a computer salesman, or an electronic department store owner, or a hacker who stumbled into a popular social app. Those were the type of boys she ran circles around in high school and college. It wouldn't be some sheik who inherited sand with oil beneath it or a corrupt politician whose only accomplishment was to steal from his own people. The prize should go to whoever grabbed it, and that would be her.

Chen was her trusted right hand. He knew

how to get things done without Gin having to soil her hands. He had to be 100% loyal to her, so she made him rich beyond his dreams and promised to double it after he completed Torrent. Any amount of money with only two commas was pocket change for her and well spent on her man. She met him on a business trip to China. He held a senior position in the Ministry of National Defense, and the Deputy Minister tasked him to help her negotiate business arrangements with their defense companies. When the Chinese assigned him to their consulate in San Francisco, he renewed his friendship with Gin and used her influence to build relationships in the U.S. She did the same to strengthen hers in China, and their arrangement grew to be mutually beneficial. She was more than willing to sponsor him when he 'retired' and applied for his green card.

"Phase two is on-point. Your social media friends are controlling the narrative. They essentially muted popular conservatives," Chen said.

"Yes, and they're happy to do it. I'm not sure any of them understand, or care, that they can influence who the voters elect President. Their self-righteousness blinds them."

"And the dependable liberals are right on cue. Their rhetoric is stoking the fires of unrest. The riots are still going in most cities."

"Oh yes," Gin said with a wide smile, "the *injustice* of it all..." She let her sarcasm linger before asking, "Are there any sustainability issues with phase one?"

"The effort in Detroit is exhausted. The riots have destroyed most of the low-income areas. Police have the central business district locked down. We are trying to steer the street captains to move to the suburbs now."

"That would stir things up. That's perfect. Any other problem areas?"

"Portland and Seattle are strong, of course. Civil action is a way of life for them. Most other cities have slowed but not stopped. There are at least weekly protests and riots."

"That is amazing to me. It's been close to four months. Frankly, we've already accomplished the phase-one objectives. The unrest physically scarred major Democrat voting blocks and sent ripples of sympathy and anger across the country. Who had this stroke of genius? Oh wait, it was me." Chen couldn't help the ear-to-ear smile that spread over his face in amusement at Gin's revelry in her own prowess.

"Yes, your wisdom is an inspiration, ma'am." He caressed her ego, pleased with his work and that of his intermediaries that made it happen.

"Tell me about phase three. Are we on track?"

"We are far into the planning and getting resources in place. There will be a slowdown of activity in Washington as the time grows close. We want to let the hard feelings simmer, so when October 1st arrives, the natives are restless and ready to explode. Experienced rioters from across the country will be sent to DC, so Antifa in those cities may ease their riots leading up to the big event."

"How many people do you expect to be there?"

"We arranged for six to eight hundred, but a social media campaign in September should incite widespread support. As soon as the antifascists and antigovernment blocs realize the march against the White House coincides with the President's thank-you celebration with two thousand of his closest friends on the South Lawn, the crowd is bound to be a sight to behold."

"No doubt, Chen."

"Have you invited the Speaker to dinner, yet?"

"I mentioned I plan to be in town October 1st, and that I'd like to see her. She joked we could enjoy watching the protests while we dine, so I'll have no trouble arranging a sit-down with her and a wealthy Democrat donor or two." Chen marveled at the boldness and influence she has with powerful people in Washington. All politicians are the same, he mused, no matter what country they rule. One needs only large sums of money to get what one wants.

"Are you ready for phase four?"

"Yes. All I lack are your instructions."

"How many days before the event do you need them?"

"Give me two weeks to build the plan with the operators so they can understand the mission parameters and develop their tactics."

"I've asked before, but humor me. Do you trust them implicitly?"

"Absolutely." Chen had contacts as deep as Gin's pockets and could arrange any covert action anywhere. It was child's play.

His revelry matched hers, but for a different reason. After November, the annals of the Ministry of State Security should display his name prominently. Never has The People's Republic of China decided the election of the President of the United States, and he will have done it single-handedly. There would be no need for the young computer hackers trying to rig the results over the internet. Chen did it the old-fashioned way — with human-sourced espionage.

Under previous American administrations, China's ambition to replace the U.S. as the world's only superpower went unfettered. China stole American technology from its universities and industry at will. It built its fleet of submarines and surface ships to rival that of any nation. It constructed and militarized artificial islands in the middle of the South China Sea to expand its territorial waters, control a significant percentage of the global shipping trade, and hoard the vast deposits of oil and natural gas beneath the seafloor. And its state-subsidized industries flooded markets with their less expensive products, making it difficult for unsubsidized western companies to compete.

The conservative President attempting reelection stood up to the behemoth People's Republic with measures to force fair trade; curb industrial espionage and keep the South China Sea open to free passage. Soon, because of Chen, that would change. Under the guise of a global economy and international cooperation, the liberals pledged to reverse those policies that protect U.S. interests. And China's push to become a superpower too strong to counter will once again go unchecked. No one needed to know about the secret political deals and growing personal bank accounts on both sides.

Chen had something else planned that even Gin was not aware of. Thanks to the prowess of Chinese espionage, he had an asset in Jersey City, New Jersey willing to spring an unwelcome surprise.

Chapter 35

It was only ten months, but it seemed as though it had been years. Mohammad brought his jihad to American soil and struck against the Great Satan in the heart of its murderous navy, and then fled to Jersey City. With a large Muslim population that blended into the melting pot that was the New York metropolitan area, it was the perfect place to hide. The original plan was to wait until the manhunt subsided and then escape to his native Saudi Arabia, but he realized his hideout presented a unique opportunity. Instead of recruiting another jihadi cell on the Arabian Peninsula and covertly entering the United States, he could do it in New Jersey. The number of immigrant Arabs and disenfranchised Americans provided a goldmine of candidates.

He was already mentoring young men and identified those who he thought may join the cause. These differed from the pious brothers in his home country. They were not willing to martyr themselves in the name of Allah, but they would strike at America, and that was important. Money, not the holy war, motivated them, but they would do his

134

bidding, and that had to be enough. Finances were not a problem for him. A rich man from a wealthy family, he kept bank accounts in the Cayman Islands that could support him for a long time.

Mohammad was in the early stages of planning his next strike, choosing his target, when he heard a knock on his apartment door. Prepared for the unlikely moment when American operators came for him, he stuck his handgun in his belt, picked up the newspaper, and made his way to the entrance. Keeping his back to the wall, he held the paper up to the eyepiece of the peephole. The sudden elimination of light from inside the apartment would signal an enemy their victim was peering through the spyglass, and it would be a good time to send a bullet into his eye. But with no shot fired, he looked through the aperture and saw an Asian woman standing away from his stoop, so he cautiously opened the door.

"Hello Mohammad," the woman greeted him as she stood in a non-threatening way a safe distance from him. At six feet five inches, he towered over her by more than a foot, and he glanced past her, searching for threats. "I am alone and *not* from the American authorities." As a Wahhabi, his traditional interpretation of the Quran did not recognize women having positions of authority, but he was in the land of infidels. He thought her well-educated as she spoke with refined English and dressed conservatively in professional attire. He said nothing, so she continued. "I have a business proposition to discuss with you. May I come in?"

"I prefer you don't. It would be improper."

"The offer must be in private." Mohammad studied the woman and then opened the door wide enough for her to enter. He allowed her to lead the way, not to be a gentleman but so he did not have to turn his back to the stranger.

"What do you want?"

"My organization understands you have plans on which the American government might not look favorably." Once again, he was silent. "We support your endeavor and offer help." Mohammad's mind raced, wondering who betrayed him. No one knew of his scheme except two of his most trusted men he recruited soon after he arrived in New Jersey.

"Why should I trust you?"

"Your mistrust is understandable, but I assure you we have similar objectives. You want to kill Americans, and we'd like to shoot certain Americans on a given date and time." The woman tired of the dance and turned to blunt discussion. "We intend to supply the rifles you need and require you to dress in the garb we provide. Escape is imperative, so you will be free to strike again as you please. We will pay you handsomely, and we both get what we desire."

"I do not need money."

"The payment can be in whatever currency you choose. Cash. Weapons. Intelligence. Your choice. This offer is obviously suspicious to you. Take time to deliberate, and I'll contact you in a few days."

It angered Mohammad someone talked to this

woman about his plans, but the possibilities a legitimate relationship might bring excited him. *Allah may have sent this visitor to me*, he considered, and he began to scheme.

Chapter 36

C harlotte and Grace ran out of patience. Kelena Zakis and her friend Noah Vann, their persons of interest, didn't call to arrange interviews, and they tired of waiting. They had the addresses of both and watched their homes. Noah seemed busy, coming and going, and was always alone. Twenty-four/seven surveillance was impractical, but the best they could tell, Kelena never left her house, so they started with her.

Charlotte let Grace handle the fieldwork. That's what a special agent does, and she was good at it. When Jace joined the team, standard procedure had him go with her. They never knew when his unique talent might prove useful. On the Kelena interview, however, Charlotte insisted on going. She was more than a little annoyed that Zakis had ignored them for so long and wanted to see the interaction between her and Jace, anyway.

Two months passed since the funeral and Kelena could not shake the depression that beset her. She wallowed in mourning for Kaitlin and for the teenager whose life she cut short. Reality wasn't supposed to be that way. She never dreamed people would die, let alone her best friend and some kid. She pulled the trigger to put a bullet in his head and end his existence, and she may as well have pulled the trigger that did the same for Kait. Kelena dragged Kaitlin into the business and got them into that situation, and it was her fault.

Kel just wanted to call the FBI and tell them it was her. She did it and deserved punishment. More than once, the phone was in her hand with Agent Madson's card in the other, but she couldn't betray her friends that way. She sucked them into this mess, and then she was going to turn them in to the authorities? No. She wouldn't do that. The best plan was to disappear. There was enough money to last a lifetime, especially somewhere like Thailand, where the cost of living a comfortable life is easy on the bank account. She'd have to live with herself and what she'd done, and that would have to be her penance.

Kelena was in bed when she jerked awake. She sat straight up and peered around her bedroom, allowing the confusion to filter away until she realized where she was. *Was that a dream? Is this real?* An urge to run, to jump in the car and drive far from where she was, nagged her. Someone was coming for her. She sensed it. Kel quietly stepped through the house, checking the locks on the doors and windows, and stopping to listen breathlessly for sounds of an intruder. Everything looked in order, and the knot in her stomach eased a bit. Tourists in floppy hats and swimsuits, carrying beach chairs and beach bags, walked by her front window, and she followed them with her eyes. Once more, she slunk to the French doors that led to her back deck and for the first time noticed the beachgoers playing in the ocean under bright blue skies painted with white wisps. It was a normal, hot August day in Virginia Beach. The scene calmed her and the anxiety dissipated, but a sense of apprehension that something was about to happen hung with her.

After a shower to wash away the last of her tension, Kelena sat sipping coffee, watching a family's vacation through the kitchen windows, dreaming she was the little girl building a sandcastle with her daddy. When the doorbell rang, her gut clenched, sending a sickness to her throat. Frozen in her chair, the bell sounded again, followed by a knock.

"Kelena. It's Special Agent Madson." The muffled voice drifted from the front of the house. Trepidation coursed through her body, and then, strangely, a wave of relief, as though she was to be freed of her burden. The release of anxiety was palpable, and it enveloped Jace as soon as she opened the door. She looked past his partners and straight into his eyes. *I'm glad you're here.*

Charlotte and Grace noticed the connection right away and said nothing. That was why he was with them.

You're feeling better.

I am.

Can we come in?

"Please join me. I was just enjoying the view of the beach." Kel led them to the informal family room overlooking the sand and ocean, offered them coffee, and introduced herself to Charlotte. *She's your wife.* Once again, Kelena locked eyes with Jace.

Yes.

She's pretty.

Thanks for saying.

I don't understand this. What's happening to me?

You are a telepath like I am.

I've never experienced this.

My mentor said you must have repressed your clairvoyance subconsciously, but my channel to you was so strong that it triggered you. He called Ike soon after the incident at the funeral.

Please tell me more.

Let's get through this interview, and then we'll talk. Kel broke contact and turned to the FBI agent.

"Kelena, I hope you're feeling better. We expected you to get back to us sooner," Grace started.

"Yes, thank you." *I didn't want to speak with you. I hear you.*

I understand.

"Can you think of a reason anyone would hurt Kaitlin?"

Jace sensed deep sorrow, and he fought back the urge to cry. Ike explained to him he was an empath as well as telepath. Many people have empathy, but some, like Jace, experience the physical response that others have to their emotions.

"No," Kel choked as tears wet her eyes. *It was my fault.*

"Do you know where she was that night?"

"No." *It's my fault.* Teardrops streamed down her cheeks. Jace quickly wiped his face. He couldn't hold it.

"Is there anything that might connect Kaitlin to the deaths of those eight gang members?" Jace had the urge to throw up right before Kelena rushed to the kitchen sink and vomited coffee — the only thing in her stomach that morning. He raced to the French doors and onto the deck. He held his breakfast but wondered what his team would think. With the connection broken by the intense physical reaction to the distress, he remained on the deck.

Charlotte poured her a glass of water and offered her a paper towel, but Kel was sobbing over the sink, in no shape to answer more questions. Nearly carrying her, Charlotte helped Kelena to the closest chair and stayed with her while Grace walked outside, more to give Kel space than to check on Jace. She said nothing. This happened before and he needed time to recover. Hader and Owais, two boys recruited by Mohammad to martyr themselves in a terror attack, affected him the same way. They were afraid and didn't want to do it. Jace felt that and wanted to help them.

Charlotte took several minutes to console Kelena and then walked onto the deck with her teammates.

"She's done. Asked us to leave."

"Yeah," Grace sighed with an ache in her heart. She knew that kind of pain she just witnessed.

Chapter 37

The drive from Kelena's oceanfront home in the Virginia Beach resort area to Charlotte's office in downtown Norfolk took 40 minutes. The team didn't wait to get there to discuss her interview.

"Ms. Zakis lives in an expensive place," Grace started. "I don't know how much money a young woman earns in the import/export business, but that's more house than an FBI special agent can afford."

"Yeah, it makes you wonder," Charlotte agreed. As a prosecutor of gang leaders, she was familiar with the large, luxurious homes they buy with drug money.

"The only thing I got from that interview is that she is in a lot of grief. That wasn't an act."

"Jace, what did you get? You two had an obvious connection."

"She lied. She didn't say much, other than it's all her fault. Kelena answered 'no' to the questions, but inside she felt guilty and responsible for Kaitlin's death. She knows what happened, but she's not saying."

"I've never seen you link that way with anyone before. Both of you seemed to be in a trance," Charlotte said, leading Jace to continue.

"I've experienced nothing like it, except with her at the funeral and today at the house. Ike said she is a telepath who had repressed her abilities, but when I sensed her thoughts at the cemetery, it opened a strong channel between us."

"What were you two doing in those long pauses?"

"Communicating. Talking, but in our minds. That was a strange and awesome experience."

"What did she say?"

"When we first arrived, she was glad we were there, and it seemed like she was expecting us. She didn't call Grace because she feared seeing me. But she was relieved we called on her. When you asked the questions about Kaitlin, a powerful wave of grief washed over her. The only thing I heard was, 'It's my fault,' and I sensed she wanted to talk but she couldn't."

"Sounds as though she knows what happened but is protecting herself, or someone else."

"Or both," Charlotte said. The conversation paused until she asked Jace another question. "What more did she say?"

"Kelena knew you were my wife. She didn't understand how we were communicating. I explained we're both telepathic, and she asked me to tell her more. She is lost in more ways than one, and

I need to talk to her — alone.

"Okay, but let's see Noah Vann first." Charlotte thought it would be smart to get a read on him before getting back to Kelena.

Chapter 38

T he Asian woman called Mohammad three days later. By then, he had formulated his plan.

"Will you collaborate with us?" she asked.

"Tell the leader of your organization that I intend to talk only to him." He didn't expect her to meet his demand, but he wanted to project strength and not to appear eager.

"That's not possible, but I speak for her. My name is Hu." The woman added the 'her' part to play mind games with him. She knew that would not sit well. Her lips pressed together, suppressing the grin that was trying to form. He had not considered that her superior might be a female, and it caught him off-guard. Hu acted for Chen, but the terrorist would not be told that.

"We should talk in person." Mohammad proceeded with his scheme.

"Yes, let's do that."

"Meet me at the Tahliya Café. It is near my apartment."

"The place is familiar to me. Thirty minutes?"

"Sixty." He needed more time.

147

Tahliya Café reminded him of home. It served freshly roasted coffee and exotic teas that Mohammad enjoyed sampling, and its private booths allowed for secretive discussions. It had become his hangout where he mentored his followers. He had no idea it was there spies learned of his intentions. He assumed one of his trusted mentees had talked to the wrong person, breaking operational security, but that's not what happened. The Constitution of the United States prevents law enforcement from spying on people inside U.S. borders without a warrant. But the Chinese spy on whatever and whoever they think might provide useful information. They tap phones, bug offices and homes, and develop friendly, even romantic relationships to gather intelligence. They do it to university professors, industry executives, engineers, politicians, and American dissidents. In Mohammad's case, they bugged the alcoves of the favorite meeting place of Arabs who may have a bone to pick with their host country. Innovative technology powers China's massive information-gathering capabilities. When its artificial intelligence heard the word 'jihad' in a booth at the Tahliya Café, the computers signaled their human analysts. Of course, the Chinese didn't tell the Americans, but they used what they learned for their own benefit.

***

When Mohammad ended the call with the

woman, he called his two most trusted followers. They were the only individuals with which he discussed a strike against America, and they both agreed to help. Fahad was a fellow Saudi who moved to the U.S. as a teenager. Jeffry was born and raised in the Bronx and bitter about his station in life. He did poorly in high school and received a diploma he didn't deserve. Barely literate, no one would hire him. Fahad attended Saudi madrassas until his father's company transferred him to New York. He sought refuge from the unkind public schools of the Big Apple in the Muslim community across the Hudson River from Manhattan.

Mohammad was confident Jeffry was the traitor with the loose tongue. His motivation was always money, and the Asian woman must have paid him for information. Fahad was a kindred spirit, more pious than he realized, and would never betray him.

He told his mentees to meet him at the café in 30 minutes. When they arrived, the three left the shop through the rear exit, crossed the ally, and entered the abandoned basement of the building next door. When he wanted more privacy or had a group larger than the few who fit in a booth, they met there. It was a bigger space that nobody ever used, and he locked it with a padlock so it stayed that way. It was a perfect place to plan and assemble for an attack.

***

"Before we begin," Mohammad started, "I have to know if I can trust you."

"I assure you we have nothing to gain from dishonesty in this arrangement."

"How am I to be sure you are not FBI?"

"You cannot, but surely you realize I don't look or sound like an American agent. As we proceed, you shall see I am a legitimate business partner."

"I have a way." He waited for the woman to ask.

"What do you want?"

"You must shoot the rogue who betrayed me."

"Why would I do that?"

"If you are who you claim, you should have no issue killing a traitor. If you are an FBI agent, you won't take a life."

Hu could not explain that no one broke faith with him. That would violate her own operational security, and that would not happen. She had no other choices in that moment, and it angered her he backed her into a corner.

"That's fine. I'll find him, shoot him, and give you a photo to verify the task complete."

"No. There is a better way."

Mohammad escorted Hu to the basement next door. She did not worry about her safety. The Chinese don't send agents into the field untrained, and her superiors recognized her as one of their best.

She found the victim of his mistrust tied to a chair, bleeding from a cut on the side of his head, and a middle eastern boy, an older teenager, standing to his left five feet away. The Arab had a gun pointed at her. She clenched her jaw as her anger grew and calmed herself by drawing deep breaths. She resented being tested. The terrorist had to push her to gain the upper hand. *What an egotistical fool.*

"Well?" she looked at Mohammad with an icy stare, trying to hide her seething.

She is getting emotional. As I suspected, she won't do it, he mused, pleased he had shown her who was in charge.

"There is one bullet in this gun. Kill the traitor." He handed her the pistol and backed away.

Hu palmed it with her naturally dominant hand. Equally proficient with a sidearm in either, the right side was also the correct tactical choice for the shot. Aware that anger affected her aim, she took a few seconds to control her breathing. Behind her, Mohammad's smile broadcast his satisfaction at her hesitation. His bright white teeth starkly contrasted with his black facial hair. He withdrew his gun from his belt, sure she could not pull the trigger, and he would have to execute her.

As she faced the whimpering man in the chair, he begged her not to shoot and screamed at Moham-mad, promising he did not betray him. Jeffry sobbed uncontrollably as she paused, looking into his eyes. Hu took two steps backward, Mohammad behind her with his gun at the ready. She raised the pistol in her right hand, aimed at Jeffry's forehead, and in one fluid motion swung her aim to Fahad's head and pulled the trigger.

Before Fahad hit the floor, Hu pivoted to face Muhammad, side-stepped his line of fire and grabbed his handgun with her left hand. In the same movement, she chopped his gun hand with the butt of the pistol she still gripped with her right. He slumped, clutching his broken wrist, his face twisted with pain. She stood back, watching as his eyes grew wide with the realization that his favored mentee was dead. He stared in that direction, seeing blood and brain matter splattered on the wall and Fahad lying in a heap with a crater in his skull.

"What did you do?!" Mohammad shouted at her in agony and shocked at how fast the tables turned.

"I did what you asked of me," she said calmly. She regained her composure as soon as she pulled the trigger. "You told me to kill the man who betrayed you, and I did." He was quiet, stunned, still making sense of what just happened. Hu gave him a moment to recover and then continued. "It is unfortunate that you distrusted me. Now you have a mess to tidy up and a wrist that needs medical attention."

"I'll clean it up." It was Jeffry. He wasn't school smart but he understood base instincts. He survived in the streets for years. The more time he had between that moment and Mohammad's next thought, the more likely he would live. "I know what to do. I've done it before."

Still disoriented, the suggestion seemed logical to Mohammad. "Yes. Do that, Jeffry."

"As soon as I'm untied, I'll get right on it."

Hu waited for Mohammad to move, but he

didn't. He had yet to clear his mind. She didn't want to give back his weapon until she was sure he gained his wits, so she unsheathed her KA-BAR TDI mini-knife from her belt, slowly walked to Jeffry, and cut him free.

"Jeffry, you do that, and I'll speak with our guest," Mohammad said, and then he held out his hand to receive the gun. She removed the magazine, unchambered the round in the breech, and handed it to him.

"You understand my caution."

"Yes. Let us go to the café and discuss our deal."

Chapter 39

Noah enlisted in the Marines right after high school graduation. He still adored Kelena, and it tore his heart leaving her behind, but he faced no future in Virginia Beach. College required money, he needed a skill to find a job, and he lacked both. But he liked the idea of being a kick-ass Marine. After combat tours in Afghanistan, he became numb to killing. It was his role, so he did it, and packed it away somewhere in the corner of his mind where he would never have to unpack it. But he had enough. He lived in a haze of no emotion. It was time to get out, so when his re-enlistment came due he said goodbye to his brothers and headed home to his mom, dad, and little sister.

Life in the states presented challenges. Society had no place for a numb Marine whose only talent was to hunt and kill terrorists. Long talks with Kelena became his therapy, and she eventually offered him the position of Head of Security in her business. He understood the nature of the Corporation, but it was better than being a zombie who spent more time alone in his bedroom than not.

That's how Noah found himself sitting in front of three federal agents inquiring about the death of one of his oldest and best friends. The special agent asked him the same questions she did Kelena, and he gave essentially the same answers. He had no idea why anyone would want to hurt Kaitlin. He hadn't seen her for a while and knew nothing of where she had been that night, and no way could she be connected to the deaths of those gangbangers.

A gunfight was something he never expected. That was stuff for the movies. Setting operational security measures and walking around with scary guns to deter stupid people from doing foolish things was all the job entailed, so he assumed. His soldier friends were ready, though. Well-trained and combat tested by the U.S. Marines, they hadn't lost their edge. The boys responded with a few expertly placed shots at fools shooting at them and they didn't bother dwelling on the recipients of their skills. They just became more daydreams to lock away in that corner with the other unpleasantries.

Noah didn't like lying to federal authorities. He respected the FBI and considered going to college and then applying to become a special agent. The deception ate at him more than offing those scumbag bangers. As a Marine, he lived the core values of honor, courage, and commitment, and his dishonesty contravened at least two of those virtues.

***

"So, that went nowhere," Charlotte said after

Noah left the interrogation room.

"I didn't expect much." Grace figured he told the truth.

"He lied." Jace took no pleasure in saying it. He felt the sense of honor in Noah and the disappointment in himself. "I saw the meth lab. There was a firefight, and he was there." Charlotte and Grace waited for Jace to continue. They heard that tone before and knew to listen. "I saw Kaitlin lying in the grass on her back, blood pouring from her chest. Noah tried to stop the bleeding. He was crying."

"If he lied and was at the lab during the gunfight, and Kelena lied and considered Kait's death her fault, then was she at the scene?" Grace thought out loud.

"Sounds like a connection to me," Charlotte said.

"Time to get Ms. Zakis in here."

Chapter 40

T he team wanted to bring Kelena into the FBI field office for questioning. That way Charlotte and Grace could observe and signal questions for Jace to ask. Being in that environment may cause her to be cautious and less likely to talk, but that was a risk they were willing to take. It surprised them she agreed to come in, but Jace said she was relieved to see them at her door when they visited, so maybe she had something to get off her chest. Jace thanked her for coming in and led her to an interrogation room.

"I assume Special Agent Madson and your wife are listening?"

"Yes." He didn't want to give her a reason to distrust him. "They're next door, and they can talk to me through this earpiece," he said, turning his head so she could see it in his ear.

"I have so many questions. What's your deal? Are you an FBI agent?"

"No. I'm a consultant hired by the Bureau and the U.S. Attorney's Office."

"For your clairvoyance."

"Yes."

"I've researched it since you said I'm a telepath, but can you explain what's happening to me?"

"We're here to discuss Kaitlin's death, but I'll try."

"I need you to help me. Have you been like this your entire life?" Jace sensed her anxiety and confusion. It was mixed with sorrow and regret, and she seemed lost. He told her everything about his journey into the realm of the mind's eye and answered her questions the best he could, and she trusted him.

Charlotte waited an hour before she prompted him to move to the subject of the investigation.

"It's our turn to interrogate, Jace," he heard her in his ear.

"Let's shift to Kaitlin, Kelena."

"Okay. But I need to understand. Can you use what I say to you not aloud, in our minds, against me or my people?"

"No, I don't think so." In his earpiece Charlotte's voice confirmed that to be true, so he assured her, "No, definitely not."

I don't care what happens to me, but I can't implicate my friends, Kel said to Jace without speaking.

"I understand," he reassured her. "How did she die?"

Those gang thugs shot her in the chest.
At the meth lab.

"How did you know?" Kelena asked him out loud. She was stunned that he was aware of the shack, and it took her by surprise.

"I've seen it. I followed your chemists there. Then I saw it in my mind, and Kaitlin..." He didn't finish, allowing her time to recover.

Yes. We were at the lab. I brought her there with some others to make a big deal about giving my cookers bonuses.

How did it happen?

Those gang people attacked us.

Attacked?

I have no idea how they found out about us or how they knew where we cooked the meth, but they roared down the trail in two cars and immediately started shooting. We had guards set. My people didn't want me going out there, so we had a security detail. As soon as they began firing, my guys shot them all. It was over in seconds. They were all dead, and the only person on my team who got hurt was Kaitlin, shot in the chest. Kel's face contorted with the painful memory as she choked back tears. The emotion clouded her mind, and the fact that she blasted the kid in the head did not surface.

Grace and Charlotte watched the video feed from the room next door. They didn't know what Jace and Kelena said, but they guessed what they must be talking about.

Noah attempted to help her. Tried to stop the bleeding. Jace prompted her to keep going.

Yes. Noah and I put her in our truck, and we left her at Chesapeake General. She was already dead, but we didn't want to leave her out in the woods. How did you find out about Noah?

We questioned him. He didn't say anything, but I saw images. He was leaning over her trying to stop the bleeding. Jace allowed her to regain control of her emotions before he continued. *So, the bodies discovered in the burned-out vehicles at the Ford plant were the members of the gang that attacked you?*

Yes. I found out later that someone suggested they take them there and burn the cars to destroy any evidence.

Kelena, a few times you talked as if you were the boss. You referred to your cookers and your guys shot the gangbangers. Does that mean you were the one in charge?

Absolutely. It's on me.

The Corporation? Jace shocked her again.

How did you...?

When we first caught wind of a gang in town that we weren't aware of, we interviewed one of your guys. Name was Joe.

A gang? We aren't a gang! Not wanting to antagonize her, he let that go without comment. *How did you know about Joe?*

A confidential informant gave us a tip. Joe said nothing in the interview, but in his head he thought of Caroni, Supply, and the Corporation.

So, you are in charge of the Corporation?

I'm Chairman, and it's my company. I started pushing pills in high school and then it grew way bigger than I imagined. My intention was to make enough money to live and pay for college, but it got to be more than I could control, and I had to keep hiring people.

Is that how you became associated with a known drug distributor like Caroni? We figured it might be his operation. Jace probed to get a reaction.

We just needed someone with experience running a lab to help with the business.

How did you find him?

He found us. He heard there was a new game in town and offered his services. Kelena didn't care for Caroni and felt no need to protect him. *He's the one who suggested burning the bodies.*

What did Kaitlin do?

Supply. We went by code names to keep our personal identities secret. She oversaw finding suppliers.

What is Noah?

Kelena hesitated. *I prefer not to say. I got him into this mess and I'm going to get him out.*

You realize we have to keep after you until we break up the Corporation, right?

Yes. That's why I don't want to implicate anyone, especially my friends. I need to shut it down and start a new life somewhere else. I have to live with what I've done for the rest of my days.

Like what? What have you done? Jace sensed she was talking about something more than she had shared.

Kelena looked into the camera recording the interview and pronounced, "I don't want to talk about it. And I'm shutting it down."

Jace understood she wanted to end the Corporation, but it left Charlotte and Grace wondering. It appeared she was stopping the interrogation with-

out having said more than a few words. They surmised it was more than that, but that's what the
video would show.

***

Between the long drives to and from the field
office in Chesapeake and her oceanfront residence,
and the lengthy interview, Kelena returned home
exhausted. But she hadn't felt as good as she did at
that moment since well before the funeral. Her head
was clearer than it had been in quite a while, and she
finally had an endgame in mind. The illicit and dangerous life would be left behind and she'd save Missy
and Noah from her mistake.

When she grabbed her prepaid phone and noticed three texts and a missed phone call from Noah,
she texted back.

'Switch to a new burner and call me on one of
my unused numbers.'

Chapter 41

"Madam Speaker, I'm so glad we could connect. How are you?"

"Everything is fine, Gin. It's good to hear from you. Thanks to you, we have enough votes to pass the tax bill."

"Madam Speaker, I had all the confidence you would do it."

"Gin, we go too far back for you to be so formal with me in private."

"Well, it's a title you worked long and hard to get, Andrea, and it's fun to say."

"Ha-ha, I still enjoy hearing it!" Gin Vandermire and her old college roommate, the Speaker of the U.S. House of Representatives, shared a laugh.

"Listen, remember I told you I'm going to be in town October 1st? I had decided to delay the trip because of the President's farcical celebration that night, but I changed my mind. Not only do I want to dine with you, I intend to throw a serious fundraiser. How's that sound?"

"That sounds wonderful, but shouldn't we avoid that date like the plague? There will be protests."

"Do you expect it to be bad? At some point, those people are bound to grow tired of protesting and go back to their normal lives."

"My security detail told me to prepare for a large event and to lie low."

"Well, you know how I love staying in The Lincoln."

"Your favorite hotel."

"And I've already reserved the Adams Room for a small gathering of extraordinarily rich people. I suspect the hotel is far enough from the White House to avoid trouble.

"You're right, of course. The nearest protesters would be four or five blocks away."

"Think of the optics, Andrea. The power you'd project answering questions on the steps of the most luxurious hotel in the city, with your colleagues by your side, would be a stark contrast to the angry mob surrounding the President."

"Gin, you are a genius!"

"Let's do it!"

"Okay, I'm in."

"Good. I'll send details to your chief of staff. Decide who you want there with you and forward me the names. I'll handle the invitations. For a display of unity, I suggest the Majority Leader, Minority Leader, and the cute new girl with the big smile who's all over the news."

"Representative Youngblood is a hard no. I can't control her and what she says. She doesn't respect the old party line. That is too dangerous."

"Whatever you say, Andrea, but please consider it. It's a fantastic idea." *Do it my way*, Gin willed. *I'm the one who calls the shots, my dear friend.*

Chapter 42

K el's purpose was clear to her now. She had to shut down the Corporation that day, and she had to warn her friends the feds were on to them. When she got home from the interrogation, she told Noah to drop what he was doing and bring Missy to her house as soon as possible. They needed a plan and had to implement it right away.

"I had two interviews with the FBI. I was with them for a couple of hours today. They know about me, the Corporation, the lab, Kaitlin's death. They're aware of everything."

"What did you say to them?!" Missy's eyes were wide with shock and her tone was accusatory.

"I didn't tell them anything!" Kelena's brow scrunched as she shot Missy an annoyed look, "at least not out loud."

"What does that mean?" Missy's voice was a pitch higher. "Is this more of your ESP crap?"

Kel took a deep breath and wished she hadn't started the conversation with such an urgent tone.

Noah spoke calmly to relieve the tension in the room and understand the cause of Kel's angst.

"What happened?"

Kel paused, annoyed she allowed herself to get sucked into Missy's drama and Noah had to be the calming influence. She used the moment to start over. "The FBI stopped by my house the other day and asked if I had information concerning Kaitlin's death."

"They called me in for questioning, too," Noah said.

"I told them I didn't know anything. Then I got sick and threw up in the sink. I couldn't continue and asked them to leave, so they did."

"My interview was the same. I had nothing for them and they let me go."

"A few days later, they asked me to come in for another interview, so today I did. I talked with Jace West. The FBI agent and the attorney were in the next room watching on video."

"Jace is the guy who spoke to you in your mind." Noah wanted to insert that into the conversation before Missy got confrontational with Kelena.

"Yes. But he told me out loud they're familiar with the lab. Mr. West had been there. He followed Joe and James there."

"They know about them, too? How?"

"Jace said the FBI got a tip from a confidential informant. He didn't get it from me. He knows Kaitlin died at the shack, too."

"How's that possible?"

"Missy, I'll tell you, but please don't get angry with me. I'm just telling you what I believe is true and what I was told. I need to emphasize none of my words incriminated either of you. Their videotape is nearly two hours long with virtually nothing on it. There is absolutely no evidence for them to use in court against any of us. They don't have a clue Missy even exists."

"Go on. What do you know?" Noah was anxious.

"To answer the question, Mr. West is clairvoyant, and he is not an agent. The FBI and the U.S. Attorney hired him as a consultant because he can read what people think." Kel braced for Missy's scoff, but it didn't come. "When he interviewed Noah, he stated he saw in his mind Kaitlin lying on the ground and Noah trying to stop the bleeding."

"He told you that?" From what he witnessed at the funeral, Noah realized there was an unusual connection between Jace and Kelena, and he believed his friend when she claimed she could sense the man in her thoughts. But he didn't expect West could do it to him.

"Jace mentioned you had nothing to say, but there were images in your mind. Were you thinking of Kaitlin when they talked to you?"

"I was. I couldn't help it. They asked how she died, and the nightmare came rushing back."

"Mr. West also said they interviewed Joe. Was anyone aware of that?"

"The cooker?" Missy shook her head.

Noah spoke up. "No. The dude should have told someone. Maybe he warned Caroni."

"If he spoke to Kaitlin, she would've informed us. I'm not sure Caroni would mention it. Besides, Jace said Joe didn't talk, but he heard some thoughts."

"Like what?" Missy's initial aggression faded, but her anxiety did not.

"Joe is how he caught on to the Corporation and Supply, and he picked up Caroni's name, too. So, for a while now, months maybe, the feds have been investigating our company." Noah and Missy sat silently, wondering if they were going to prison. "I'm not sure how they first found us out, but Jace said they got wind of a new gang in town, and somehow that led to Joe."

Missy's stomach tightened, and she felt her heart in her throat. "How much do they know?" she squeaked.

"I repeat. There are no verbal statements against us, and I'm unaware of any physical evidence. If they had something, I assume we'd be in jail. I'm confident they've learned nothing of Missy. Her name, or even her position, hasn't come up. They saw you at the funeral, Noah, and when they interviewed you, Jace sensed your thoughts. That's all they have. Jace's psychic readings cannot be used in court. But they figured out who we are and what we're doing. They know I'm Chairman; Kaitlin was Supply; Noah was at the lab; we had a shootout, and the eight gang members they found burned in the cars were the people that attacked the lab. He asked me what you did, Noah, but I explained I didn't want to say. I'm pretty sure I revealed nothing related to you. I was adamant everything was on me, and I refused to give up my friends."

What Kel conveyed to her old classmates stunned them, and what it meant for them had not sunk in. She knew what the FBI let on to her, but was there more they didn't tell her? What else have they learned?

"What do we do?" It was Missy.

"I made it clear we are done. Jace warned me they'd keep after us until they broke up our organization, so I told them I'm doing it. I'm shutting down the Corporation."

"But I can't imagine we'll just be let go," Noah said. "We left nine murdered people in our wake. They won't quit until we're in jail."

"The FBI has no evidence, and it'll stay that way if none of us talk, and we end everything now. If we keep going, they're bound to get what they need to put us away for a long time."

"Shit." Missy and Noah said it simultaneously as they realized that they're in deep trouble and had to work to dig out of it.

"This is what we do." Kel's clarity spoke with authority. "First, we get on our burners and call our managers. Order them to stop everything immediately. The FBI is watching, so just stop now, or we'll all go to prison. I want to give every individual in the company $10,000 severance pay. It's important the managers tell everyone."

"That's a lot of money, Kel."

"Yes, but we have a ton. Ten grand should be enough to tide them over until they find something else to do and *not* continue to do business as the Corporation. That'll get everyone in trouble."

"We don't need to worry about my dealers," Missy agreed. "All of them have jobs or are students. That kind of cash ought to make them happy to move on with their lives without us."

"Good. What about security, Noah?"

"That should work. The jacks and jills are clueless, anyway. My core guys will be more than willing to forget those bangers and find the same kind of job somewhere else. For Caroni's people, I need to think. There are only a few of them, but they may be a little more difficult to satisfy. Most of the others are just independent suppliers who can easily unload their product to other dealers."

"What about us?" Missy was worried.

"We're rich. We stashed money in safe deposit boxes and offshore accounts, some of it is laundered through the import/export company, and some of it isn't. Stay here and take your chances with the feds or leave. I haven't decided yet. Part of me wants to stick around and go to college. There's no way they can touch me unless one of us talks — or Caroni does. He's the only person who can burn us. He may be our biggest risk, and the authorities understand that."

Chapter 43

"Yeah, that's him. Surprise, surprise." Grace identified Caroni as Slick in a photo Charlotte retrieved from an old case file. Law enforcement suspected him of being involved in the local narcotics trade, but they never got enough evidence to take him to court. "So, Ms. Zakis told us she wanted out and is closing the Corporation, but she had Caroni cutting a deal with a presumed drug dealer at about the same time." Grace mused out loud and voiced it more as an open-ended question than a statement.

"I'd bet she wasn't aware of it," Jace said. "She was out of touch both times we talked with her."

"I'm inclined to agree with Jace," Charlotte added. "From what we've observed, she went into a severe funk when Kaitlin died, and the organization kept operating without her."

"We need to get eyes on Caroni."

"And on Noah. It looks as though he's close to Kelena, so he must be near the top of the food chain in the Corporation."

"We know where Noah lives and found a last known address for Slick, so we'll start there," Charlotte directed.

"What about tapping their phones?" Jace remembered a year ago Grace and Charlotte used recorded cell phone conversations to help track down the terrorists. Charlotte answered.

"We have nothing to bring to a judge to get a warrant to listen in on Noah's calls. All we've got are your telepathic readings, and that's not legitimate probable cause. We may secure one for Caroni. A special agent observed him in what looked like a business arrangement with a suspected dope dealer. That could be enough but convincing the judge would be difficult. Seeing Caroni with Dealer-Girl, who we never witnessed making a drug buy, is probably too shaky. We need to find more probable cause."

"Yep," Grace agreed. "I'll assign a surveillance agent to each of them."

Chapter 44

SAN FRANCISCO — AUGUST, CHINATOWN

After meeting with Mohammad, Hu flew to San Francisco to brief Chen. For his security, she was one of only two people who reported directly to him. He trusted her completely. That she was a Chinese 'diplomat' provided ultimate protection. Immune to prosecution if apprehended by American authorities, she would have no reason to give them information about him or anything else. In the worst case, she'd be on a plane to see her family in China in a matter of days.

The two met in a private dining room in the back of a restaurant favored by the local Chinese immigrant population. The proprietor knew him only as the wealthy man who tipped extraordinarily well and who desired privacy. Chen preferred to speak with her in English. There were few, if any, people nearby that understood it. The owner and staff, and most of the customers, spoke their native tongues.

Hu explained her negotiations with Mohammad. Chen thrived on information and insisted on knowing everything. His brain needed it. Removed from dangerous fieldwork long ago, he enjoyed living vicariously through his young protégé. As his superiors promoted him into the upper echelon of the Ministry of State Security, he became more valuable as a political operative.

"Was the victim disposed of discretely?" Chen asked with a gleam of envy in his eyes.

"Yes, sir. The boy who I did not shoot said he knew what to do, but I made sure he did it properly. I directed my protection shadow to see to it. He reported to me that the fellow drove the body to a dangerous part of the city, several blocks from where we were, and put it in a trash dumpster. No one can trace the remains to them, or me."

"Good. You handled the situation as I would. I am pleased with your display of cunning and skill."

"Thank you, sir."

"Tell me what happens next."

"Mohammad agreed to all conditions. He has a four-man team, and he chose to lead them himself. In a week's time, I intend to give him ten AR-15 short barrel rifles with twenty 30-round magazines, and 1500 rounds of ammunition."

"That is much more than they need."

"It is part of his payment. I instructed him to use only one magazine each to allow him and his men time to exfiltrate. Firing more than that takes too long. I impressed upon him his team must remain anonymous, and escape is mandatory."

"Perhaps we should supply them with only the 150 rounds required."

"My people and I should be far away from the

east coast before October 1st, and I don't want to return to pay the remainder of our fee. But to ensure operational success, I plan to deliver only 200 before the assault and place the rest of the ammunition in an undisclosed location for Mohammad to retrieve after his assignment is complete."

"Excellent thinking, Hu. What is the plan for infiltration?"

"I will outfit his unit with ballistic vests, helmets, face masks, and black clothing so that they blend with the protesters. Tactical sling bags that look much like the backpacks carried by the black bloc fools will conceal their weapons. He and his team will deploy to pre-determined strike points throughout the crowd to achieve maximum confusion at 9:05 p.m."

"What is the exfiltration strategy?"

"After they empty their magazines, they will drop their weapons and flee. I mapped individual escape routes that include discrete locations to shed their tactical gear and black clothing. Then they'll muster at their vehicle for the drive from Washington back to New Jersey. Mohammad will be on the road before authorities understand what happened."

"The AR-15s are to be left at the scene?"

"Yes."

"Genius, Hu."

Chapter 45

"C hristian, I'm uncomfortable with this drug deal. That is not what I do. If I get caught, they'll put me away for a very long time. Besides, we don't need meth to fight for our cause." Now that Jaana was back home and pondered Zo's request, carrying it through seemed less than thrilling.

"I'm the same way. It didn't feel right when he asked, but the situation intimidated me too much to say no. I'm sorry for getting you into this mess."

"What do we do? I don't want to go to Norfolk and pick up the drugs, and I don't want you to do it either. Even if it's a legit buy, we'd have to drive to DC with it in our car. Then what do we do with it when we get there? He'll probably have us distribute it for him too. I'm not doing this."

"That's fine. I have no desire to be a drug dealer. I'll call Zo and tell him to close the deal himself. You'll have to contact this Supply guy and set it up, and then we'll wash our hands of it."

***

Zo looked forward to getting out of the city for

a day or two. He was tired of listening to his social justice warriors whining about the injustice in the United States. More than once he almost exploded, aching to shout at them to 'get over it and find a job you lazy bitches,' but he couldn't do that. They were paying him far too much for him to ruin his payday, but their privileged, misguided asses ate at his core.

He left the family farm when he was 17 with eight dollars and two quarters — every cent he had — in his pocket. Each day he worked whatever odd job a friendly business or homeowner was willing to give him so he could buy something to eat. He slept in the woods or under an overpass, only to wake up hungry in the morning and start the routine again. He had nothing but the clothes on his back and the will to live.

Zo's life changed when an Army recruiter noticed the strapping young man washing the windows of the storefront next to the recruiting office. By then, he was 18 and allowed to join the military with no one's permission but his own, and he did. After serving ten years, a former platoon commander recruited Staff Sergeant Alonzo away from military life, and he joined his friend in the private sector.

As a security contractor, he earned much more than a squad leader in an infantry unit. His free time was his own, and the assignments were interesting and diverse. Zo was a self-made man, proud of his success and content with his life. Most jobs were easy to accept and carry out with no conflict with his conscience, but the antifascist one was tough. He pulled himself out of the gutter without handouts, and they could too. The only consolation was that he was getting paid a butt-load of cash. Whoever contracted with his company must have had more money than they knew what to do with.

The drug buy was different. Not that he and his mates didn't break laws for other jobs, but that was more bending the rules for honorable causes. Buying a huge amount of meth for these deadbeats was flat-out wrong. When the organizer from Portland agreed to do it, Zo felt the burden lift from his conscience, but the guy just reneged, and he would have to do it himself. At least he had a reason to take off for a couple days. The drive to Norfolk could easily be a day trip, but why not relax and spend some time at the beach? It would be a great excuse to grab a haircut and a shave — he preferred to be high and tight and clean-shaven. He'd blend-in in the military town and look more like a soldier than a drug dealer.

Zo just needed to take precautions so that he's not caught in a setup, get it done, and move past it. The plan did not include spending a decade of his life in prison.

Chapter 46

"Kel, we have a problem." Noah was on her pre-paid phone, and he did not sound happy.

"What is it?"

"Caroni…"

"What did he do?!" She cut him short, fearing the worst. Her anxiety swelled thinking about Caroni. He knew too much and could bring Security, Distro, and Chairman down.

"It's not like that." He could hear the resentment in her voice. "He made a sizable deal with someone from out of state, and they're coming for it sometime this month. He was all proud of himself. Says he has the crystal ready to go. He just needs to make the exchange."

"Damn it. I knew we shouldn't have given him Supply. He's going to mess things up for us." She felt the blood rushing to her face as anger tried to rear its head, but Noah calmed her.

"It's one last sale. We already have the stuff and would have to get rid of it, anyway. We might as well sell it to the person who ordered it. And it will take care of most of Caroni's crew — 50K."

Kelena was quiet, working through the new hurdle in her mind.

Noah tried to reassure her by giving her an update on the status of the Corporation. "Except for that, we are at an all-stop. Everyone knows the FBI is on to us and to lie low. Joe worked all night to clean the lab. It's gutted and wiped with bleach, and he trashed the equipment in dumpsters across three cities. There weren't a lot of chemicals left, and he dumped those in the woods. The only loose end is Caroni's deal."

"I want to be careful with this sale. We don't need to get caught in an eleventh-hour snare. Tell me details."

"I 100% agree with you. It smells a little fishy, and we need to take extra precautions. Caroni says he met with a pretty girl from Portland, Oregon and she agreed to a deal for a pound of ice for $50,000."

"Portland? Why would someone from the west coast buy dope in Virginia?"

"That's the weird thing. She said there's a huge protest in DC on October 1st, and the meth is for the protesters to keep them going the whole day."

"Still doesn't make sense. Why Norfolk? Why us?"

"Caroni told me he got a call from Distro. One of her dealers was meeting with someone who wanted a good amount of crystal. A dealer from Richmond was there and introduced this buyer to our person. Our girl has been doing business with the guy for a while, selling him meth and he sells it up there."

"So, he's probably legit."

"He said the pretty girl's name is Jaana, and she was in Richmond and Norfolk recruiting people to go to the protest at the White House. Whoever she's working with in DC told her there was a cheap source of good ice down here, and to buy some."

"Okay. Still not warm and fuzzy about this."

"This is another weird part of it. Jaana called Caroni and said she couldn't meet with him and a guy from DC was driving here to do the exchange."

"Now we're back to real fishy. I don't like it."

"I considered telling him to cancel it, but the last thing we need are bangers from Washington, DC looking for us."

"When's it happening?"

"Supposed to happen at the end of the month."

"Let's spring some unexpected wrinkles that only you and I know about. The first wrinkle is for Caroni to phone his contact and instruct them to be here in three days. I don't want to wait. Tell him to deliver that message and see how they respond. If they call off the buy, that's cool with me. We'll be in the clear and just dump the stuff. If not, we'll figure it out."

"That sounds good to me. Missy told me she's shut down too. The only other loose end is to distribute severance to everyone. We'll need to do that discretely."

Chapter 47

"She told us she would shut it down. I guess she did." It frustrated Charlotte they couldn't find hard evidence against the Corporation.

"Kelena must have made a phone call as soon as she left our interview. Our agent on Noah Vann said he's done nothing unusual and doesn't talk to anybody beyond a casual greeting. He works out and runs every day. Fortunately, our surveillance agents train for those kinds of things. She followed him into the gym and ran behind him, and says he didn't say a word to anyone. He gets takeout and makes grocery store runs — normal stuff. Not a single thing suspicious."

"And Caroni?"

"Same thing. Although, it took a while to find him. He wasn't at his last known address. Our guy reported he doesn't leave his apartment much. He's gone to a bar a few times, but the agent went inside and said nothing was going on there. They are both sealed tight."

"Kelena is back to being a hermit in her comfy, oceanfront home?"

"Yep."

"Did we get the warrant for electronic surveillance?"

"No. Not enough probable cause. I didn't even try for Zakis and Vann. But I got one for Joe Harkness?" Grace said, ending the sentence with a 'remember the interview with the cooker?' inflection. "Based on the tip from my CI, the judge granted it."

"And?"

"Nothing. Not a peep. If they're communicating, they're using burner phones or another way we're not aware of. And we never determined the identity of James, Joe's partner."

"What about the meth lab?" Jace asked.

"Abandoned. The shooting must have spooked them. It was empty and wiped clean. We found what looked like bloodstains in the grass. Those samples are with forensics. I assume they will match to some of the dead eight."

"Maybe Kaitlin, too," Jace reminded his team. Grace and Charlotte had nothing more to say, both considering where to go from there. "Now what do we do?" He broke the pause.

"I've asked NPD and VBPD to pass along any intelligence they get from the streets. They said they are hearing the local gangs buzzing. Suddenly their suppliers are feeding them all the product they can handle, and there's not much crystal on the street."

"Already?" Jace was in disbelief.

"It only takes hours for dirt to fill the voids," Charlotte mused. "Looks as though the Corporation evaporated."

"So, we move on?"

"No, we still have nine murders. It'll take a lot of effort to find enough evidence to bring charges for those. We'll have to start at the bottom and work the streets; see what our CIs can tell us."

"Wait, what about Mil? Has she reported anything?" Grace remembered she asked her to call them if she saw something suspicious.

"I called her yesterday. No more Dealer-Girl, and no more Slick."

"She hasn't even seen Dealer-Girl?"

"Nope. Gone."

"That's not a surprise, I guess. What do we do with the tails on our three favorite drug kingpins?" Grace understood surveillance agents were in high demand. If their current leads were dry, the boss would reassign them.

"Cut them loose," Charlotte said with a sigh of resignation, and her lips pressed in a frown. "We'll bring in the players we know and try to pressure them into talking. Not much more we can do."

Chapter 48

"I'm doing it!" Kelena practically shouted at Noah. She removed herself from the nitty-gritty of the drug trade long ago. His job was to protect her and her identity, and now she insisted on completing the last and probably the most dangerous deal of the Corporation's history. "I do not trust Caroni. We are done with him, or he's going to land us in prison."

"I'll do it then. Please, let me do it," Noah pleaded.

"No. That is not happening. I've gotten you into a pile of crap, and I'm getting you out. If you make the sale and it's a trap, you'll go to the federal pen for a large chunk of your life. I can't be responsible for that. I have to get this done."

***

The new twist in the drug buy made Zo even more uncomfortable than he already was. Not only did his buyer back out, but the seller insisted on doing it weeks sooner than originally planned. The last thing he wanted was to go to prison for some lousy job. Packing up and leaving was an option, but his pride wouldn't let him. He never backed out of a commitment, and he wasn't going to start, so he figured out a way to do it that didn't land him in jail. One of his street captains was not that bad-looking. He'd ask her to travel with him for a two-day trip to the beach.

The dude from Portland told him to buy a prepaid phone and text the message, 'Hello, I'm Nero,' to a number he gave him. That made sense to him. In his business, they used only disposable mobile phones. That left him with a better vibe about the whole thing. Do cops insist you use burner phones?

***

"It's him." Kel and Noah were lounging on her oceanfront deck enjoying ice-cold Shock Tops when her prepaid cellphone dinged. "Ready?"

"Yep. Tell him step one."

Kelena texted, 'This Thursday drive to the Waterside Marriot on Main Street in downtown Norfolk. Arrive before noon. Do not reserve a room. Do not check-in. Text me when you are in the lobby. Acknowledge, please.'

Close to 200 miles and three hours away, Zo typed, 'Acknowledged,' and hit the send arrow. *So it begins.* The app on his smartphone told him it would be a sunny and warm September day in Virginia Beach — perfect weather for sun, sand, and surf.

***

It flattered Zo's street captain girl that he invited her on his getaway to the beach. She knew the Antifa girls secretly crushed on him, and she made sure they were aware he told her to bring a bikini with her. When he picked her up Thursday morning in his rental, an Audi SUV, he was clean-shaven and groomed, looking quite GQ in his casual business attire. At first, she peered past him, searching for the Zo she expected, and her heart fluttered when she realized the guy who stepped out of the fancy car appearing as if he just left a men's fashion shoot was her date. Her attraction to him annoyed her. He looked like the type of successful, well-off man Antifa railed against. Still, she was glad she styled her hair and wore a sundress for the drive to Norfolk. Zo's involuntary grin gave away his sudden vision of a pleasurable night. She was a lot prettier all cleaned up than on a normal Antifa day.

***

"Nero's here," Kel called Noah.
"Good. We're ready for him here."
"Okay. I'm texting him step two."

Zo and his girl parked in the Main Street Garage across from the Marriot and entered through the main entrance. The girl's jaw dropped for a second before she could catch herself. She hadn't been in such a luxurious place since she was a kid, and she felt good on the arm of a handsome man standing in the lobby of a fancy hotel.

Zo maneuvered her to an overstuffed chair and sat in his own alongside her. Then he removed the new burner phone from his pocket and texted, 'I'm here.'

After a brief pause, the reply told him what to do next. 'Check-in at the front desk under the name Nero. We already paid for you. Don't show any ID. Go to the room.'

"Smart," Zo said aloud, impressed by the security measures of his business associate. He had a much better feeling going into the deal. *These people aren't acting like cops.*

"What?" Girl asked.

"Oh, nothing. Let's check-in. By the way, my name today is Nero, so don't act confused."

She wanted to ask why but didn't bother. It just added to the excitement of her adventure.

Kelena and Missy watched from a window of the guest business center. They noticed the good-looking couple walk through the entrance, but neither one of them thought it was Nero until they saw him take out a cellphone and text. When he lowered his phone, Kelena's dinged. They glanced at each other with wide eyes. That must be him. The two were the only people in the lobby. When Kel texted back and he studied his cell, that confirmed it. But they wondered who the woman was. They lingered for 15 minutes, alert to anyone who might follow

Nero or who looked like cops. Kelena gave Missy her burner and wallet, and then Missy left the hotel. Kelena climbed the stairs to the fifth floor carrying nothing but a Virginia Beach logoed beach bag. Once there, she stopped to catch her breath and to monitor the room she rented for Nero.

The paradisiac, contemporary décor of their room overlooking the Elizabeth River enthralled the girl, and she realized right away there was only one king-sized bed. She blushed with anticipation and glanced at Zo with a coquettish grin, hoping they'd not bother with the beach that afternoon. He noticed the flirty look, and they began their playful dance, allowing themselves to enjoy the courtship. As he finally stepped toward her, a knock at the door startled them both. She tilted her head and gave him a questioning gaze, but he shrugged his shoulders and answered it.

When she was sure she was alone, Kelena took a deep breath to steady her nerves, walked to the hotel room, and knocked. When Zo opened the door, she greeted him as confidently as she could muster.

"Hello, Nero. May I come in?"

The fetching women in front of him caught him off guard. Her long, chocolate-colored hair and bright blue eyes did not fit his image of a drug dealer. As he stepped aside to let her enter, he noticed she was tallish for a woman, and she wasn't even wearing heels.

"And you are..." he left the statement open for

her to fill in the blank.

"Call me Kirk," Kel said with a grin.

"Ha-ha," Girl laughed nervously, wondering who the pretty woman was violating her romantic moment. Zo looked at her with a wrinkled brow. She saw the confusion on his face. "Kirk. Nero. Star Trek! Get it?" She was a leftist antifascist, but she enjoyed movies and caught the reference to one of the sci-fi franchise's recent movies.

"Ah, not really." He turned to Kirk and waited for her to start the conversation.

"I hope you two brought your beachwear," Kelena started.

"I have a bikini," Girl blurted awkwardly, still jumpy about the cute, unexpected guest.

"Good. Nero, will she be coming with us?"

This twist took Zo off-guard. He invited her thinking if he were uncomfortable with the situation, he would have her make the buy — a kind of sacrificial lamb if the deal went south. But Kirk was changing the scenario, and he didn't know what was next. Girl was clueless what was happening, and she'd be no good at this point. "Yes, she's coming with us."

Kelena turned to the young woman and saw her face was flush. *Ugh-oh, I must have interrupted something.* She smiled to herself. "So, who are *you*," she asked, emphasizing 'you' so the question didn't seem accusatory.

"You can call me Uhura," Girl said with almost no hesitation. Kel laughed out loud, and Girl joined her, but he didn't catch the joke. His face remained expressionless except for a slight, puzzled wince.

"You are too funny," Kel said, still giggling.

"Let's get on with it." Zo was a little annoyed but wasn't sure why.

"Get on with what?" At that point, Kel sensed Uhura didn't know what was happening, and she felt at ease. What cop brings a date to a drug bust?

"Okay. Please follow my instructions." This was the part of the scheme that made Kel uncomfortable. Noah insisted on doing it to ensure they had no hidden listening or tracking devices. She considered winging it and completing the exchange right there. She could avoid the embarrassment of what came next, and she was sure that the couple were not police. Unfortunately, she didn't have the ice with her, so she decided she may as well let the plan play out.

"We're going to the beach," Kel started, and saw the objection on Uhura's face. *She really does not know why we're here.* Kel shot a glance at Nero with a 'what were you thinking?' expression. She turned to the girl. "This won't take long. We'll conduct our business and we'll be done. You have the room for the night, and you'll have the rest of the day to yourselves."

"How're we doing this?"

Kelena faced Uhura. "Change into your bikini. You too, Nero. Please put on your suit." Girl didn't move, frozen with apprehension.

"It's okay. Let's just get this over with." Zo reassured her.

"Uhura, you can change in the bathroom if you want, then bring me your dress. Don't take too long."

Girl only took a minute and returned to see Zo in his underwear and the shapely intruder in a one-piece swimsuit. Kirk reached out for her dress, so Uhura handed it to her.

After examining the frock for tiny electronic devices, Kel asked the girl to twirl in her skimpy bikini. The suit barely hid what it should, and Kel wondered if it was even legal to wear it in public. She gave Uhura her clothing and told her to put it on, and she gladly complied. After doing the same with Nero and allowing him to check her clothes, all three were decent and ready to go.

"As you can see, I have nothing with me except this empty beach bag. Both of you leave all of your personal things: phones, watches, wallets, behind. Only bring what you need to complete our business and put it in the bag. Do you have it?" Nero nodded. Uhura's jaw dropped, and her eyes grew large when Zo took more money than she'd ever seen out of his suitcase and placed it into the bag.

Chapter 49

T he group looked like nothing more than guests leaving to enjoy a late summer day in the sun. Zo followed Kirk with his girl on his arm as they exited the Marriot through the lobby. When Missy saw them, she pulled her rented, black Hyundai sedan into East Main Street traffic and stopped directly in front of them. Kel opened the passenger side door for Nero and Uhura and then climbed into the seat next to her friend. As the doors closed, Missy drove away. With no instructions spoken, she took them to the end of the block, turned left, and then again into the parking garage across from the hotel. She parked next to a white Nissan Pathfinder.

"Okay, let's go," Kel said as she got out of the Hyundai and into the driver's seat of the Nissan. She put on the floppy hat and sunglasses that were waiting for her and handed shades to Nero. She noticed another pair of women's aviators and grinned. *Missy thinks of everything.* And she gave the glasses to Uhura. Within two minutes, she was on Interstate 264, headed for Virginia Beach.

By that time, Kelena was sure Noah's elaborate

plan had too many twists. She was convinced that Nero was who he claimed to be, a buyer of a half kilo of crystal. But she had no choice other than continue with the ploy and meet Noah where he waited with the meth. If, by some chance, Nero and the girl were cops and signaled to their handlers that they were going to Virginia Beach, they'd be wrong. The subterfuge veered the white Nissan off I264, onto Interstate 64, headed north to the Chesapeake Bay. Kel exited the highway, took a circuitous route through the streets of the northern part of Norfolk, and pulled into a condo complex on the bay in East Ocean View.

Kelena invited her guests to exit the car and walk to the beach. "Get your stuff," she said, and Nero understood that meant to bring the money. She grabbed a blanket from the back of the Nissan and strolled along the sandy path through the dunes and onto the shore of the Chesapeake Bay. She walked a hundred yards east and spread the blanket next to a woman already sunbathing. Kel told him to put the bag with the $50,000 alongside the sunbather's bag. Zo knew the plan when he saw the other tote, identical to the one he held in his hand. When he bent over to drop it in its designated place, he realized the sunbather was the same person who drove the black sedan. Kel motioned for everyone to sit.

They sat quietly at first. Kel lifted her chin to the bay breeze and let it blow through her hair, and noticed the girl doing the same. For a moment, the tension of the day left her, and she felt almost free, but she sensed Nero's anxiousness.

"We're just going to sit awhile," she said, intending to calm him. As each minute passed, it became more and more unlikely that the buy was a setup. That was true both ways, and Nero seemed to understand that too. The four were alone. It was early afternoon on a workday. Most residents of the community were still at work, and tourist season ended a couple of weeks earlier on Labor Day weekend.

After 30 minutes, Missy stood up, picked up her blanket, and walked east along the beach. As Zo expected, she left her tote behind. With the serenity of the warm September sun and the cool bay breeze broken, Uhura spoke up. She was eager to get back to their planned getaway.

"Zo, can we leave now?" She didn't realize she used his real name. He did, but he didn't react. *Maybe Kirk didn't hear it.* His mind raced, though. If they found out who he was, they could trace him to the job. They could find out about the riot, the diversion, everything. As the thoughts and images stormed through his head, his demeanor remained cool and collected, but he wanted to get the meth and leave. Kelena felt the turmoil and saw the visions. She had these sensations before with other people over the years but didn't understand them. They were fleeting and meant nothing to her, so she dismissed them. But this was different. After talking with Jace and researching what he told her, she realized what was happening, and was not ready to let go of that moment on the beach.

"Isabella. Is that your name?" she asked the girl.

"Uh, yes. How did you know?" Kelena sensed her alarm and suspicion but found the experience exhilarating. She knew Bella's name. It just came to her, and that was so cool.

"I guess Nero must have said it." She called him 'Nero,' attempting to soothe his nerves.

"My friends call me Bella."

"It suits you. A cute name for a pretty girl."

Zo regained his confidence and had enough of the chit-chat. "We need to finish this." His voice was stern, and Kel figured it was time to complete the transaction. Even though she felt sure it was a legitimate deal, her heart rate jumped a few beats. It was the moment of truth.

"Okay. Get up so I can grab my blanket." They stood up. She shook off the sand and continued, "You take her bag and I'll snag yours." She picked up the tote with the cash and handed the Pathfinder keys to him. "I programmed directions to the Waterside Marriot into the GPS. Please park it in the same spot where we found it. Don't break any traffic laws," was her last instruction in a motherly voice.

Before he laid his hands on the bag with the pound of crystal meth inside, Kel looked at the girl and said in a sing-song way, "Nice meeting you, Bella!" and walked east — the same direction in which Missy had left. Zo grabbed his bag and hurried west, back to the Nissan, with Isabella in tow.

Noah's thought was the cops wouldn't move in

for the bust until their undercover agent could confirm he had the drugs, and she had the money. They didn't have wires, so they would have to wait until their guy covered the 100 yards along the beach to meet them. Meanwhile, Kel went in the opposite direction. She walked to a condo they rented for the weekend and disappeared inside. Missy took the cash and exited out the sliding glass doors to the back patio, crossed into the parking lot of the complex next door, and drove away. Kel and Noah sat at the kitchen table and had a celebratory beer, giving Missy enough time to get to Kel's house before they left the condo.

The elaborate plan was for nothing. Zo and Bella weren't undercover cops, but it eased Zo's mind, too. As Kel stepped him through the procedure, he figured the police wouldn't set up such an extravagant scheme for a drug bust. It took a couple of hours, but it was over, and he still had a night with Bella in a luxury hotel.

Chapter 50

Z o escaped from his annoying assignment at a place called Down Range — a bar in nearby Arlington that serviced a particular clientele. A separated Navy Seal and former security contractor who decided he aged out of the profession used his savings to open the establishment to cater to fellow operators and other rough men. There were plenty of them in the DC area, some still on active duty, many contracting out their skills, and a good number were retired.

Zo found comfort by hanging with brothers who understood combat, and the adventurous women who dared enter the bar. And it was common for him to see familiar faces there, guys he served with in some form or fashion. Ice was one of them. Operators rolled with a single name. Some preferred their proper surnames, but most used the nicknames given to them by comrades in warfare. They assigned a brother's handle based on an identifying characteristic or notable circumstance. Zo's was a shortcut of his actual name — Alonzo. Ice's derived from his propensity to kill with no thought or emotion. It didn't bother him. He had ice in his veins, so said his mates.

Both worked for the same contractor and occasionally trained with each other. Ice showed up at Down Range the previous week, and he and Zo drank together most evenings. Zo never liked him that much. He was more arrogant than most extroverted operators, and his reputation as an unremorseful killer made Zo feel dirty. But most times, he was the only guy in the place Zo recognized.

It was an especially boozy evening, and neither of them felt like getting up from their seats at the bar and going home. Zo was one of those guys who got quieter the more alcohol he drank, but Ice was the opposite, and that night he was talking.

"So, what does the company have you doing here in the city?" Zo asked.

"I have a big job coming up in a few weeks, *huge* job. But I no longer work for them," Ice bragged.

"You don't work for Stealth-Tempest?"

"Nah, man. I'm solo. I'm freelancing, and you would *not* believe the money." The truth was that he made the company nervous. Ice was a loose cannon, and they couldn't afford the scrutiny if, or more likely when, he got overzealous in his work, and they stopped using him.

Ice's new employer was very clear that silence was mandatory. Operational security was critical to mission success, but the beer and bourbon oiled his jaw and he kept working it.

"I'm talking retirement money, man. I can retire on this one gig alone. You wouldn't believe it if I told you. But I'm not retiring. I got a lot more left in me."

"Okay, I'm dying to know. How much cash?"

"Guess." His bleary-eyed companion wanted to play a game.

"High five figures." Five-figure salaries were normal for Zo, so he figured it had to be at the top end of that range.

Laughing, Ice enjoyed pointing his right index finger upward. "Higher."

"Six figures?"

Up went the finger directed at the ceiling, with a broad, satisfied smile on his face. "Higher."

"Seven figures?!" Zo was incredulous. Either Ice hit the jackpot, or he was full of crap. He could only describe Ice's grin as 'shit-eating.' The braggart said nothing as he read Zo's expression, looking for the inevitable awe Ice inspired in him. Zo had to ask. "Doing what?"

Still smiling like a Cheshire cat, he couldn't resist. "Weeeell, let's just say I'm going to do what I do best," drawing out the 'well' to tease his audience. Zo wasn't drunk enough to not understand the implication, so he probed.

"What's that?"

"You know, they call me Ice for a reason. Turn on the news October 2nd and you'll see what I'm talking about. I'll disappear for a while, but I may be back here someday."

***

Zo didn't bother checking in with his street captains the next day. His hangover got the best of him, and he didn't sleep well the night before. Ice's words echoed in his mind.

Chapter 51

"How did it go?" Noah asked as soon as Missy left the condo with the money, and they cracked open their Shock Tops. They had 30 minutes to kill, and he was eager to hear how his covert transaction went.

"Exactly the way you planned it. It couldn't have gone better. But I was sure early on they weren't cops."

"Who was the woman?"

"She was the buyer's girlfriend, and she had no clue they were there for a drug buy. No police officer brings his girl on an undercover operation. I could have made the exchange right there in the Marriot."

"Yeah, but we had no way of knowing for sure." He wanted validation for his spy movie-like plot, and Kel gave it to him.

"Worked to perfection, and it was fun. It seemed to me Zo and Bella liked it too."

"Those are their names?"

"Bella let it slip at the very end. She was ready to get back to the hotel room," Kelena said, giving Noah a big smile. They both chuckled. "I'm relieved that's over."

"We're almost out, Kel. I'm so glad you made this decision. Missy is too. None of us meant for our lives to go this way..." Noah realized he touched a nerve with her, so he didn't finish his thought. She felt guilty about everything, and he just reminded her that Kaitlin had no life to change. The hurt on her face was obvious as tears welled in her eyes.

"But we still have loose ends." Caroni worried her. He would sing like a songbird if the feds applied pressure to coerce him to talk, especially if they offered him a plea deal. Jace told her the FBI knew he was a drug distributor.

"Yeah, we'll deliver the 10K to everyone. Most of the folks are front-line, white-collar dealers that worked for Distro. Missy can get it to them easily enough. It'll just take time."

"And the supply side?"

"Most of our product came from suppliers who only dealt with Supply, and he already informed them we are out of the business. We only had one grower, and he had a jack and jill helping him. They were more like independent contractors than employees. Their only contact was with Kaitlin, and then Caroni, who funded the operation and took delivery of their crop. They've been told we're no longer in the market and to sell to other dealers. That leaves the lab guys — Joe, James, Tiny, and Bubba who, unfortunately, witnessed the gunfight, and they've seen our faces."

"Very loose ends."

"Yep. I can give Joe and James larger severances and ask them to disappear for six months. Not sure they'll do it. I've talked with a friend in the security business. He's willing to employ Tiny and Bubba as low-level muscle, and they'll be several states away."

"And the loosest end of all?"

"He scares me too. He knows almost everything. And the cops know he's dirty."

Kel took a deep breath and slowly exhaled in a drawn-out sigh. It wasn't over, but her thoughts were elsewhere. She needed to talk with Jace West.

Chapter 52

CHESAPEAKE — FOURTEEN DAYS BEFORE THE AS-SASSINATION, FBI FIELD OFFICE

"**H**ello, Kelena," Jace greeted her as he walked into the interrogation room.

"Thanks for seeing me, Mr. West." She wanted to have a private, unrecorded conversation with him, but they insisted on doing it in the FBI field office. No way did she intend to give an official state-ment, so it seemed unnecessary. But she had to tell somebody. "Are Agent Madson and Mrs. West next door?"

"Yes."

"Could you come in, please?" Kelena said into the camera mounted in the upper right-hand corner of the room. "I'd rather you talk to me face-to-face." She saw no reason for them to be covert about it.

After Grace and Charlotte greeted her, she ex-plained why she requested to talk with Jace. "I know something bad is going to happen. I need to tell someone in the FBI, but I'm not sure who to call. Seems to me you three are the only ones who will take me seriously, but I can't tell you how I know this."

Grace took the lead. "Okay." The way the investigation played out frustrated her and Charlotte, and they were eager to hear what Kelena had to say. "What's on your mind?"

"You guys are aware I'm like Jace, right?"

"Yes."

"I had no idea until I sensed he was in my head at Kaitlin's funeral. Then a tidal wave hit me. It all came at once, and it was overwhelming. Then I realized I had been doing it most of my life. I just ignored it. It took Jace to wake it up."

"We understand." Charlotte spoke to her in a kind voice. It didn't matter law enforcement considered the young woman in front of her to be a drug gang leader. She had experienced the turmoil Kelena must be going through. Besides, she couldn't bring herself to hate her as she does the murderous, amoral, scumbag thugs that sell women and children. "Go on."

"Obviously, you believe what Jace does is real, or the FBI wouldn't have hired him."

"That's right."

"So, that's how I know what I'm about to tell you."

"What's on your mind, Kelena?"

"On October 1st at 9:00 p.m., there will be an assassination attempt on the life of someone in Washington, DC." Kelena said it calmly and with confidence, as though it were fact.

The three interrogators expected an admission of her drug felonies. After all, she told Jace it was all on her, and he sensed she struggled with a great deal of guilt. Kelena's statement took them by surprise.

Grace and Charlotte showed no reaction. They worked long enough in the darker side of society that nothing surprised them. On impulse, they both looked to Jace with the expectation he would confirm or dispel the claim. Kelena followed their gaze and peered at him too, knowing validation was coming.

He realized they waited for him to speak. "She believes what she is saying is the truth. I can't say it is or it isn't, but to her, it's fact."

The four sat in silence, considering the weight of the knowledge they now possessed. Neither Grace nor Charlotte doubted the revelation. They never found Jace to be wrong. Grace's mind raced ahead, wondering how to present it to Headquarters and if they would take it seriously. The feeling was familiar. Less than a year ago she struggled to convince her Special Agent in Charge to devote more resources to prevent the terror attack that she, Charlotte, and Jace knew was imminent. Their 'conjecture' was only good enough to continue the investigation, but not get help to stop it. Charlotte stayed in the moment and hungered for more information.

"You need to tell us everything."

Kelena drew a deep breath and told her story. "I was with a man for a couple of hours yesterday."

"Thursday."

"Yes."

"What's his name?"

"Zo. That's all I got."

"Who's Nero?" Jace asked, hearing the nick-name in his mind.

"That's just what I called him. We weren't using real names..." Charlotte's unspoken accus-ation interrupted Kelena's train of thought.

"*No*. That's not true, Mrs. West." The idea that she didn't terminate the Corporation, as she said she would, annoyed Kelena. She paused to let the irrita-tion pass. "I shut it down."

"Sorry Kelena, but I'm a federal prosecutor. You understand why I would think that, right? Please, go on," Charlotte said, hoping she remedied her faux pas.

"Anyway, Zo and I and his girlfriend were sit-ting on the beach. That's what triggered his rush of emotion. It was just a normal day, and then Isabella, his girl, slipped and called him by his name. Zo pan-icked inside and these thoughts rushed through his head, and I heard them all."

"What thoughts?"

"There's going to be a huge protest October 1st outside the White House. Zo is supposed to turn it into a crazy riot at 9:00 p.m. as a diversion. Then, someone he knows intends to kill somebody. I felt a lot of trepidation, like he doesn't want to do it."

"Who's the target?"

"I never got a name, and I don't think he knows. It was clear to me he creates a big distraction, and then his friend executes a hit. Sounds like a whole conspiracy thing going on."

"You very well may be right," Charlotte said in agreement. "Can you get in touch with Zo? Do you think he'll talk to us?"

"I'm not certain, but I have a number."

Chapter 53

S ecurity's primary mission was to protect Chairman and her identity. Noah cared deeply for Kelena, and his loyalty to her was unbreakable. He would do what he had to do to keep her from being hurt or going to prison. That was his job. That was his commitment.

Caroni and his meth lab crew were the biggest threats to Kel's and his safety, so he felt an urgency to wrap up those loose ends. He and Caroni met with Tiny and Bubba. Noah paid each of them $10,000 and saw them off to their new employer in Florida. Working for a security agency seemed cool to them, and they wanted to get out of town. After all, Noah said the FBI in Norfolk was looking for them.

The cookers were a little more expensive to handle. Joe and James both thought they might just lie low for a while and go back to their normal lives. Noah agreed it was a great idea but maybe do it somewhere else. He offered to pay them an additional $40,000 each to vacation for six months in the Caribbean, and they flew out the next day.

The one threat left — the one that may well

put Kelena and him in prison for a long time — was Caroni. He ran the meth lab for the Corporation and witnessed the gunfight where nine people died. He conspired with Security's crew to desecrate human remains to destroy evidence. He would benefit by cutting a deal to testify against them should the FBI threaten him.

"So, what are your plans?" he asked Caroni. "Where are you headed?"

"I think I'll vacation in Costa Rica for a few weeks. It's nice down there, and cheap. They like Americans."

"Are you leaving anyone behind? Anybody going to miss you?"

"Nah. My Mom and Pops died young, and my girlfriend left me a long time ago."

"Sorry to hear that. What kind of cash will you need?"

"I'm thinking you gave Joe and James 50K each, and I deserve more than that."

"Yep."

"So, how about $100,000?"

Noah had no problem with paying off Caroni with 100K. It was worth getting him out of the country for a year — but not a few weeks. He knew too much and could hurt Kel too badly.

"Okay. I have that with me in my bag of goodies."

Also in his bag was a KA-BAR — the legendary combat knife first adopted by the United States Marine Corps in World War II and still produced today.

U.S. Marines are trained to be proficient with it, and Noah was a Marine.

Instead of removing $100,000, he gripped the KA-BAR and used the force of his entire body to thrust its seven-inch blade into Caroni's heart in one powerful movement. It is a strong, straight knife designed to kill, and penetrating the sternum was no problem. Caroni was dead in seconds. He was too much of a liability.

Noah's father took him camping in northeastern North Carolina when he was a kid, and he thought it was a good time for an overnight trip to his old stomping grounds. He brought the body with him, built a bonfire, stoked it all night, and destroyed the evidence just as Caroni himself would have done. In the morning, Noah packed up the bones and dumped them into the river on his way back to Virginia Beach.

It was something else he would have to lock away in that corner of his brain, he told himself.

Chapter 54

SAN FRANCISCO — FOURTEEN DAYS BEFORE THE ASSASSINATION, GIN'S OFFICE

"So?" Gin provided Chen with the details of phase four of her plan. "Can your men get this done?"

"It won't be too difficult, although your parameters insert a higher degree of difficulty."

"How so?"

"Avoiding collateral damage requires a certain level of precision. That means using tactics and care we would not need otherwise."

"For example?"

"There will be security personnel there. My team must use nonlethal force to disable them, and that takes more skill and patience than shooting them before they realize they are under attack. And that is before we get to the primary target."

"But your men can do it."

"Yes. But if we didn't need to be careful not to harm others, the job would be much simpler."

"I was concerned that may be an issue. How dangerous might it be?"

"We'll use the best shooter to enter the room.

He will be accurate. There could be minor collateral damage, but nothing life-threatening."

"When will it happen?"

"The distraction outside the White House should be in full force at 9:00. We'll go at 9:30."

"I'm concerned security might get antsy if they see the riot getting out of hand and may want to end the affair early."

"Then we'll be in position at the top of the hour and ready to move any time after. That won't be a problem."

"It's imperative no one gets caught. We can't have anyone blabbing to the FBI."

"None of the operators know who they work for or why they are executing the assassination. They only care about the paycheck, which is substantial. And they understand if they do not meet mission parameters, they will not get paid. Nothing can be traced to us."

"Besides that, Chen, the most important thing, the entire reason for the operation, is public perception. Voters must think it was a vast, right-wing conspiracy. Otherwise, the whole thing is a bust — a dismal failure."

"I have a few tricks up my sleeve. Their handler will drop hints to lead them to credit wealthy capitalists with funding the hit — just in case."

"Chen, you always impress me."

Chapter 55

C hen trusted Hu. She was the perfect insulator between him and law enforcement, so she was only one of two people who took her orders directly from him. Janco was the other. Chen met the Afrikaner decades before when he worked at the Chinese embassy in Pretoria.

As a young man, Janco trained to be an exceptional soldier in the South African Special Forces, and the 30-year Angolan civil war molded him into a hardened combat veteran. Chen recruited him to run covert actions against the Russian-supported People's Movement for the Liberation of Angola. As a SASF operator, he spent more time than he could remember fighting the MPLA and Cuban troops, so he had no moral or ethical issue with killing the same people, except earning a lot more money doing it for China. He became a mercenary loyal only to his homeland of South Africa and to Chen. In those years, Chen and Janco formed a personal bond, and Chen fed him a continuous stream of lucrative jobs since then. Hard as nails, Janco miraculously escaped many hopeless binds, and he wondered if he were living on borrowed time. He would never admit to anyone to working for Chen, and besides, he knew his friend would use his resources to extricate him from any trouble, legal or otherwise. They were too valuable a duo. Their loyalty to each other steeled over the years from the mutual benefit the relationship brought them.

Chen asked Janco to execute the October 1st assassination. Even at 61-years old, he was still in top form and liked to lead most missions himself. But he understood his commitment to protecting Chen required his discretion in this particular matter, and he contracted with his favorite team leader to have all the fun. He thought it important to give his best men the most lucrative assignments.

Janco flew to San Francisco to meet with Chen, who briefed him on the mission, stressing the parameters set by Gin. He was clear. Only one person is to be killed, and his unit needed to assume it was rich, white conservatives who wanted her dead.

Chapter 56

G race had that same sinking feeling she had a year ago. She told her boss she believed a terrorist attack in Norfolk was imminent, but he said her conclusions were conjecture. She had enough circumstantial evidence that he allowed her to continue the investigation. Back then, she couldn't tell him they built much of the case on Jace sensing the terrorists' thoughts. In the end, the after-action review of the incident concluded his clairvoyance was vital to finding the jihadis and determining their target. That's why they hired him. But there was no corroboration that the assassination conspiracy was real. This time, the team brought their concern to Grace's Special Agent in Charge and Charlotte's superior, the U.S. Attorney for the eastern region of Virginia. They made the joint decision to hire Jace in the first place and create their unique team.

"This suspicion is so flimsy it is virtually non-existent," the SAC said, looking at Grace. She reported to him, and it would be his responsibility to report the conspiracy up the chain to headquarters in DC. "Do you have any evidence other than this psychic thing?" Although it probably wasn't meant to be, Jace considered it a shot directed at him. His face flushed with embarrassment, and his imposter syndrome, something he fought every day to repress, came rushing to the surface.

Grace squirmed in her chair. "No sir, not yet, but October 1st is just two weeks away and we needed to inform you." She wanted to defend Jace and added, "We've never known Jace to be wrong."

"I'm not questioning Mr. West's ability. He's proven himself. But as I understand it, he didn't read the source of the information. It was this Kelena person who did that."

"Yes sir, but Jace confirmed she was telling the truth. She believed what she said."

"And let's not forget," Charlotte added, "Kelena came to us with this intelligence, even though she knew we suspect her to be an illicit drug distributor."

"Still, that doesn't mean she's right. She thinks she sensed something. That's very thin ice for us to act," the SAC said. "Bring me more."

"If Zo gives a statement…"

"Then I'll consider that a tip from a confidential informant. And I'll be more confident in it if Jace thinks he's telling the truth."

Chapter 57

VIRGINIA BEACH — ELEVEN DAYS BEFORE THE ASSASSINATION, KELENA'S HOME

Z o was paranoid walking that 100 yards along the beach in East Ocean View. While he didn't believe it was an intricate setup by the police, he'd find out for sure when he and Isabella got back to the Pathfinder. His relief was obvious when they safely parked the Nissan in its designated spot in the parking garage. Once they returned to the hotel room, his date drew all his attention, and it stayed that way until they returned to Washington the next day.

He forgot about the phone he used to text the pretty drug dealer. It was in the pocket of his jacket when she told him to put on his swimsuit, and he hadn't touched it since. At first, he thought the faint ringing was coming from the apartment next door, but when it didn't stop, he tracked the source to his closet. Zo found the phone where he had left it and figured it was just a misdialed call, but the number on the screen — the only one the phone had ever connected to — was familiar.

"Hello? Who is this?" he answered. His curiosity got the best of him.

"Hi, Zo. It's Kirk. I'm surprised you still have this phone." Kelena called him Zo intentionally. She wanted to signal to him she was serious and needed all the credibility she could get.

"Why are you calling me?"

"To start, I want you to know my name is Kelena."

"Well, I thought Kirk was a strange name for a woman." Playing along, he wondered what the call would bring.

"I'd like to meet with you — in DC. I can drive up tomorrow to discuss an important issue." Kel had no idea how to broach the subject.

"I'm not interested. That business was a one-time thing, just a part of my current job, and I want nothing more to do with it." Kelena was glad they weren't recording the call. She feared Zo would say something incriminating, so she refused the tap.

"I recognize that. It's not what I do either. It was an unusual circumstance."

"I thought you took a lot of silly precautions. I found it almost comical."

"Yeah, but it was fun."

"What do you want to talk about?" That was the question she wasn't sure how to answer. If she blew it, she'd lose the opportunity to reach out to him.

"Zo, I think you're a decent guy. I felt it."

"Okay?" His inflection hinted to her to continue.

"I assure you I'm not a cop, and I didn't talk

to anyone in law enforcement about our deal. Hopefully, you realize that by now. No one knows anything."

"Why did you call?" Zo's tone became short and defensive.

"I'm a good person too, and I'm worried about you." She paused but got no response from Zo, so she proceeded. "I sensed you don't want to be involved in the upcoming assassination in Washington."

"What?" Zo wanted to hang up. But if he did, the alarms in his head would go unanswered, and he needed answers.

Kelena explained her clairvoyance and reading his thoughts about October 1st. She told him she felt his turmoil, that he's a patriot and a good person at heart, and he didn't want to be a part of the plot.

His stomach turned. How could she know all that? Everything she said was true. There was no way for her to know any of it, particularly his anxiety that he hadn't mentioned to anyone.

Kelena let him think and then threw him her pitch. "You are *not* in trouble. No one knows about the drug buy. Do the right thing and meet with me."

"How will that help?"

"I'll have friends with me who can stop whatever is going to happen at 9:00 that night."

Chapter 58

CRYSTAL CITY, ARLINGTON, VIRGINIA — TEN DAYS
BEFORE THE ASSASSINATION

"I want you to understand I'm a patriot, a proud
American. I was a soldier for 10 years and
would never do anything to hurt our country." Zo
agreed to meet the day after Kelena called. She, Jace,
Charlotte, and Grace drove together to a pizza place
near Ronald Reagan National Airport. Zo picked the
location presuming it was far enough out of DC
that none of his acquaintances would see him there.
Kelena told him they were some sort of team from
the FBI, and he was good with that, even thankful
because he had been frozen with indecision. They
decided for him.

"We understand that," Charlotte said.

"That's why I agreed to this meeting. I couldn't
sleep and didn't know what to do."

"Tell us what you think will happen on October
1st. Kelena said there may be an assassination."

"Yes. I'm a security contractor now. I hang out
at a bar where other operators go and ran into a guy
I trained with a few times. We call him Ice."

"Ice?"

"I never found out his real name. That's his operator nickname. His team tagged him with it because he is a cold-blooded killer. He'd kill anyone and not think twice about it. No remorse. I've been drinking with the dude at Down Range, but I don't like him. He scares me, really."

"Down Range?"

"The bar in Arlington where I hang. He told me he's independent now and has a huge contract — unheard of money — to assassinate someone."

"How much?"

"Seven figures, he said. That's crazy pay. He was drunk, and he talks and boasts big time when he's drinking."

"If he was drunk, are you sure he wasn't feeding you a line of BS?"

"He doesn't do that, but he loves to boast. I knew he was telling the truth, so I questioned him about it. He didn't give me details, but he told me to look at the news October 2nd."

"So that's why you say it will happen on the first. Kelena said 9:00 p.m."

"Not sure it'll be 9:00, but I put two and two together and figured that's what will happen."

"What do you mean?"

"I'm getting paid a ton of money — a lot more than I should for such a simple job — to create a diversion in front of the White House at 9:00."

"How?"

"There's going to be a huge protest. A riot. Antifa turds. I've been helping them get organized and I'm supposed to have them crazy by then."

"How are you to do *that*?"

Zo hesitated, not wanting to admit to breaking any laws. He bought the meth, and his superiors expected him to distribute it the night of the riot. His handler told him to make sure his antifascists had the weapons they needed, but he couldn't bring himself to do that, so he gave the money to his street captains and let them buy what they wanted. But he realized that was a copout. Blood would still be on his hands if cops got hurt. Zo had to free himself and explained everything to the team. He remembered Kelena said she revealed nothing concerning their deal, so he took care not to divulge where he bought the crystal. But Jace sensed it as clear as if he spoke the words, and Grace and Charlotte are very smart women. They didn't have to hear him say it to figure out where the drugs came from. They'd decide how to handle Kelena later.

"Daniel," Charlotte used his given name, "can we count on your cooperation from this point forward? We'll need you to have any chance at stopping the assassination."

Chapter 59

CHESAPEAKE — NINE DAYS BEFORE THE ASSAS-
SINATION, FBI FIELD OFFICE

"Okay. Go. I want you to stay near the White House so you can monitor things close-up," Grace's SAC told the team. "I'll tell headquarters and the Washington field office that you're coming, and we have an assassination conspiracy coordinated with a potentially violent riot. Report to the Special Agent in Charge of the Counterterrorism Division when you get there." His words were clear and calm, but he fired them in staccato, sure of his decision and showing urgency.

The boss considered Zo's statement to one of his agents as though it came from a reliable CI. Jace confirming it was legitimate, at least in the inform-ant's mind, was sufficient for him to send his team to DC. Typically, the field office would forward the information to HQ and offer no other support, but this was different. While the Norfolk SAC had con-fidence that the danger was real, those who hadn't experienced Jace West personally may be less so. He learned his lesson in a bad way when he failed to take the terror threat, brought to him by Grace a year ago, seriously enough. He didn't want to spare the resources then and he feared his counterpart in Washington would be of the same mind now. Besides, there was an operational reason for the Norfolk crew to follow the lead. The CI trusted them and might not trust a new, unknown agent from another field office.

Grace secured two suites in a hotel a block away from Black Lives Matter Plaza. She normally would not stay in those higher-priced places, but with an endorsement provided by the FBI, she got them a bird's-eye view of where they expected the riot on Friday.

They checked in to their rooms that night. Although it was late, Grace texted Zo. 'We're in the city. When can we meet?'

Chapter 60

Mohammad was not keen on taking direction from a female, but he was in a different reality from where he was a year ago. As a Wahhabi devoted to the ultraconservative interpretation of the Quran, he still committed himself to Osama bin Laden's jihad against the United States. He stayed in America to continue to strike the Great Satan from within. That meant he had to adjust his tactics to carry on his mission. If doing the bidding of a woman who provided needed resources was in his interest, then so be it. Besides, she showed herself to be strong and unflinching in her quest by killing the traitorous Fahad, and he respected that.

Hu met with him one more time before he struck the Americans. To make sure he understood the value of his attack, she explained the deleterious effects it would have on the U.S. Government and how it would weaken its stature around the globe. She had no worry that he might divulge information if he was captured. A man with his devotion to the holy war would never aid his enemy and allow himself to be taken alive if he could help it.

"You know the importance of this undertaking we have asked of you." Her statement was more of a question. She needed him to affirm that he would complete the assignment as instructed. "The Americans must believe that your assault is the work of their so-called white supremacists."

"I understand. My attack will prompt American voters to elect Democrats whose policies weaken the U.S. military and favor foreign governments." The people Hu wanted him to kill were not targets he would have selected, but those will come later with the help of his new supplier of weapons and intelligence. They were still infidels and deserved to die.

"And you get to shoot Americans while reducing the influence of their government in the Middle East. That is the purpose of your jihad, yes?"

Mohammad agreed with her. An intelligent man with a university degree, he understood geopolitics quite well. His goal was to rid the Middle East of the U.S., and he saw the genius in Hu's plan, but his motivation was more immediate. She was an easy source of guns, ammunition, and explosives, and the intelligence she promised him would lead to more substantial attacks on the American government in the future. That's what he wanted.

Chapter 61

The team's only genuine lead to the assassination was Ice. Every evening since they arrived in DC, they sent Zo to hang out at Down Range, hoping Ice would show and let slip more information other than he's in town to kill somebody. After the fourth day of no trace of him, they began to worry. Was he keeping a low profile preparing for his hit? Had he gone into hiding? Their questions were soon answered.

On the first night, Grace, Charlotte, and Jace sat in a van, each eager to watch the video stream coming from Zo's electronic surveillance device while he waited in the bar. Those were five hours wasted that repeated themselves the next night. Jace made better use of the time on the third. He explored the vicinity around the White House, Lafayette Square Park, and BLM Plaza, hoping to see or sense something that may give clues to what lay ahead. Grace and Charlotte spent two more days witnessing women trying to get unusually friendly with the lonely Zo who sometimes forgot it was being recorded.

Their patience paid off on the night of day five. A couple hours into their vigil, Ice swaggered through the bar's entrance. Zo noticed and waved him over. As he strolled like a peacock toward his comrade, Zo whispered under his breath.

"He's got that shit-eating grin on his face," he said to the women in the van. "This will be a piece of cake." They didn't give him an earpiece. They figured it would be too easy for Ice to see and know why it was there, but Charlotte told him out loud anyway, "Don't get cocky. We've waited too long for this." Zo let an hour pass to let Ice pour a few beers down his gullet, and then probed the way he had practiced with the FBI agent and the prosecutor.

"So, what are you doing out tonight?"

"I'm giving myself a night of drinking before the big job. Then I'm going to take a few days to clear my head."

"Ha-ha! That doesn't sound like you. Ice is always ready to go."

"Yeah, but this assignment will take some precision, so I'm making sure. Don't want to screw up *this* paycheck."

"Is it really that serious?" The women in the van watched as the blonde man with his hair combed back with more than enough product, flash a toothy grin.

"You bet, brother."

"Seems like a whole lot of money for what we do."

"This is different." Ice finished a fresh draft in one gulp and signaled the server for another. "If it were just a break and blast, it would be quick and easy — in and out in seconds. But the customer wants us to be careful."

"What do you mean?"

"Well, let's say we have a room with ten people in it. A particular person needs killing. Two shouldn't be harmed and it's ok to injure the others, but no serious damage. Those are the parameters."

"Any room for me? I could use cash like that."

"Nah. We have a small crew. That's all we need, but I'll keep you in mind for the future if they hire me again."

"That's cool. I have a job that night, anyway. Getting good money for not doing much of anything."

"Friday?"

"Yeah, I'm babysitting those Antifa squirrels while they riot."

"Haha! Why do they have a babysitter?"

"At 9:00 I'm supposed to make sure they get crazy to divert police attention to them. Don't know why."

"Dude! I think we're on the same team."

"What do you mean?"

"That's when we move, at 9:00. We were told the cops would be too busy with the riot to respond quickly. We do the hit and exfil before anyone knows what happened. You're my diversion, man!"

"Wow. I wonder who's paying for all this. They

must have a ton of cash."

"I think it's a bunch of Republicans."

"Republicans? Why would they fund Antifa to riot at the White House?"

"They don't care about Antifa. They need the distraction."

"I don't get it."

"I'll just say the GOP would want our target dead, not the Dems." Zo nodded, more acknowledging Ice than understanding what he meant.

"So, I'll be on the front lines on Pennsylvania Ave getting gassed and having rubber bullets shot my way. Where will you be?"

"Can't say. My team leader is a hard ass, and he'd literally shoot me if he knew we were having this convo. Let's just say I'll only be a few blocks away rubbing elbows with important people."

"Like where, Smiley?" Charlotte said to the video monitor in the surveillance van. "Tell us where."

"Zo needs to be careful here. If he asks too many questions, then Ice will suspect something," Grace said, more to will the outcome than to tell Charlotte what she already knew.

Zo tried to think where he might mingle with big wigs in Washington, but there were scores of places. There were influential and powerful people everywhere. The bar had gotten crowded and warm inside with operators entertaining their friends with stories told over the din of country-pop. The two sat silently for the first time since Ice arrived and ordered a fresh pitcher of cold beer. They drank slower, enjoying the refreshment rather than to enhance their buzz, and pondered their conversation. When women in tight jeans and low-cut tops cozied up to the boys, Grace and Charlotte knew the intelligence gathering was done.

It was another hour before Zo remembered he had a wire and excused himself to return to the van for a debrief. As he stood to leave, a thought struck him.

"Hey brother, you need a ride? I can get you back to your hotel."

"What is he doing? That wasn't part of the plan," Charlotte said.

"Smart. Good thinking. He's trying to find where Ice is staying to help us track him," Grace answered.

"Nah. I want to stay here with the ladies for a while."

"You sure dude? You have something coming up," Zo tried to coax him.

"I'm cool. I'm only two blocks away."

"Perfect." Grace was impressed.

Chapter 62

WASHINGTON, DC — FOUR DAYS BEFORE THE AT-
TACK, LAFAYETTE PARK

W hile Charlotte and Grace finally recorded
their elusive target confirming what
sounded like an assassination conspiracy, Jace
strolled the site of the expected Friday riot. As they
did during the protests over the summer, the rioters
would probably gather in front of the White House
on Pennsylvania Ave and Lafayette Square, and
likely overflow into Black Lives Matter Plaza on the
opposite side of the park.

September had always been Jace's favorite time
of year to visit the nation's capital. Cool breezes
blowing through the streets and parks comple-
mented the warm weather. Trees started to turn
colors, and the crowds were thinner with the kids
back to school. The architecture and pleasant green
spaces gave him a calming pride, and the historical
significance of the city left him inspired.

There were still plenty of tourists walking
around the White House enjoying the views and
beholding the sights. Jace joined them, but he had
to remind himself he was not there to sightsee. He

walked slowly and lingered near people who seemed to stop and study, rather than admire. He thought he would snap a picture of anyone who looked or made him feel suspicious. Everyone had cameras lifted to their eyes, so snapping a photo would draw attention from no one.

It was on Pennsylvania Avenue that he noticed a tall man with a black, closely cropped beard and a dark complexion. The man was taking video, not of the White House or its grounds, but the streets and sidewalks nearby. He stood with his back to the iconic residence and pointed his camera phone outward, sweeping it from his right to his left in one panoramic, 180-degree view. That was odd. Most tourists take their photos pointing the other way. Shots of people on a street or in a park do not elicit memories of visiting one of the most famous buildings on Earth.

Then Jace's stomach knotted. His heart pumped oxygen-laden blood to his brain and muscles, heightening his senses and preparing his body for danger. Why did this guy give him an adrenaline kick? If Jace were a tourist, he would turn and walk away, choosing flight over fight, but he wasn't. He was there for a reason and sensed Tall Man was it. He strode toward the stranger as nonchalantly as he could, his phone ready in hand. Jace angled to a place 15 feet in front of his subject and raised his camera as if to photograph the White House. As he recorded the scene, Jace made sure Tall Man was in the frame when he moved his own camera, exposing his face. Jace's urge to flee intensified as a dark sense of doom crept through him, around him, enveloping his soul. The deep, murky green aura that Jace had experienced only twice previously enshrouded the imposing figure before him. Each time, he was with Bilal, the pious commander of the terrorists they exposed a year ago. Although it was a cool evening, sweat wet Jace's forehead, and he felt weak. He lowered the camera to steady his hands. Mohammad, Bilal's spiritual leader and the jihadist who created the Norfolk terror cell, was standing just a few yards from him. Jace had never been in his presence but recognized him from photos and sur- veillance video. And his evil energy left no doubt.

***

"But you said we'd leave here late in the after- noon, arrive in Washington around seven, do the deed, and then go home. All in the same day. You didn't say anything about going ahead of time."

"Trust me, Jeffry," Mohammad said, "one never goes to battle without proper preparation." With Fahad out of the picture, he relied on Jeffry to be his second in command. "Our plans are detailed but not sufficient. I need to scout the area."

"What are we going to do there?"

"We shall duplicate the drive there. Determine where to park the vehicle, where to position each of our soldiers, and take videos of our escape routes so they won't look unfamiliar to our men. Don't worry. We'll be tourists among the thousands. And we will leave the city the same day to simulate our escape."

***

It was fortunate Mohammad and Jace had never met. He paid no attention to the man who had walked towards him. To him, he was just a tourist taking a photo of the White House behind him.

Chapter 63

T he urge to call Charlotte and Grace was almost overwhelming. Jace wanted to leave so that he could talk freely but thought he should focus on Mohammad. He walked to the fence in front of the White House pretending to take in the view and spied him from the corner of his eye. Jace felt more awkward as each minute passed and was about to leave when Mohammad's phone dinged. He looked that way and saw him walk across Pennsylvania Ave and into Lafayette Square. That was the direction of the hotel, so Jace followed. Mohammad crossed H Street NW, climbed into a minivan on BLM Plaza, and it drove away, but not before Jace snapped a photo of the rear of the van as it pulled into traffic.

"We're headed back now," Charlotte said into the phone. "Meet us there." She looked at Grace. "Jace says he saw Mohammad. He has video."

"Well, hell. *This* has turned into a night."

Stunned, they sat in their car in silence. They assumed he had escaped to Saudi Arabia and never expected to cross paths with that man again. Grace's hand subconsciously moved to cover her inner thigh where scars marked the wounds from bullets fired by Mohammad's jihadis, ripping her femoral artery and coming within minutes of robbing her of life.

Confirming an assassination conspiracy was too important to take a back seat, but Grace and Charlotte could not resist looking at Jace's video. They hurried to the hotel room and burst through the door, startling him.

"Are you sure it's him?" Charlotte said without greeting her husband.

"Sure as I can be." He had it loaded on his laptop and watched it on the 15-inch screen. He stepped aside, hoping they'd look at it and tell him he was wrong. The two Joint Terrorism Task Force members had spent more time studying photos and videos of Mohammad than he did.

His teammates viewed the clip, replaying it several times. Finally, Charlotte paused it at the frame in which the subject looked straight into the camera. Jace knew from their sighs and deflated posture that he was right.

"That's a pretty good shot," Grace said.

"Yes. It is."

"I'll grab some photos and video from our case file for comparison." With a tight lip and blank stare, Grace exhaled.

"It's him," Charlotte said in a tone of resignation.

"I know."

Chapter 64

"It certainly looks like there's an assassination planned," Grace briefed the Special Agent in Charge of Counterterrorism in DC and handed him a thumb drive with the undercover recording of Ice with Zo.

"Give me a quick rundown," the SAC said. He gave the memory stick to a man already seated at his conference table. "I'll have my deputy take the lead on this," and he introduced DSAC Smyk to Grace, Charlotte, and Jace as they each took a chair.

"We wired our CI with video and audio. The guy he's talking to is a security contractor named Ice. We don't know his identity. Ice states he is part of a small hit team with orders to kill someone of importance at approximately 2100 hours Friday. It will be at a location blocks from the White House, possibly in a room with a group of ten people. The target is a Democrat." Grace paused to let the information sink in.

"Get on it now." The SAC turned to his deputy. "Use everyone you can."

"There's more. There's another video on that drive. Mr. West recorded a known terrorist on Pennsylvania Avenue and Lafayette Square last night. His name is Mohammad al-Qahtani and is responsible for the terror attack in Norfolk a year ago."

"The attack you sniffed out."

"Yes. We thought he escaped to his homeland, Saudi Arabia. We were wrong."

"What's he doing here?"

"Unknown. There's one more thing." The SAC stared at Grace with a look that resembled irritation. He didn't reply, so she continued. "Both the CI and the subject stated there will be a diversion in the form of a riot at the White House to cover the hit at 2100."

The boss waited for her to finish and then said, "Is that it, Special Agent Madson?"

"Yes Sir."

"Are we looking at a three-element attack?"

"Possibly, Sir. And we have three days to figure it out."

***

DSAC Smyk gathered his assistant and field agents in their briefing room and explained their assignment and its urgency. Grace and Charlotte did most of the talking, and Jace provided the context of his video of Mohammad. Most agents were aware of the unit from Norfolk. They'd been briefed as part of their continuing awareness and lessons-learned process, and the individual awards bestowed on the key personnel were well-publicized. The DSAC split his people into three groups, each focusing on one element of the threat expected on Friday, just a few days away. It made sense that Grace's team would take on Mohammad. They knew him best. They felt less empowered when the DSAC assigned the assassination plot that they uncovered to another team, but they had a personal stake in finding the terrorist that eluded them, and that was the task they wanted.

Chapter 65

It was late in the day when they left the FBI field office and the team headed back to their hotel. The plan was to freshen up and then meet for dinner to discuss their next moves. Jace's immediate assignment was to hurry to the restaurant and grab a table.

"Boss! Jace!" It was a déjà vu moment that sent chills down his spine. He turned to find Millicent Jackson speed-walking towards him. Her broad, white smile broadcast to all within sight that she was glad to see her former employer and friend. Finally recovered from the trauma of a year ago, the young woman with the infectious grin, always cheerful and caring, was back.

"Mil?!" Jace and Charlotte loved Millicent like a daughter. They became close over the past 12 months and spent plenty of dinnertimes with her and her parents. But hearing her call out to him from behind, as she did that one time in the MacArthur Center Mall, chilled his soul. It was that moment two summers ago that started the odyssey that left people dead, wounded, and traumatized.

"What are you doing here?" she said as she wrapped her arms around him and squeezed.

"Charlotte, Grace, and I are working a case. What are you doing here?"

"I'm here with Mom. She was invited to the party at the White House on Friday and I'm her date! I'm so excited."

"Wow, what an opportunity. So, you and Octavia are staying here?"

"Yes. You guys are too? We need to meet up."

"Well, I was just going to get a table…"

"That's where I'm headed. Mom should already be in there." Millicent grabbed Jace by the arm and pulled him into the restaurant in time to hear her mother request seating for two, and Mil blurted from behind to make it for five. Grace and Charlotte walked up a moment later, and after the warm greeting of good friends, the hostess led them to their table.

Jace began the conversation. "Mil says Octavia got an invitation to the shindig at the White House and they're both going Friday." Charlotte and Grace are practiced in not showing emotion. It serves them well in their careers. But both paused for a split second and shot a look at him before replying, and Octavia noticed. A respected and highly successful attorney in her own right, she was an expert in reading body language.

While they were aware of the celebration on the White House lawn during the riot, they let the Metropolitan Police Department and the Secret Service handle the safety of the people behind the iron fence. But Mil and Octavia being on the grounds, and the return of Mohammad brought back frightening memories. His plan in Norfolk was to shoot hundreds of rounds from AK-47s into a crowd of thousands, killing as many Americans as possible. Was he thinking the same for Friday — into 2,000 guests of the President of the United States?

"What time is that thing supposed to end?" Charlotte asked.

"Nine o'clock," Mil said. Her eyes were bright, and her energy level was a little higher than usual. She was excited to go to the White House.

"What's going on?" Octavia knew her friends were holding something from her and Mil, and she trusted them enough to ask them straight up.

"Oh, you know, we expect a riot outside the fence, and that's a bit worrisome." Charlotte saw no need to mention Mohammad. That would bring back traumatic memories for Mil.

"They told us a protest from Antifa is likely, but no one mentioned rioting."

"We have intel it could get nasty around 9:00," Grace said.

"That's why we're here," Charlotte added. "We're helping to follow up on some leads."

"Will it be dangerous?"

Jace spoke. "It may be, but you'll be safe on the grounds." He wanted to sound reassuring and not ruin Millicent's excitement. "Have they told you anything about leaving after the function?"

"Just that we'll be using the gate at the south end of East Executive Ave. That's a short walk from the hotel."

"We'll check what plans MPD has for the White House guests when they leave and keep in touch with you."

***

"So, what do we have so far?" Charlotte started as soon as they finished dinner and the Jacksons left for evening sightseeing. That was routine for the threesome. She liked to think out loud with her partners joining in.

"We got a hit on Mohammad's van from Jace's photo," Grace said, looking at a message on her smartphone. "It's from a rental company in Jersey City."

"New Jersey?" Jace said, scrunching his face in curiosity.

"Who rented it?" Charlotte asked.

"A corporation named Orient Xpress. Someone at the office is running it down for us."

"Mohammad was standing at the north fence of the White House but filming outward toward the park and along Pennsylvania Avenue — not the Residence itself," Jace said. "To me, that means whatever he's planning is in that immediate area of Pennsylvania Ave."

"What if Jace found him when he was finishing his recon? Mohammad may have scoped the pedestrian gate or the southern fence before Jace saw him," Grace said. "The protesters would want to disrupt the outdoor party, so they'd try to get as close to the South Lawn as they could."

"There's bound to be roving bands of rioters around the entire perimeter, but they need news footage to show their riots near the iconic front entrance to the mansion. I figure that's where most of the action will be. We'll hear what the other teams are doing in the morning briefing and what precautions they plan to take for the guests leaving the party just when the protest turns into a frenzied riot," Charlotte said.

"That can't be a coincidence."

"So, what's Mohammad's game?" Charlotte brought the discussion back to their primary concern.

"The last time, he preferred to attack with automatic rifles, so we ought to consider that's his plan this time," Grace said.

"We know he'll have help. He did before, and he jumped into a van driven by someone else. So that's at least one other person."

"Who's his target? The only thing that makes sense is that he's going after the uniformed Secret Service and the MPD on the fence line under the cover of the protest."

"I agree. Taking potshots from the south trying to hit the party on the lawn is just stupid. It's too far away, and the angle isn't right. He wouldn't do that."

"So, what are we doing?" Jace asked his more experienced teammates.

Charlotte laid out the plan. "Given the stakes, we cannot afford to have Mohammad in the city, so we have to put out an all-points bulletin from New Jersey to DC to stop the van and detain whoever's in it. We'll find who rented it and pull that string, too. Make sure the cops along the fence line know they're targets, and they wear body armor. We need as many law enforcement undercover officers as we can get among the rioters near the police barricade, ready to take down shooters."

"I have a very uneasy feeling about this," Grace said. "We don't know what he's up to. He could be involved in the hit for all we know."

"Or, more likely, part of the diversion. We'll coordinate with the other two units in the morning, and I want to talk to Zo again, too."

"Is that it?" Jace asked.

"We'll need to be out there, scanning the crowd."

Chapter 66

WASHINGTON, DC — TWO DAYS BEFORE THE ASSASSINATION

"Andrea, I'm in town and can't wait to see you. Everything is set for the fundraiser."

"Do we still have our donors lined up? The talk of a protest didn't scare anyone away?"

"No one ran away. They're all attending. I had lunch with Ephron Huffman and Vlad Miller today. They're already here and are eager to give you money."

"Thank you, Gin. This was such a great idea."

"All are in from your side?"

"Yes, your darling is coming. I had to promise her a big campaign boost for the election, and she promised to be good, but I don't know what you see in her. Representative Youngblood irritates me to no end. She's so unpredictable."

"That's why we need her. Your show of strength and party unity will be a stark contrast to that fool in the White House under siege. It's going to be grand. When do you plan to announce the press conference?"

"I'll push the release at 6:30. We'll be on the

front steps of The Lincoln at 8:00. I'll give the cameras as much time as they want, and we'll be in the Adams room for cocktails and rubbing elbows before 9:00."

"That sounds perfect, Madam Speaker. I hope you don't mind. I brought a reporter from the San Francisco Chronicle for some of my own publicity. It wasn't hard persuading her to jet away for a few days on my Gulfstream 650. I'll tell her about your press conference after you announce it."

"That's fine. The more the merrier."

"This will be *so* much fun!"

***

"Yes, Ma'am?"

"We're all set, Chen."

"What time?"

"Play it by ear — after 9:00."

"Very well."

Chapter 67

The DSAC ran the morning briefing of the 20 agents and analysts who made up the task force working the conspiracy.

The assassination unit had a breakthrough. Thanks to Zo's quick thinking to offer Ice a ride home from Down Range, they located where he was staying and verified he was in his room. The would-be assassin was now under 24-hour watch by a team of surveillance specialists. Highly trained in their art, the agents were confident that their subject would lead them to his co-conspirators and would have no clue that he had done it. If the FBI were to foil the assassination, they needed Ice to deliver the hit squad to them before it moved on its objective. They still did not know who the target was or where the attempt would be. The default plan was to stage tactical teams in every direction within a few blocks of the White House and identify potential meeting places in that radius. If it came down to a desperate, last-ditch assault, the hope was that they would have a response team a minute from the scene.

The riot unit worked closely with the Metro PD and the Secret Service. Their task was nothing new and preparing for an incursion on the White House by mobs was routine. Federal officers would be on standby to reinforce the police line around the perimeter. And the FBI had a dozen undercover agents who moved among protesters all summer and gathered information on individuals who appeared to be habitual rioters and leaders of the unrest. They'd monitor those suspects throughout the night and pass intelligence to the FBI Command and Tactical Operations Center. The goal was to handle whatever was thrown at them so they did not become the distraction to law enforcement expected by the assassins.

Days earlier, when the Norfolk crew briefed the Counterterrorism SAC of the conspiracy, the Attorney General asked the Mayor of Washington to activate the National Guard to help control the situation around the White House, but she declined. As a Democrat, she had no desire to appear to cooperate with the Republican administration and lose the support of the BLM activists in her city. That forced the Department of Justice to call agents from federal law enforcement agencies across the country to back up the MPD and Secret Service. With the cooperation of ATF, ICE, Park Police, and several others, the riot unit was ready to help protect the President and his house.

As the leader of the terrorism unit, Grace briefed the room what they knew about Mohammad. They believed, based on observed behavior, that he'll target the police line north of the grounds, but the function at the White House posed a particular concern. While inside the fence, the guests will enjoy the safety provided by the Secret Service, but outside the property, on the streets of the city, they'll be exposed to attacks by terrorists and rioters. Besides ensuring the visitors' gate at the south end of East Executive Ave was fortified, the riot unit had no plan to address that matter and promised to have an answer by the next brief.

After the meeting, Grace and her unit huddled in a corner of the briefing room. "I just don't have warm and fuzzies about this. We're assuming a lot. The only thing we know for sure is Mohammad was scoping the north side of the grounds. It's hard to believe he's collaborating with professional assassins. The bottom line is we're in the dark, and I'm getting nervous about it. Have you found the van, Darcy?" She looked at the analyst assigned to her from the Washington field office.

"Not yet."

"Our only hope of figuring this out is to find that van and whoever rented it."

"There's a special agent in New Jersey working on it and he knows the urgency. I'll phone him right after this."

"Okay. Call me either way." Grace turned to her Norfolk team. "Let's go talk to Zo."

Chapter 68

With the thump of wheels of the Boeing 737 Max landing on the runway at Washington Dulles International Airport, Jaana's stomach fluttered in anticipation of the event the next day. One hundred of her hand-picked Antifa rioters from Portland flew with her, and another 100 from Seattle. She didn't know who chartered the plane, just that Christian told her where to be and when to catch the flight. The group climbed into motor coaches waiting for them and were driven to inexpensive hotels near Falls Church, Virginia. Other buses unloaded throngs of protesters at lodging within an hour of the White House. Area restaurants flooded with young people and buzzed with excitement. Tomorrow was their big day.

Jaana and her leadership were expected at the planners' meeting that evening. Even though Christian didn't make the trip, he had an Uber waiting for them in time to drive to a hotel in Rosslyn where the DC organizers rented a ballroom. She and the other travelers from across the country couldn't help but be impressed with the accommodations and organization of their 'convention.'

***

"Zo doesn't want to meet until later." Charlotte had texted him to say they needed to talk.

"What? Why?" Grace snapped. The three of them were feeling the pressure. The riot was 24 hours away, and they had no hard clues about what Mohammad was up to or even if he had anything planned for the next day.

"He said he has to attend an organizers' meeting for the protest later and he'll tell us about it when he gets out. Should be around seven. I told him we couldn't wait that long, and we'd call him in a minute."

"Good. Dial him up."

Grace, Charlotte, and Jace were in their car, ready to drive to wherever Zo wanted to meet, but that wasn't working out.

"Hey," he answered, knowing who was on the line.

"Hi, Zo," Charlotte said. "We need to hear everything concerning the riot, but right now we have a few questions that can't wait."

"Go ahead."

"We're following another lead and we hope you can help us. Is there an element to the diversion that you haven't mentioned? Something besides the riot itself?"

Zo thought of the crystal he's supposed to give

the rioters. He felt dirty buying the stuff and even dirtier at the idea of giving it out to the 'kids.' "I told you about the meth. Not sure there's anything more to tell you."

"Is there another diversionary attack led by someone else? An attack that will happen during the riot?" Charlotte got to the point. Time was running out.

"Not that I'm aware of. There are a lot of people coming in from all over the country, but as far as I know, they're just protesters. Whoever is paying for this is flying-in rioters."

"No rumors of an attack other than Ice's hit?"

"That's right."

"Okay, thanks Zo. Call us after your meeting," Charlotte said, ending the conversation.

"Someone with a ton of money is funding this whole thing." She summed things up. "They're bringing in rioters, paying pros to organize it, buying a lot of meth, supplies, and weapons, and hired a hit team to take out somebody they want dead. None of that adds up to Mohammad. That's not his game."

It was the evening before the expected finale, whatever that may be, and Grace, Charlotte, and Jace were no closer to knowing Mohammad's plans. Back at their hotel, they tried to relax while they waited for their confidential informant to call. At the least, Zo might give them information they could pass along to the riot unit.

After dinner, Grace attempted a little humor with a hint of desperation mixed in. "Why don't you take a nap, Jace?" She pursed her lips, but they curled into a grin.

"What? I'm fine. I don't need a nap." It annoyed him that she thought he needed to rest, but Charlotte got the joke and smiled. The afternoon before the terror attack in Norfolk he felt troubled and tried to ease his mind through meditation. He fell asleep and had a vivid precognitive dream that led them straight to the jihadis and their target. With her suggestion of a snooze, Grace, half-joking, half not, hoped he'd do that again.

Jace saw the smile on his wife's face, and Grace's implication hit him like a gut punch. He and Charlotte had a similar, subtle sense of humor and their lives together included plenty of laughs, but that joke at that time fell flat with him. Being an engineer and a man of science, he had trouble accepting his clairvoyance at first, and was still sensitive when it appeared someone passed judgment on him. Grace didn't intend it that way, and he understood that, but he thought he had not been contributing as he should be. The quip hurt. "Oh. I get it," trying to chuckle to hide his feelings.

"Sorry. Bad joke."

"That's okay. But you realize it doesn't work like that, right? It just happens when it happens. I can't do it on demand."

Zo's call broke the awkwardness in the room, and Charlotte quickly answered.

"There's nothing new for you, but I have details you might want to know."

"Go."

"We've bused or flown in around 800 of Antifa's best. Combine that with the locals, there will be approximately a thousand actual rioters geared up and armed. There should be a few thousand more coming in to protest the President's party, so you're looking at about 3,000 to 4,000 unruly people outside the fence. The black bloc will bring their shields and helmets and ballistic vests and everything else — firebombs, mortars, and blunt weapons like bats and hammers. Some intend to bring industrial lasers, batons, and blades. They have battle plans drawn and it will get very nasty."

"Any guns?" Charlotte asked.

"We told them *not* to bring guns and none of the organizers bought them any. We stressed that all the cops carry weapons, and if anyone shoots at them, there's going to be dead protesters everywhere and the riot will end. They understand that. Most are experienced with this crap and know what they can get away with and what they can't."

"Are you going to be there?"

"No. I'm staying away. It's going to get hairy and I don't want to be anywhere near there."

"And the meth?"

Zo hesitated. Technically, he didn't give it to anyone. He understood he'd be guilty of distribution, but his street captains were expecting it, even looking forward to it. He wanted to just throw it away and wash his hands of it. "I think they have it." Those words sounded silly as soon as they crossed his lips.

"You think?"

"I stashed it in the room they use for training, and it's gone. I didn't give it to them or tell them it was there. But I can't find it now." Charlotte didn't push it. There were more pressing things to worry about.

"Training room?"

"I didn't mention that?"

"Noooo?" she said with an accusatory inflection, prompting him for more information.

"These black bloc people are serious. Every day they aren't protesting or rioting, they train. They form small groups and use squad tactics to attack their targets — like police cars. The shield lines practice when and how to hold and when and how to fall back. They have commanders on the streets with them, coordinating troops and giving orders. If you pay attention to those videos of the riots on the internet, you can see it. They know what they're doing. Nothing is random. They are trouble."

Chapter 69

T he morning briefing was much the same as the
day before. The assassination unit reported Ice
went out for dinner the previous evening but returned to his hotel without interacting with anyone.
And he hadn't left his room as of the time of the
brief.

Grace called the leader of the riot unit after
they hung up with Zo the night before and passed
the intel to him. The MPD and Secret Service dealt
with similar tactics all summer long. What she told
them was not new, but the sheer number of rioters
with weapons was disconcerting. Their strategy for
White House guests exiting the grounds was to release them through the gate in intervals and escort
them past the throng of protesters. With the uncer-
tainty of Mohammad's intentions, they decided it
was a bad idea to expose all at once two thousand
of the President's friends to the threat outside the
fence. The large group of people leaving the estate
would be a juicy and easy target for terrorists looking to make a political statement and send shock

waves through the American psyche. That tactic did nothing to ease the anxiety of the Norfolk team. As far as they were concerned, it wasn't much of a plan. There would be a relatively small number of law enforcement officers available to protect innocent partygoers as they swam through the crush of demonstrators. At least it eliminated what would be a very desirable objective for someone intending to shock the world, or a mob taking out their anger on their vulnerable 'enemies.'

Grace reported to the task force they had no additional information regarding Mohammad, and their one lead was the vehicle in which Jace photographed him four days prior. The bottom line was that it was a crapshoot, and they did not know what a known terrorist was doing in the Capital.

***

Mohammad directed his followers to meet him in their basement meeting room where he ran through the mission one more time before they left for DC. He trusted only three of his mentees with the operation — Jeffry and two others. After he agreed to the arrangement offered by Hu, he didn't have time to recruit and train jihadis in which he could place his faith. In fact, thinking of them as jihadis was an insult to Allah. One was an Iranian Muslim from the Jersey City community and two were Americans who had no allegiance to their government. None of them were pious men. All of them were interested in the large wad of cash that would come when they completed the job. Through his loyalty, especially after the Fahad incident, Jeffry had earned the position of second in command.

Mohammad reviewed the critical aspects of the mission insisted by Hu. They would carry only one magazine with 30 rounds. Each will push their way to their assigned points of attack, and at 9:05 p.m. expend their ammunition as fast as they could towards their targets. Killing was not important, but the shock of the strike itself was paramount. And their escape was essential. They were to throw their weapons to the ground, and run their predetermined exfiltration routes, shedding their black bloc clothing at the designated places before heading to the waiting van. Mohammad added a contingency that he expected they would need after the earlier reconnaissance trip. He decided it might be difficult to find a spot to park in the location required by the exfil plan. If that were the case, Jeffry would stay with the van and make sure he was in the right place at the right time to facilitate their disappearance.

When their review was through, Mohammad collected their identification and placed them in a shoulder bag to remain in the vehicle. They loaded their gear into the rear of the minivan, Jeffry took the driver's seat, the rest climbed into the back, and they were off for Washington, DC.

***

The day had worn into late in the afternoon, and Grace huddled the terrorism unit together in the FBI field office to discuss their play for the up-coming evening. They sat quietly in a small con-ference room at the end of a long hallway, away from the Command and Tactical Operations Center. The trepidation was thick. There wasn't much they could do at that point but react to Mohammad's next move. When the analyst's smartphone erupted with the clattering of an old-time alarm clock, the team startled in unison, and they each stared at Darcy as she answered. She recognized the voice of the caller and signaled with wide eyes and hand gestures she was receiving news of something important.

"Okay, thanks," she said into the phone. "Call me with an update as soon as possible." She ended the one-sided conversation and told her teammates, "New Jersey State Police stopped the van on Inter-state 95 headed south. They detained the passen-gers, and our guy is on the way."

"Who's in the vehicle? Do we know?" Grace's tone reflected the urgency of everyone in the unit.

"No. Nothing yet. Special Agent Barnes just got the call."

***

It was a long, straight stretch of I95 near the town of Auburn. A New Jersey state police officer pulled off the highway onto the right shoulder of the southbound lane. His task, like all other troopers on duty, was to locate a blue Chrysler minivan. Trooper Transue was on heightened alert. Someone's pants were on fire in Washington and wanted that van and whoever was in it.

The sun sunk low in the western sky, and the patrolman was nearing the end of his shift. He wasn't as attentive as he was when he began his day, and he fidgeted in his seat, trying to ward off the fatigue. Just as he looked away from the highway, he caught the bright blue blur of a minivan speeding by him at 65 miles per hour. He missed the number, but he saw it was a New Jersey license plate — exactly what he was on the lookout for — so he flipped on his light bar and pulled his cruiser into traffic.

***

Mohammad sat in the second-row seat behind the driver. He thought it best that he stay hidden behind the dark tint of the passenger windows. They stowed their AR-15 short barrel rifles in their tactical bags in the back. He felt bare without a weapon, so he carried his sidearm in a belt holster. He had Jeffry buy handguns for his entire crew in case they needed them to escape pursuers after their strike, so they all had guns clipped to their belts.

All four terrorists saw the blue lights flashing behind them. Jeffry reflexively tightened his grip on the steering wheel, and beads of sweat formed on his forehead. In a controlled voice, Mohammad told him not to panic. He had been in a similar situation before, and the police sped away, apparently after someone else. But he reached for his weapon that time a year ago and did the same this time.

***

When he approached his subject from behind, the tag number was clear. Trooper Transue double-checked the all-points bulletin and verified he found their quarry. As he pursued the van with his lights on, he radioed dispatch to announce his find. The dispatcher alerted other units in the area and directed them to back up Transue, and she cautioned, "Be advised, consider the suspects armed and dangerous." At that call, the trooper's heart rate elevated, and his head cleared.

He expected his target to flee and mentally prepared for a high-speed chase, but the van slowed, pulled onto the shoulder, and stopped. He followed but kept a safe distance from it. The trooper stayed in his cruiser to call in his status and waited for backup to arrive. Procedure dictated that he approach a vehicle with dark tinted windows, and suspects thought to be armed, with at least one other officer. But the people in the van didn't wait for procedure.

The driver, an extremely nervous young man who became impatient with the cop, exited his van and began walking toward the patrolman. Officer Transue had no choice. He got out of his patrol unit and drew his nine-millimeter service weapon. He pointed the gun at the kid advancing on him and ordered him to halt.

***

"It looks like we caught 'em," Darcy reported to the group. "Our special agent is on site. The trooper who made the stop was forced to shoot the driver, who died at the scene. State police took two other suspects into custody, and he'll question them as soon as he gets to the station. He said it was nearby, and he'd be there in a few minutes."

"Did they get Mohammad? Who did they kill?"

"Special Agent Barnes indicated the driver was a young, white male. He hasn't seen the passengers. The troopers took them before he arrived."

"The driver I saw across from Lafayette Park was a young, white kid," Jace said.

"I want to know the description of the other two suspects ASAP," Grace told the analyst. Charlotte glanced at her teammates. Their ever-darkening look of frustration over the course of the day had just been replaced by the glimmer of relief.

***

The minivan was a late-model Chrysler Voyager with a jazz blue, glossy pearl-coat finish. Mohammad found it pleasing and thought law enforcement would not suspect jihadists to drive away in a beautiful, new family vehicle like the flashy blue minivan. Besides, they had little choice. Someone at the rental company must have liked the color because all its Voyagers were jazz blue with the pearl-coat finish. They asked him to return the van they had driven to Washington. Their records showed a technician failed to complete a maintenance inspection and they preferred to finish the safety check to ensure the car was safe rather than wait for the renter to bring it back. It was a minor annoyance, but Jeffry had time to take it to the lot and make the switch.

Chapter 70

"T ango is on the move, headed to the elevator," the FBI agent surveilling Ice's hotel room reported to his colleagues on their radio net.

"Copy that," the special agent running the team responded. "Everyone acknowledge." He directed each member of his unit to state that they knew Ice was moving, and they did.

"Tango is in the lobby. He's wearing a navy-blue suit, white shirt, and blue tie," came the radio call from the agent stationed nearby. "He's rolling a small, black suitcase but is otherwise empty-handed." The FBI equipped its surveillance operatives with high-definition body cams that transmitted video of what the officers saw to their teammates and the command center in the field office.

"That doesn't look like he's going to an assassination," one of the dozens of staffers manning the CTOC observed. After a brief pause while everyone watched the huge screens at the front of the room, another person joked, "Maybe he's invited to the afterparty." Grace, Charlotte, and Jace rushed down the hall to the ops center when they heard Ice was on the move and took seats in the observation gallery. They didn't see who made the joke, but they saw the stern glare it drew from the Special Agent in Charge.

"It's 3:00 p.m. That's a bit early for him to leave the hotel," said DSAC Smyk, the man leading the task force. "If the hit is at 9:00, then where is he going?" No one answered as they eyed the video feeds from the ten or so surveillance agents that were part of the Ice operation.

"Tango is still in the lobby. He's looking outside. Appears to be waiting for his ride." The agent tailing Ice reported.

"Copy. Mobile units standby."

The tail guessed right. Their subject left the hotel and climbed into a large, early model Mercedes sedan. It was clean and looked well-maintained. "That's an Uber," a voice in the room reported. Following the car to the Rosslyn metro station, a two-mile drive east on Lee Highway, was simple. But the surveillance team didn't expect him to take a car to somewhere so close to his hotel, and they didn't have agents waiting there to pick up the tail.

"That's smart," said the ASAC of the surveillance unit. "He took a five-minute ride to the Rosslyn station when he had the Court House metro just around the corner from his hotel — an easy stroll."

"Think he knows he has a tail?" Smyk asked.

"No. He's a pro taking normal precautions."

"Are we going to lose him?"

"No. We had three mobile units on his tail. Two just followed him into the metro." The ASAC monitored the video feeds and saw the units drop off undercovers right behind Ice before they made their radio calls. "And we have ghosts at each of the metro stations within five blocks of the White House. He won't lose us."

"What if he gets off the subway somewhere else?" Jace whispered to Charlotte and Grace. They didn't answer, and the worried twist of her lips and scrunched nose Grace shot him didn't ease his concern.

Ice timed his ingress into the city to coincide with the rush hour of the afternoon. Traffic in Washington at the end of the workday is mind-numbing, and people crowd rail stations and bus stops by the time 3:00 p.m. arrives. Following someone through a subway commute is difficult, and he knew that. Not that he thought he was being tailed, but he was an operator on a job and a professional is always careful. He figured nobody could follow or make sense of his route to connect with his associates. From the Silver Line out of Rosslyn, he transferred to the Red Line at Metro Center, and just one quick stop later jumped on the Green Line at Gallery Place. He exited the metro at L'Enfant Plaza. Commuters making transfers and entering and exiting the railway mobbed all three places. There was no way anyone followed him. He smiled that toothy grin of his as he walked a few blocks southeast, in the opposite direction from the White House, and into the lobby of a high-end hotel. But he wasn't done with his fun little game. Once he entered, he hurried to the mezzanine that overlooked the entrance, shielded himself behind decorative foliage, and watched for characters that looked like a tail. After 30 minutes, he was sure he was in the clear and called a Lyft, met it in the parking garage in the basement, and drove away.

"Well?" asked DSAC Smyk to his ASAC running the surveillance.

"We're still trying to pick him up at L'Enfant Plaza. We followed him through the maze of the metro and lost sight of him there. My team is sweeping the area and will find him," the ASAC said confidently, but he knew his guys had blown it. Once a pro loses his tail, it usually stays that way.

Chapter 71

J ace watched as the task force's only two leads vanished into air. The FBI lost track of Ice, their only lead to the assassination that they knew would happen at around 9:00 that night. And Mohammad's minivan turned out to be a bust. Police stopped the van in Jace's photo, but it wasn't Mohammad. Three teenagers from New York decided they would make their fortunes delivering drugs up and down the east coast. Unfortunately for them, they rented the vehicle Jeffry had returned to the rental company to complete its maintenance inspection.

Hours before, they picked up a package from a house on Staten Island for delivery to a residence in West Baltimore. They were on their way to make a quick thousand dollars for each of them when Trooper Transue stopped them. Inside the minivan, the mood turned tense as soon as the teens realized a police cruiser was trailing them with its blue lights flashing and it wasn't leaving. The two passengers, not thinking clearly and full of bravado, pulled handguns from their belts. Afraid of what might come next, the driver got out of the van and walked to the cop, hoping to smooth things with him before his friends panicked. But a gunshot cracked from somewhere behind him and the officer reacted by squeezing the trigger of his own nine-millimeter.

Jace, dejected by the failures of the day with no recovery for the good guys in sight, decided he had to step up. There was only one play left, and if they were to win the game their only option was for him to throw the Hail Mary.

"I'm going to the hotel," he told his teammates. He looked at Charlotte, and then to Grace, and they knew what he met.

"Need to be alone?" his wife asked, making sure he didn't want her to go with him. He nodded.

"I'll get you an escort. The protest is forming around Pennsylvania Ave and I don't want you to have to deal with it." Grace already had her phone to her ear.

"Call us. Either way. Remember, we're hitting the street at 8:00."

***

Jace thanked the young Agent Shackleford as he got out of her car and stepped to the hotel doors. In front of him were Millicent and Octavia, waiting for him to notice them.

When their eyes met, Octavia spoke first. "Mil and I are walking to the White House," she said in an expectant tone. Jace looked at Mil, her smile as bright as ever, and she seemed to bounce out of her heels in excitement.

"Hi, guys." He promised he would keep them informed regarding the riot, but he was so wrapped up in the day that he forgot to call. Octavia raised her eyebrows in anticipation. "The protest isn't too bad right now, so if you stay a block over before heading to the gate, you'll be fine."

"What about at 9:00?"

"The Metro PD plans to escort small groups from the grounds past whatever crowd is out there. Keep at least two blocks from the White House until you get back to the hotel."

"Are you okay, Jace?" Octavia sensed his tension.

"Do me a favor and call me when it's your turn to leave. I'm not sure where I'll be, but if I can, I'll meet you outside the gate."

"We will." Jace's apprehension made Mom nervous. Millicent had seen it before in the minutes leading up to the terror attack that had consumed her life over the past year. The flashback drained some of the day's excitement as she felt her chest tighten.

***

The hotel room was eerily quiet. Charlotte was usually there with him, making the suite seem warm. Now, he was by himself and the lives of people he didn't know may be in his hands. His insides felt tied and twisted, and his thoughts raced. *It's okay*, he told himself, *you know what to do.* After the accident that day in June over a year ago, he learned to meditate to calm his mind, and Ike taught him how to use that technique to nurture precognitive dreams. It was a long shot. Last time, he worked hard at it, and it took emotional contemplation to open his consciousness to see what was to come.

Jace laid on the bed, put in his earbuds, and played the jazz mix his kids made to help him relax. His breathing and the music relieved the tension within minutes, but the day's events still sped through his mind. That was good. That's how it worked. If something were to present itself, it would be because his thoughts were already there.

***

He stumbled through the mob of black, noise coming from all angles. The black bumped and jostled him, pushing him in directions he didn't want to go, but he forced himself forward. His eyes stung, and it hurt when he breathed. He became aware of the bag slung over his shoulder, practicing how to open it in his mind, wondering if it was 9:05 yet. Then he heard the pow-pow-pow. Single shots fired in rapid succession. He felt panic, but swung his pack around, unzipped it, and removed a small rifle. It looked like a toy. He pointed it at the mass and pulled the trigger. The sea parted, and he ran. Down a street. Paranoid. He saw the rifle in his hand and threw it. He remembered. He was supposed to drop it on the ground. And he was more at ease the faster he fled.

The athletic men wore sharp-looking suits. He

admired the way they looked, and confidence oozed from his being. There was a bulge under his jacket, and he knew it was another toy-like weapon. Large paintings of presidents hung from the walls, and French doors with ornate woodwork and opaque glass drew his interest and of those with him. 'Adams Room' was scrolled onto the brass plate adhered to the right-hand door.

***

Jace heard ringing in his ears, like the phone hanging on the kitchen wall when he was a kid. It rang again, and then again. Startled awake, he sprung to his feet, and his earbuds alerted one more time, bringing him back to reality.

Chapter 72

TWO HOURS BEFORE THE ATTACKS

"**H**ey. It's 7:00 and we'll have to get ready soon. Did you grab something to eat?" Charlotte didn't want to appear too expectant, so she started with small talk. Jace took a moment to clear his head and didn't respond. She could tell over the phone. It had worked.

"Eat? No." Jace was processing, and she waited. She put her cell on speaker so Grace and Darcy could hear.

"What did you see, Jace?"

"There will be shooters in the crowd of pro-testers." Charlotte understood not to ask questions right away. Jace needed to focus. "At least two. They will use mini rifles, single-shot — semiautomatic." Darcy knew about the team from Norfolk and realized what was happening. She was fascinated. "They'll shoot at 9:05."

"Who is their target?"

"Protesters. I didn't see uniformed police."

"After several shots, I ran. I was supposed to drop the weapon, so I threw it and kept running down a street." Darcy squinted and looked confused, but she didn't interrupt.

Grace whispered in her ear. *"His precog dreams come in the first person. He's sensing what one of the shooters is feeling or thinking."*

"Anything else?" Charlotte asked.

"Yes. I was in a room with presidents."

"Presidents?"

"Paintings. Washington, Jefferson, Lincoln. And there were fancy French doors — elaborate woodwork and etched glass. I was with big men in expensive suits. And there was a brass nameplate on the doors."

"What did it say?"

"Adams Room."

"What else?"

"That's it." Charlotte gave him a minute to think. In the past, he recorded his precognitive events in a journal and she knew better than to disturb him until he decided he was done. After a long pause, Grace brought everyone back to the urgency of their situation.

"Jace, I sent a car for you when Charlotte called. Agent Shackleford should be downstairs waiting for you. Take a minute to freshen up and then get over here."

Chapter 73

T he jihadis' trip to DC was uneventful except for a close call with a state police officer. The trooper pulled behind them in traffic with his lights flashing, but then he sped by, apparently responding to an emergency somewhere else.

They arrived around 7:00 p.m., just as Mohammad planned. The protest had formed by then, allowing them to scout the perimeter and get comfortable with the lay of the land. He thought the idea of parking the van was a nonstarter but realized as they toured the area that they could do it easily. From his reconnaissance trip earlier in the week, he expected finding a place to park close to the center of Washington would be impossible. But that Hu woman who developed the plan must have been remarkably familiar with the city. The time of year and the evening hour thinned the number of vacationers and sightseers, and the warning of unrest kept residents from visiting their favorite restaurants and shops near the White House. The parking garage on I Street was open, so Jeffry pulled their vehicle into the structure and parked in a spot next to the stairwell to the ground level.

Since they had plenty of time, the four of them walked their egress routes and found the hidden alcoves tucked under building archways or behind vegetation where they could secretly strip off their black clothing worn by the shooters. They would emerge from those hideaways in clothes that sightseers might wear and walk to the parking garage and the van inside. Mohammad designated Jeffry as the getaway driver and kept him with their transportation. He would drive the family minivan away from the commotion and safely home to Jersey City with the others, who may have been seen in their escape, behind the dark tinted windows.

At 8:00 p.m., the shooters covertly checked their weapons, pulled on their black bloc coveralls and gear, and walked to the protest. The first snag in their plan was almost immediate. When they approached 16th Street, police in their riot kits marched toward them, sandwiching BLM rioters between themselves and the jihadis. Mohammad led his men to detour on 17th Street and south to the edge of Lafayette Park. There they diverted to their assigned positions. Ali pushed his way to the northeast corner of the horde, Mohammad to the center, and Tomas to the northwest. They burrowed halfway into the mob and waited.

Chapter 74

As soon as Jace closed the car door, the young agent flipped on her emergency lights and siren and sped toward the field office. It was a straight shot down H Street to 4th that typically took seven minutes. She made it in five and escorted him to DSAC Smyk's office where the task force leadership already gathered around the conference table. Grace was at the table, and Charlotte sat in one of the chairs lined against a wall.

"Jace, time's running short and we have nothing to go on," Smyk said. "Special Agent Madson says you may have something."

Jace explained his precognitive visions to the larger group. It was obvious from the body language and unfriendly looks that the Washington field office personnel didn't think much of him and what he shared. He had confidence in his ability and history had proven him right several times, but doubters in decision-making positions ate at his credibility. He had begun to resent the implications and spoke with a firm but not yet adversarial voice.

"So where is this fancy place with presidents on

the wall?" Smyk led the ensuing discussion. He read the after-action report and investigation into the terror attack in Norfolk and understood what Jace had done. Regardless of the looks around the table, he was going to follow Jace's leads. Besides, he was out of options. The question was directed to the entire room, but he looked at Jace.

"I don't know where," Jace said, "but I believe it's in a high-end, possibly historic hotel. And from what Ice told our CI, it's within a few blocks of the White House."

"Where is this hotel, people? We need to find it now. Seems to me the quickest way to do that is to call hotels near the Residence and ask them if they have an Adams Room."

"Ice was wearing a business suit when we lost him," the Assistant SAC leading the assassination unit said. "That makes sense if you believe West's little story."

"Get the word to our tactical teams that the bad guys are likely wearing expensive suits, and find that hotel."

The ASAC looked over his shoulder to a special agent sitting along the wall. That was a signal to get on it, and the agent hurried away.

"What do we make of what I assume is a coinciding terror attack?" The DSAC quickly moved the discussion forward.

As the leader of the terrorism unit, Grace spoke up. "I think Mohammad al-Qahtani will have at least two shooters, maybe more, interspersed in the mob of protesters. They'll carry backpacks, like hundreds or even thousands of others, but they'll conceal short barrel rifles in theirs. At 9:05, they'll remove their weapons, shoot into the crowd, and then run away. The gunfire is bound to create chaos on the streets and confusion and indecision in the MPD and Secret Service. They will already be in the middle of trying to control a dangerous riot."

"How do we prevent that?" DSAC Smyk asked his team.

The men at the conference table were quiet, so Grace gave her opinion. "At this point, there's not much we can do. We need to get as many agents in the field as possible, scanning the crowd for shooters. We'll distribute photos of al-Qahtani. The terrorists will carry their weapons in tactical bags similar to the backpacks used by the black bloc, but they have a distinct shape to fit a short barrel rifle. Everyone needs to know what they look like and search for those, as well as for Mohammad."

"That's worse than looking for a needle in a haystack," one of the task force leaders sitting at the table scoffed.

Charlotte was a straight-to-the-point person and had little patience for people who said or did unhelpful things. The attack was imminent, and she needed the honchos to get moving. "Got any better ideas?" she asked pointedly, directing it to the 'haystack' agent. Grace smiled inside. That was one reason she loved Charlotte, but she didn't want her superiors to see her satisfaction. Charlotte was not part of their chain of command. By extension, she worked for the U.S. Attorney General, the overseer of the FBI. Even though she held no authority in the room, she didn't hesitate to use her implied power.

The haystack agent didn't reply, and neither did anyone else. "Alright, Grace. Get on it." The DSAC issued his orders and glanced at the riot unit lead. The plan was his to implement.

"Grace, my people are already in the crowd, and they aren't briefed," the leader of the riot team said once they got to his office.

"How do you communicate with them?"

"They have two-way undercover comms. We can talk to them from the CTOC. We'll redirect their priority from checking subversive activity to stopping the terrorists. They know what tactical bags look like. Heck, all of them probably own one, so that won't be an issue."

"But we can't get them photos of Mohammad?" Charlotte asked.

"No. The best we can do is broadcast his description."

"Let's do it now."

"Okay, anything else?"

"You have to be here to direct things in the command center. We need to be in the field, and we need tactical gear," Grace said.

"I don't know about sending two civilians into the hornets' nest. That's not a good idea."

"No, it's not." She flashed back to the first time

the three of them went toe-to-toe with Mohammad. She had to do it then, and it had to be done now. "But we're the only ones who have seen al-Qahtani, and you need all the eyes you can get."

"Fine. No weapons, though."

"I'm a federal officer and permitted to carry in DC," Charlotte said, not looking for approval or a weapon, but setting the special agent straight. He didn't respond, and she didn't want him to.

Chapter 75

T hroughout the afternoon, cars, buses, and subway trains disgorged thousands of protesters
and rioters onto the streets surrounding the White
House, and more walked to 1600 Pennsylvania Ave
from wherever they lived or lodged. The people motivated to take part ranged from activists offended
by the President's blunt personality to antifascists
intent on insurrection, believing the time had come
for America's 'unfair' capitalist society to be replaced
by socialism. Antifa factions clad in their black bloc
clothing and riot gear mixed with the black t-shirts
of BLM demonstrators, creating an obsidian sea in
front of the White House, around its gates, and to
the south. Many answered the call on social media
to protest the President while he gathered with supporters, but hundreds came ready for revolt. Recruited, trained, and equipped, they were prepared
for this day.

Jaana was one of the recruited, and she brought
with her 200 black bloc troops experienced in making political statements through chaotic and violent
spectacle. They were good at it and had many years

of practice. Each of her soldiers was grouped with those less versed in the art of turmoil. All had specific roles and carried gear in their hands and backpacks particular to their tasks.

Jaana brought Piper, her second in command, as well as the other Antifa faction leaders from Portland. She thought it imperative to bring her entire leadership for continuity of control. The Seattle street captain and she agreed it was best they operate separately, but coordinate through liaisons. Each chose a trusted third to swap with each other to make it easier to communicate between their command structures.

Following the battle plan, the Portland crew headed to the north, in front of the White House, and the Seattle contingent moved to the south. They coordinated through their liaisons using two-way radios. The southern unit's mission was to push through the pedestrian gates and occupy E Street NW along the grounds' fence line. Once established, they would launch fireworks above the South Lawn to disrupt the President's celebration. Jaana's troop was to get as close to the iron fence as possible and lob mortars at the White House itself. It would make for spectacular news footage, which was the point of the riot.

At 15 minutes before 8:00, the Portland and Seattle companies were in place and ready to make their assaults, but they waited for their support protestors to gain strength. The DC captains and their Antifa factions coordinated the effort, guiding throngs to Pennsylvania Ave and E Street, freely distributing Zo's gift as they did. Jaana was in awe of the operation. She guessed that with her 100 and their share of the antifascists from other cities, she had about 500 trained rioters interspersed among 2500 protesters, and the southern unit had the same. If all went as planned, they would direct a two-pronged assault on the White House with 3,000 social justice warriors from the north, and 3,000 from the south. With those numbers, they could even breach the fence and attack the building itself, she mused.

She looked at her watch and felt an urgency. Time was slipping toward 8:00. She knew they had to start soon if they were to be in a position to disrupt the party scheduled to end at 9:00. They realized it would take a while for the guests to leave, but she and the Seattle street captain wanted to create havoc at just the right moment.

Over the din of her 3,000 protesters gathered on Pennsylvania Avenue shouting slogans and obscenities at the Metro PD and uniformed Secret Service, Jaana heard sirens scream behind her. She yelled to Piper, "What is that? It's too early for the cops to move in. Nothing's happened yet."

"It's BLM. They're rioting on BLM Plaza!" The DC captains watched the operation's rear perimeter from strategic locations and monitored the chatter on police scanners. Their job was to keep Jaana and the Seattle command aware of law enforcement movements behind them. Piper was in direct radio contact with them.

"Are our shield lines in place?"

"Yes."

"Good! It's time!" Jaana's eyes gleamed with excitement, and her heart pounded with a sudden adrenaline rush. "Tell all line squads to push forward to the barricades." She flashed a look at the Seattle liaison, signaling him to relay her move to his street captain to the south.

The DC antifascists had done a decent job staging supplies and handing out shields and umbrellas to those who agreed to use them. They joined the shield lines and followed the orders of the leaders in the field. The shield holders were the tip of the spear. They formed a line facing the police, and when ordered, would advance towards them. Their task was to push the cops back and absorb any counters like baton strikes, rubber bullets, and pepper pellets. Those holding umbrellas were to ring the rioters and open their 'weapons' to hide the identities of their comrades breaking the law. They were also handy in protection against targeted crowd control sprays.

Jaana positioned herself, along with Piper and the Seattle third, near the front and center of the forward assault. She needed to be able to see first-hand how the battle progressed. "Do the fireteams have targets?" Piper had an earpiece in her right ear and a microphone wrapped to her lips. She toggled her radio and spoke loudly into her mic to overcome the cacophony, receiving responses just seconds later.

"Fireteams have targets!" she shouted.

Jaana surveyed her front line. Behind their barricade, the cops were only two deep, and she had a throng of 3,000 ready to mow them over. She had to be careful to coordinate her teams' actions. One powerful surge may elicit the early use of tear gas, rubber bullets, and other non-lethal force which might cause her ranks to break and the mission to fail. The police formed their temporary barriers into a long rampart of conjoined rectangular pens making advancement more difficult, but Jaana and her leaders had a solution for that. The ballet had to be intricately choreographed.

"Seattle fireteams are ready!" the third said.

"Tell Fireteam 1 to execute."

Piper relayed the orders on their radio net, and the third did the same. Antifa's battle plan called for the fireteam to torch a police cruiser, or another worthy target, on the northeast corner of the White House fence, drawing MPD and Secret Service attention. Five minutes later, another fireteam would do the same on the southwest perimeter, and then other teams were to hit the northwest and southeast. With the authorities' scrutiny drawn to the corners, the shield lines would make their big push to get close enough to the fence for their ballistic squads to launch mortars.

Fireteam 1 had plenty of targets from which to choose. The MPD positioned multiple vehicles at the vertical cylindrical barriers that stretched across Pennsylvania Avenue to prevent people from driving near the White House. FT1 organized protesters to the 15th Street side of the parked patrol units and then chose its victim. Using squad tactics, it used hammers and bats to batter a police car, drawing attention to themselves. One teammate rushed forward, smashed the target and then ran away to avoid arrest, and then another did the same. Amid that diversion, a third rushed to the opposite side of the cruiser, shattered its back window and similarly retreated. A fourth followed close behind, pouring lighter fluid inside, and the fifth squadmate threw in a torch, setting the car ablaze. Within seconds the fireteam was gone, leaving the herd to cheer the wreckage and menace law enforcement responding to the incident.

"Fireteam 1 reports objective complete," Piper announced to the small command unit.

"Cool. Mark the time," Jaana ordered. "We wait five minutes, then tell Fireteam 2 to execute."

***

The Command and Tactical Operations Center in the FBI field office was fully manned. They had three actions in play simultaneously. Their top priority was preventing the assassination — of whom they did not know. Their next concern was the potential terror attack expected to occur at the same time as the hit, and the third was the riot that was already in full swing. The Secret Service oversaw the riot response around the White house while MPD had to handle whatever spilled into the rest of the city.

The air in the CTOC was thick with tension. There was no chatter in the room except for the voices on the radio channels. The FBI was no closer to preventing the attacks than it was a week ago, and none of the field teams reported progress.

"There's a second fire," a sober voice called out, "southwest of the White House."

Chapter 76

T he U.S. Capitol Police provide 24/7 protection for leaders of Congress, including the Speaker of the House of Representatives and the majority and minority leaders of both chambers. Earlier in the week, the FBI notified them of a threat against a person or persons unknown, but that was nothing new. The number of vague threats against members of Congress made the situation the norm rather than an exception, so it was business as usual for the security details protecting Speaker Andrea O'Shea and her guests. Besides, putting a lid on the hyper-political Speaker was impossible. They'd have to tie her up and barricade her in her home to keep her from attending a fundraising event, and that wouldn't happen.

Five blocks away from the White House near the historic Ford's Theater, she stood on the steps of The Lincoln, an exclusive hotel reserved only for the wealthy. As she addressed the gaggle of television and newsprint reporters, the faint sounds of sirens wailed from the direction of the President's mansion. She couldn't have asked for a more perfect backdrop to her speech. The Majority Leader of the House, the Minority Leader of the Senate, and media darling, Representative Youngblood, were behind her as cameras whizzed and clicked, recording the performance.

"And while the President and 2,000 of his accomplices in the racial and economic divide of our country celebrate their privilege, they are surrounded by rightfully angry citizens expressing their displeasure. Fires burn around the White House as we speak and the President hides behind makeshift walls and lines of police in riot gear. We leaders of Congress are meeting tonight to chart a way for this nation to get out of the mess he created." She finished her prepared and practiced remarks, spitting out the last words in feigned disgust, and on-lookers and reporters clapped their approval.

Gin watched from inside the window of a private sitting room off the lobby of the hotel. The press asked the Speaker and her colleagues the expected leading questions, allowing them to continue to berate the President and call attention to their own leadership. When the media had their fill, they directed their attention to their favorite congresswoman with the youthful skin, styled chestnut hair, and gleaming white smile. They clambered to record whatever words she uttered. Gin allowed the corners of her mouth to curl into a subtle smile, and she darted a knowing eye towards Chen. And then she continued to watch her servants perform.

***

Two hours earlier, handsome, prominent-looking men entered the main entrance to The Lincoln. Five strapping gentlemen arrived one by one, a few minutes apart. They wore professional business attire and carried expensive leather briefcases. When the doorman inquired about the nature of their visit, they named a wealthy hotel guest who had left their names with the front staff. He had reserved a small, private room to host an important corporate meeting. The men, including one in a blue suit, with blond hair and a broad, toothy grin, gathered in their chamber down the hallway and around the corner from the Adams Room, and waited. They ordered no service for their conference and asked the staff to give them privacy. It was not an unusual request for meetings held in The Lincoln.

***

It was a surprise to Jace, but not Grace and Charlotte. The special agent in charge of the riot unit led them to a tactical room full of black bloc gear.

"These are things we've needed to stock up on in the last year or two. Antifa has become much more active in DC." He didn't say it, but Jace understood that meant the FBI infiltrated street actions. "All of this is commercially available stuff that rioters wear right down to the style of shoes. We have ballistic vests, goggles, helmets, backpacks, and gas masks. Hurry and get dressed and we'll wire you with comms."

"Will Special Agent Shackleford drive us over there?"

"Yes. She's at your service, but I don't want her undercover. She's too new. Where are you three going to be out there?"

"I think we should focus on Pennsylvania Avenue," Charlotte said. "That's where Jace saw Mohammad scoping the streets and Lafayette Square Park."

Grace agreed. "Yeah, we may as well throw our eggs in that one basket. It should increase our chances of finding him."

"Octavia and Mil will leave the event sometime after 9:00," Jace said. "They promised to call me when they're at the gate. If I can, I want to work my way there to make sure they escape the mob."

"I get it, but we'll have to play it by ear, okay? You may be right in the mix of stopping a terror attack."

***

"All fireteams report mission complete," Piper yelled over the cacophony of chanting, screaming, and sirens. MPD must have used pepper spray against the squads that burned the police vehicles. Jaana felt a slight burn in her eyes and throat. It was time to make their forward push before the cops went full crazy with the tear gas and rubber bullets. She'd taken non-lethal projectiles in the chest, back, and legs before. Those were unpleasant experiences.

She knew the protesters would disperse in panic if law enforcement decided they had enough and aggressively deployed their riot-busting weapons.

"Cutters forward!" Jaana staged squads with bolt cutters behind the shield line. When ordered, 30 of them were to cut the metal rope and straps at waist and ankle level holding the barrier pens together. Jaana and her troops had reconned their areas of responsibilities earlier in the day, and each knew exactly which ties were theirs to snip. The shields would hide their handiwork from the authorities. The fence circling grounds held the southern unit farther from the White House, so they had no penned barricade to deal with and no need for the maneuver.

"Cutters in position!" Piper responded.

"Tell them to cut." It took what felt like hours to her, but the cutters finally reported they completed their task, and the police hadn't reacted. "That means they didn't notice," Jaana sighed with relief. "Order the shield lines and ballistic squads to get ready."

This was the critical part of the operation. When ordered, the front line had to pull apart the pens and move forward rapidly. There were concrete barriers on the other side of the barricade, and Jaana's plan was to use the shields and the concrete to protect her ballistic squads from projectiles and sprays. Those mortar teams would follow their protectors, set up their tubes, and fire as many shells at the White House as possible before the cops moved in to disperse the mob. Once the cops realized what was happening, they'd advance swiftly and with full force. They would not tolerate ordinance, even fireworks, lobbed toward the Residence. Everything had to happen very fast.

She equipped her rioters with goggles and gas masks to allow them to linger long enough to complete their parts of the mission, but most of the protesters didn't have the best gear. She needed them to cloak her troops, but once bullets, pellets, and gas flew en masse, the horde would disintegrate into chaos, exposing her Antifa soldiers. Getting thrown in prison for attacking the White House was not part of the plan, so they'd have to drop their weapons and run.

The DC organizers instructed Jaana and her counterpart to the south to trigger their ballistic squads at 9:00. That was easier said than done, but they held their ground and waited.

***

"Special Agent Shackleford, drop us off at our hotel and we'll walk from there," Charlotte told their escort. "You won't be able to get much closer than that anyway." Grace was in the front passenger seat and snuck a peek at Charlotte. It was a 'what are you up to?' look.

"Angie, you can leave us there, then circle the area until we call you. It'll be an hour or more, so stay a safe distance from the protest," Grace said. "You can park if you want to, but not too close."

Charlotte held back and watched the agent drive off before she started to the hotel entrance. "Just need to grab something. I'll be right down."

Grace had an idea what Charlotte was after but wasn't sure she wanted to object or not. Charlotte returned in less than five minutes.

"Okay, I'm set," she said, and handed Jace his Walther PPK. She already holstered her Smith & Wesson on her belt under her jacket.

"Shit, Charlotte! I don't know about that. Jace doesn't have a permit for that in DC."

"We're inserting ourselves into a terror attack. He's just as proficient with it as I am."

Grace looked away and began walking towards Lafayette Park. "You two remember how to use the radio?" She didn't wait for an answer. "Jace, you take the east sector, I'll take the west, and Charlotte has the in-between. You'll have to move around, but don't be conspicuous. Don't forget, there will be other undercover agents in there with us. The first thing you do if you see something is call it in. And do NOT draw your sidearms unless a terrorist has a weapon in his hand. We don't want a UC taking you out thinking you're a bad guy."

***

The Heckler & Koch MP5 is a nine-millimeter submachine gun of German design. It is one of a few weapons favored by special forces for covert, close-quarters combat. It is small, has a retractable stock, and conceals in a briefcase of the kind carried by the handsome men to their business meeting. At 8:55 p.m., Janco's hit team removed and readied their HK MP5s.

Their orders were to limit collateral damage. Had that not been the directive, it would have been easy with fully automatic weapons. They could have surprised and killed the security detail, entered the Adams Room, sprayed the guests with bullets, and in 30 seconds or fewer they'd be gone before anyone understood what had happened. But the mission was more complicated than that.

Chapter 77

"I t's the Speaker!" Someone rushed into the Command and Tactical Operations Center and shouted.

"What? Where?" The outburst startled DSAC Smyk and the rest in the CTOC. It was an analyst assigned to the assassination unit.

"I heard the Speaker had just given a speech on the steps of The Lincoln, so I called. They have an Adams Room and she's there right now."

"Warn the Capitol Police," the DSAC ordered his assistant in a clear and firm voice. He wanted to shout in excitement but fought the urge. Everyone knew the situation, and he needed to be a calm leader through the crisis. "Where's our closest tac team?" The agent overseeing the deployment of the Special Weapons and Tactics teams pointed to an 'S' icon on an aerial-view map of the area around the White House.

"We have one right here," he said, "E Street North West and 13th."

"That's three blocks away from The Lincoln. Get them there." Without responding to the DSAC, the agent pressed a button to activate the microphone on his headset and dispatched the FBI SWAT unit. "Damn. That's just around the corner from HQ. Is there anyone over there that can respond?"

"No sir, but they're looped in to the CTOC, so they know what's happening."

"Tell the tac team they only have a minute."

***

"This is it." Jaana's heart was pounding, and she felt lightheaded. She had years of experience clashing with police and attacking federal buildings in Portland, but nothing like this. This was much bigger, so much more consequential. They were about to spark a historic change in America, and she was giving the orders. She faced her small command team and put her right hand on the shoulder of her liaison to the leader four blocks to the south. She looked him in the eyes and then shifted her stare to Piper. "Shield line and ballistic squads execute. Go now!" Her charges spoke into their radios, and she turned to face their symbolic target.

She expected to see fireworks almost immediately. Although farther away from the White House, the southern crew had an easier time getting as close as they could get, and their mortar teams could execute within seconds. It would just be a matter of running forward, setting the tube and aiming it, dropping the shell down the cylinder, and lighting its fuse. Moments later, it would launch towards its target and then explode in fiery colors. The explosion would be harmlessly high in the air. If it went off near people on the ground, the concussion and the flaming tentacles of the explosive could inflict injury. But the point of the display was to startle and disrupt the President's gathering, and to signal to the nation the time for change had come.

In Portland, Jaana had directed her ballistic squads to level their tubes and fire at police lines. Not to hurt the cops, but to scare them and cause them to break ranks and run. That would be a victory and allow Antifa to march unencumbered or burn whatever deserved their wrath that night. She did not direct her people to take aim at the White House, but she didn't tell them not to.

***

Jace, Charlotte, and Grace pushed through the mob. Searching faces did them no good, especially since masks covered most. There were two ways to find their quarry. The first was to focus on the backpacks. Those who didn't have a bag were of no concern, and they dismissed demonstrators with inexpensive bookbags — the type of packs kids carried to school. Tactical bags designed to carry weapons had a subtle but distinct difference. They were well-built, expensive looking, longer, and less wide than most daypacks. Made for covert carrying, some could be difficult to recognize. But the team figured the normal, everyday antifascist wouldn't spend the money on something that a shooter would buy to hide a short barrel rifle, particularly one intended to allow quick access to the weapon. The second and most promising clue to finding the terrorists, at least their leader, was to look for tall men of slender build. Mohammad was around six feet five inches. The last time they saw him, he had a slim and athletic frame.

Charlotte was the first to find a target, and she believed it to be him. He stood taller than most everyone else in the crowd and drew her attention as soon as he caught her eye. He didn't have his prominent beard, and she couldn't see much of his face, but he had the kind of expensive covert carry bag she had seen before. Designed to be slung over a shoulder and across the back, it easily swung around to the chest, unzipped, and allowed a weapon to be in hand in seconds.

She triggered her comms switch and reported to the CTOC and her team. "November-2," she identified herself using her call sign, "I have probable tango Mohammad al-Qahtani in sight." That got everyone's attention. Her shirt collar concealed the mic wrapped around her neck. Its transducers sensed the vibrations in her throat and transmitted her voice clearly, despite the din of the protest that enveloped her. She spoke as though she was having a conversation, but not even protesters standing next to her could hear over the noise. She tried to relay her location, but the best she could do was that she and her subject were in front of the portico in the middle of the crowd.

Jace looked at his watch. It was only a minute

or two before 9:00, and he desperately searched the horde for suspicious-looking backpacks. Grace did the same and placed her hand on her service Glock 19 Gen 5. The shooting could start any moment and maybe she'd get lucky and take out the shooter before too much damage was done.

***

Janco chose Lode, another former South African Special Forces soldier, as his on-site team leader. They served together in the Angolan civil war and Janco persuaded him to go private and work for him. He trusted him as much as he trusted himself. Lode may have lost a half-step from his peak physical condition, but his years of covert operations made him smarter and cooler under pressure. They had visited The Lincoln when they planned the op and chose the meeting room to launch the attack. It had a back exit that allowed them to circle around to the front lobby without being noticed.

After blabbing to the media, the target finally entered the Adams Room with the rest of the guests. It was 9:00 p.m. and Lode was ready to go, but he waited for security to settle into their positions before he surprised them.

There were six uniformed Capitol Police at the hotel. The three congressional leaders each had two assigned to them. A couple posted themselves on the steps to the main entrance, two near the Adams Room, and the last two began patrolling the lobby and meeting room area on the first floor. Lode smiled. That made his plan easier to execute. They would grab the individual rovers one at a time with no one noticing. That left two operators to take care of the cops outside and two to disable the officers by the ornate French doors. After they incapacitated the guards, he'd burst into the fundraiser, double tap his target in the chest, spray the rest of his magazine around the room for good measure, and scare the crap out of everyone else.

One minute after 9:00 he told his operators to subdue the roving security and bring them back to their meeting chamber. The ball was rolling. That meant they'd be out of the hotel and exfiltrating the area in less than 100 seconds.

***

Jaana's shield line ripped apart the barricade as they had trained that morning. The police on the other side had no way to react, as their hedge worked both ways. Checked by the opposite side of their own blockade, they couldn't reach the rioters to push them back until they had destroyed the pens and advanced to the concrete barriers.

The shield team held their positions with the help of their anchors. More insurgents used their weight to lean into their comrades on the front line and to hold steady against the onslaught of cops and batons.

It wouldn't be long before the MPD and the Secret Service sent in their reinforcements with rubber bullets, bean bag guns, and pepper spray. And then the tear gas canisters would fly.

As Jaana watched her soldiers battle, fireworks fired from the south burst in the air behind the White House. If not for the violence playing out in the streets, a tourist might think the President's celebration was ending with a Fourth of July flair.

Time seemed to slip away, and she quietly begged her ballistic squads to hurry. They only had a minute or two left.

***

The evening was all Octavia and Millicent had hoped it would be. It started with speeches by the Vice President, First Lady, and President — all in one place on the same night. Chill bumps formed on Mil's arms as she soaked in the inspiration from the event that stirred thoughts of running for office once she graduated from law school. After the keynote, the staff served hors d'oeuvres and cocktails while she and her mom mingled with others invited to the President's celebration. The protests outside the fence offered little distraction from the affair.

The fireworks seemed like a perfect ending to the event and a prompt to the guests it was time to leave the grounds. Octavia was the first to notice the men and women of the protection detail were not pleased. Their faces betrayed their alarm as they hurried everyone to the gate. It became obvious to the visitors on the South Lawn they were objects of an attack when shells exploded on the ground nearby rather than high in the sky.

The Secret Service took no chances. They couldn't have thousands of people on the grounds when the President himself may be the target of an assassination attempt. The guests had to be expelled in a hurry, regardless of the angry and growing crowd waiting for them on the other side of the fence. And uniformed reinforcements had to move immediately on those firing the mortars.

***

Hu instructed Mohammad to wait until 9:05 to execute his attack but he worried the scene had become too volatile and fluid. If he waited five more minutes, the police may have already begun dispersing the protesters, leaving him exposed. He covered the scenario with his men during their training. If they heard him fire his weapon, or any gunshots, they would empty their magazines and run.

***

It was impossible for Jaana to see her mortar teams through the crowd of black bodies that had swarmed around the rioters to shield them. The thousands of protesters were not told of the Antifa plot, but when they saw it unfolding in front of them, they rallied to help. She kept her eyes to the sky, hoping any second to see fireworks above the north entrance of the White House. That was their mission, and she would consider it a failure if her squads couldn't launch any shells.

The first mortar exploded high above the iconic facade, then another, and another. All three of her ballistic squads started firing, and Jaana felt enormous relief. She had been running on adrenaline for hours, and now that the mission was a success a light-headed fatigue wrapped around her. The job was not done, though. They'd keep rioting until the cops swept them off the streets.

The fourth mortar shell hit under the portico, hitting the executive mansion. Mortar Team 1 had lowered its tube. The other two teams followed, and their shells exploded against the White House walls. They were attacking the President's home, and the horde of protesters roared with approval.

Jaana knew that would elicit an entirely different response from the MPD and Secret Service — potentially a deadly one.

***

"Where's the tac team?" DSAC Smyk asked.

"They're on-site, sir. They're taking positions around the hotel."

"There's no time for that. They've got to move. Now!"

The on-scene commander of the SWAT unit knew what he was doing. He didn't appreciate someone back in the office giving him orders. Tactical decisions were his to make, and he was going to follow protocol. The safety of his men came first and that meant establishing a tactical advantage before moving on an unknown adversary. At that point, he wasn't even sure that there *was* an adversary. Two Capitol Police were just standing around outside, business as usual.

The moment he looked up from his radio and back at the officers, a brilliant explosion came from the lobby of The Lincoln. The policemen fell to the ground, surprised and confused, but they recovered and rushed inside, reaching for their sidearms.

He ran toward the hotel, reacting to the blast, just as quick bursts of automatic weapons cracked from the entrance, and the commander dove for cover. The USCP tumbled backward and down the steps, writhing in pain on the sidewalk and struggling to breathe. SWAT agents left their positions from either side of the door and pulled the officers out of the line of fire.

Inside the hotel, the hit team executed their plan to perfection. With the roving watch out of commission, Lode sent two men out the rear exit of their room and to the front. They waited around the corner from the lobby for their signal to move on the cops outside. Lode exited the main door behind his other two teammates. They paused as his point man lobbed a stun grenade at the men guarding the ornate French doors.

A stun grenade shocks and disorients anyone unlucky enough to be in the room when it goes off. Fragments that tear through human flesh when it explodes are not part of its design. The loud noise and bright light rock the senses and incapacitates rather than kills.

At the sound of the blast, both teams advanced from the safety of their positions. The triggermen in the lobby surprised the guards running in from outside with carefully placed MP5 fire, peppering their ballistic vests and avoiding vulnerable parts of their bodies. Their intent was not to severely injure, but to blow them back through the doors, stunned and perhaps unconscious. The two operators ahead of Lode rushed the officers staggered by the grenade, grabbed them as they lay debilitated on the floor, and dragged them into the entrance vestibule. That removed them from their post, separated them from their sidearms, and obstructed the front door for any first responders trying to enter the hotel.

Lode entered the Adams Room. The dazed guests had only enough time to rise from their chairs, allowing him to find his target. It was easy. She was the only attractive young woman in the room. He carried the semiautomatic version of the MP5 so he could better control his fire. Congresswoman Youngblood, the media darling, caught Lode's first two rounds in her chest. He skipped the standard, finishing round to the head to avoid the mess. She was no threat, and it wasn't necessary.

Twenty-eight bullets remained in his magazine, and he made a good show of it. Carefully spraying them around the room, he added more drama, administering flesh wounds to some others. He particularly enjoyed giving the Speaker of the U.S. House of Representatives, the third in line to the presidency of the United States, a couple of MP5 kisses. Nothing serious. She was on the do not harm list, but the fun was too much to resist.

***

The thud and bang of the mortars firing and exploding surprised Mohammad. He looked toward the White House, temporarily mesmerized by the bursting colors in the air. When he saw the shells detonating against the walls of the most revered building in the nation, he realized his time had run out. The Secret Service would consider that an attack on the President and respond with over-whelming force, leaving his strike team much more vulnerable to police action. He had to act and use the impending pandemonium of bullets, gas, and flee-ing, screaming people to cover his escape.

Without removing it, he maneuvered his bag from his back to his chest, unzipped it, and reached inside. The throng was still cheering the fireworks in a frenzy, and Mohammad had to shove them to keep from being jostled by the rabble. As he ripped apart the Velcro straps holding the AR-15 in place, Charlotte realized bloodshed was imminent. She had no time to trigger her comms and call it over the net. She found her nine-millimeter, pulled it from her belt holster, and inactivated the thumb safety in one smooth motion. The rifle was in his hand and pointed at whoever was in front of him as she took her tactical stance to fire. Charlotte was six feet be-hind him and there were as many people between her and her target. He fired single shots in rapid succession. *Semiautomatic, just like Jace said,* registered somewhere in her consciousness. Protesters next to Mohammad pushed and trampled those near them to escape the danger. He spun as he had trained his men to do to make sure everyone around them was clearing away, giving the gunmen paths to run. It would happen so quickly that they'd empty their magazines, drop the rifles, and flee with the crowd. No one would know who the shooters were.

By the time the last protester between Charlotte and the terrorist left her field of vision, his rifle pointed at her. He did not expect to see a firearm aimed at him and the surprise forced a heartbeat's hesitation. Charlotte, staring down the savage end of an AR-15 in the center of a deafening calamity, froze for that same fraction of a second. And then there were gunshots. Mohammad jerked, and trained his weapon to Charlotte's right. Her eyes followed the barrel of the rifle and saw a woman, dressed the same as she, in a shooting stance and firing a handgun. He returned her fire, and Charlotte's instinct told her to squeeze the trigger.

***

Rob was a uniformed Secret Service officer. He swelled with pride when he got the job to help protect the most important man, and building, in America. He was in the wall of police on Pennsylvania Avenue, standing between the rioters and the iron fence protecting the grounds. His training insisted that he remain calm in every situation. The

President's life might depend on it. But after hours of racial slurs, obscene insults involving his mother, frozen water bottles, urine, and more hurled his way, his professionalism eroded. In the minute it took him to realize the insurgents in front of him had landed explosives on the White House, he became enraged. It happened on his watch and was an unacceptable personal affront. Rob charged the rioters' line where the mortars were firing, and dove. He sliced between shields, breached their anchors, and tumbled into Jaana's first ballistics squad. Their tube fell sideways, and the lit shell shot along the line, hitting Mortar Team 2, exploding in their faces. The cheers at the fireworks and taunting of the police turned to screams of horror as the blast ravaged a dozen of Jaana's insurrectionists, some with gruesome injuries.

Rob rolled forward as he tumbled into the ballistic squad, sprung to his feet, and wielded his baton as though he were a ninja, lashing at the unending legion of black. His compatriots had no choice but to follow, jumping the concrete barriers and crashing into the now retreating shield line. The police reinforcements advanced in a pincer movement from both ends of the avenue, loosing tear gas and non-lethal projectiles at will. The protest disintegrated into a screaming, crying, stumbling mass, fleeing in every direction.

**

Lode and his four operators retreated to their

meeting room, slung their MP5s over their shoulders, and donned the large windbreakers that Janco staged in the closet a day earlier. They hung perfectly forged credentials around their necks, ran to the rear of The Lincoln, and exited into its parking lot just before SWAT officers rounded the corner and took tactical positions near the exit. To the tac team, the five 'agents' in their blue field jackets with bold yellow 'FBI' emblazoned on the back must have run there from the FBI Building less than a block away. The SWAT commander ordered his unit to enter the building, and the imposters in the parking lot climbed into a waiting panel van and disappeared.

***

On the east side of the protest, Jace heard gunshots to his west. Worries for his wife flashed in his head, but he had confidence she could defend herself. She had been through it before. More rifle fire, this time much closer to him, demanded attention and pushed those thoughts to the back of his mind.

Ali heeded his instructions as Mohammad began shooting. He pulled out his hidden AR-15 and squeezed the trigger, rotating his body in a full circle to rake people aside and make his escape. Jace was 20 yards away and could only witness the slaughter in front of him. Struggling against the rush of the panicked crowd, he pushed his way towards the shooter, stumbled over a fallen protester, and unholstered his PPK. By the time he had gotten to within 15 feet, Ali had swung past him, depleting most of his magazine.

Jace and Charlotte practiced many times at the tactical ranges around Virginia Beach, learning how to move and shoot and distinguish bad guys from the good guys. That muscle memory kicked in. He regained his balance, took a stance, pointed his weapon at the shooter's torso, and fired twice. He saw Ali fall to the ground just before he found himself on his back, struggling to breathe. The MPD moved on the protesters on Pennsylvania Avenue from 15th Street. Jace and the shooter were near the police line. When the fireworks exploded on the White House, and Mohammad opened fire, their commanders ordered them to advance. Two rubber bullets hit Jace's ballistic vest as soon as he pulled the trigger of the PPK, and tear gas followed. The projectiles knocked the breath from him and as he tried to inhale, the cloud of irritant blanketed him. Unable to see through burning and tearing eyes, vomiting while he choked and gasped for air, Jace was down.

***

Jaana's position deteriorated into uncontrolled, tumultuous mayhem. Cops jumped her shield line and were wreaking havoc in front of her. Behind her, dozens lay injured by what sounded to her like machine-gun fire, and the people of her second ballistics squad were screaming and convulsing on the ground. Her medical teams provided a fleeting sense of pride amongst the horror. She witnessed one crew rush to the mortar casualties and another hurry to give aid to the gunshot victims despite the onrush of police and the rain of tear gas canisters and rubber bullets. There was nothing left for her to do. When she realized her second in command and the Seattle third were still by her side, she turned to them, water in her eyes and cheeks glistening wet.

"Run! Piper, get out!" Piper balked. She'd leave when her best friend left. Then Jaana ran to her injured comrades, tears flowing wildly from emotion and worsened by the gas that hung in the air. She arrived to see her med team sobbing while they tried to administer first aid to bloody and mangled faces and limbs. Realizing her medical volunteers were overwhelmed, she cried for help. Within seconds police officers kneeled to give aid, drawing from their own med kits and calling the emergency on their radios.

"People are shot over there!" Piper shouted, pointing to the bodies 30 feet behind them, and more cops rushed to those injured.

***

Charlotte noted just below her consciousness that the rifle fired again, but it was not at her. Someone firing at Mohammad from her right drew the weapon's ire. Her half-second hesitation ended, and she sent nine-millimeter rounds from her S&W Shield into Mohammad's torso. The tall man fell backward. The beginning of an exclamation squeaked from his throat before her bullets cut it short. The AR-15 SBR tumbled from his hands. Charlotte, still in her shooting stance, stood ready to empty her magazine into the terrorist — she had done it before — but he was on his back, no longer a threat to anyone. The sounds of crying, screaming humanity, and the bitter taste of tear gas jolted her from her trance-like focus. She knew it was him but had to make sure. She walked to the body on the ground and watched for his chest to rise and fall with life-sustaining breath. To her satisfaction, it didn't. She kneeled next to him and pulled off his mask.

"Bastard," she said as she recognized the face.

"Charlotte." It was a pained voice, but she knew who it belonged to. "Damn it. They got me again. This is getting old." Grace was several feet away. She was sitting on the pavement, propped up on her uninjured arm, bleeding from the shoulder. Charlotte rushed to her side. "I saved your life, though. Asshole was about to plug you full of holes. Those AR-15 rounds go right through our soft armor."

"Oh my God, Grace!"

"I'm fine. Just under my collar bone. That's it. You got him?"

"Yes, it's him. Did you call for help?"

"Umm. No. Good idea." Grace triggered her mic. "November 1. I took a round to the shoulder. Request assistance. Shooter is down."

"Copy, November 1," a professional but amped voice from the CTOC acknowledged. "What's your location?"

"Right in front of the White House, and can you tell the boys to ease up on the tear gas? It's getting rather unpleasant around here."

"Hey. I saved *your* life," Charlotte teased Grace, trying to distract her from her wound.

"That's true. But I saved you first."

"Now, if you could just *stay away* from terrorists' bullets..."

***

The communication networks in the FBI CTOC burst with hectic radio calls just past 9:00 p.m.

"Well? Is she okay?" the DSAC practically yelled at his special agent monitoring the SWAT team.

"On-scene commander reports the Speaker is alive, but she has minor flesh wounds."

"Thank God," Smyk whispered as he let out the breath that he didn't realize he held.

"He also reports two more wounded, and..."

"What?"

"They killed Representative Youngblood." The man in charge of the task force said nothing, pondering what he just heard. No one else spoke. That meant they failed. Even though the killers didn't get the Speaker, a member of Congress was assassinated. He had no time to contemplate the repercussions. The room erupted in voices and radio calls.

"Secret Service is reporting fireworks mortar shells over and into the White House. POTUS is in the bunker."

"UCs north report semiautomatic rifle fire."

"MPD chatter confirms."

"Damn it. I need situation reports from our people on the ground," said the DSAC. "Now." The personnel manning the radios requested sitreps from the agents in the field, and while they listened, all eyes were plastered on the big screens in the front of the room. They watched in real-time as MPD moved in on the anarchists from each side of Pennsylvania Avenue. The tear gas and smoke were so thick in some areas that it obscured the aerial video feed from the drones. Those in the CTOC could see, though, three locations with dozens of bodies sprawled on the ground, and rioters running away in every direction.

"Deploy our medical units," the DSAC said in a calmer but commanding voice.

"Sir, November 1 reports she's down with a round to the shoulder. November 3 is in pursuit of an armed suspect."

"Where?"

"South on 15th Street."

***

Jace rolled over and managed to get to his hands and knees. In between retches, and through watery eyes and wheezing for air, he crawled on the pavement looking for his PPK. He didn't see it as much as he felt it under hand, and a wave of relief washed over him. It would be a decidedly bad thing if he lost his handgun that he wasn't supposed to have in the U.S. Capital. He holstered the Walther in his belt and crept toward the terrorist he was sure he shot twice.

He rose to his knees and sat on his haunches. Still coughing, but better able to take in air, he wiped the water from his eyes. Blinking and wiping, Jace saw his shooter, but he was on his feet about 10 yards in front of him, stumbling away. "Body armor," Jace said out loud, but there was no one near enough to hear him. He stood up, wincing at the pain in his ribs, and gave chase.

Tear gas, smoke, and a sea of black-clad bodies running indiscriminately to everywhere obscured the sightlines of the advancing police in their riot gear and face masks. They were still several yards from Jace by the time he got to his feet and began to run. He was just one of thousands to them, and their job was to disperse the rioters, not to arrest them. They were unaware of what played out a minute before.

A large group escaped Pennsylvania Ave on 15th Street. Some running north, and some south, turning the first and nearest corner to get away from the gas and bullets. Out of the cloud and the clammer of the noise, Jace felt better with each breath and each step. The crowd of fleeing protesters was still thick. He had to push his way through while trying to keep the terrorist, who was gaining speed, in sight.

The first thing you do is call it in. He could hear Grace's instruction in his head. He keyed his mic, "This is November 3." He labored to breathe from the exertion and the effects of the gas. "I'm chasing one of the terrorists south on 15th." Jace saw the rifle bouncing on the strap slung over the terrorist's back. "He has a gun." Then he realized the shooter and the mob were running straight to the East Executive Ave gate where 2,000 guests of the President were to leave the White House grounds. "No," he grunted, and he ran faster.

***

Mil looked through the fence as she walked towards the exit with her mother and 1,998 other people. As they got closer, she became more aware of the angry faces and the chants of filthy slogans directed at them.

"Mom. They're not going to make us go out there, are they?"

"I think so, Hon," Octavia said in a pensive voice. "It'll be okay. Jace said they would escort us away." Her lack of confidence did not soothe Mil's apprehension.

"It looks crazy out there. I'm calling him." After holding the phone to her ear for close to a full minute, Millicent hung up. It was obvious to Octavia he didn't answer. "Mom, they're getting attacked out there." She looked outside where guards shooed guests through the gate. "Mom..." Her eyes were wide, and her jaw dropped, staring at the chaos created by supporters of the President abruptly expelled into a throng who had just been gassed and shot at for protesting him.

"Maybe they'll let us pass, Honey." Octavia tried to comfort her daughter, but she saw the anger. She didn't believe the mob would leave them alone.

She stepped in front of Mil when they approached the gate. "The police are supposed to escort the guests past the demonstrators. Where are they?" she shouted to the uniformed Secret Service officer urging her into the crowd.

"They're busy. They can't come," is all he said as he waved her through. She grabbed Mil's hand and pulled her into the swarm as people dressed in black screamed obscenities in their faces and blocked their way. She had no choice but to push past them. Octavia was a tough-as-nails defense attorney and had little patience for bullies. The scowl on her face and the hard shoves as she plowed through protesters were real, and her aggressiveness intimidated most.

Mil inherited her mother's empathy and care for others. That's why she decided to go to law school — to stand for justice like her mother. And she also came by her toughness. Octavia was an athlete throughout her youth. Quitting was never a consideration, and she loved a physical workout. It cleansed her body and mind. So, when her daughter was seven years old, Mom found a sport they could do together. Through the years they switched martial arts disciplines for the variety and thrill of it. More than a decade of study made them both well-practiced and physically fit, and no fun for an opponent in the ring, or a cretin on the street.

Ali, the terrorist Jace chased south on 15th Street, was lost. He was to empty his magazine and run north to the van waiting in the parking garage only a couple of long city blocks away. But when the chaos started, and someone shot him, he just ran in the direction he faced. Now he didn't recognize where he was, so he thought he would move in the safety of the crowd until he figured out what to do. When he slowed with the mob and tried to catch his breath, he heard a woman scream.

"Gun! He's got a gun! He's the guy that was shooting at us!" The pack parted, running from Ali, and he remembered. *I didn't drop the gun.* He felt it dangling under his arm, caught in the shoulder strap of the tactical bag. As he pulled the rifle up to his chest to untangle it, someone stepped in front of him. He reflexively looked up and glimpsed a beautiful young woman. Her stunning emerald eyes framed by wavy black hair were the last thing he saw before everything went dark.

Holy cow, it works, was Millicent's first thought. Her instructors taught things that can gravely injure or kill, and she couldn't practice them at full speed on people. As the crowd parted, screaming and running, she turned to find a man with a rifle three feet in front of her. Without hesitation, as she practiced thousands of times in the gym, she stepped forward with her left foot, punched with her right hand, fingers back and folded tight, leading with her palm, and struck the gunman under his nose with an upward force. The palm-hand strike driving up and into the nose with the torsion of her entire core stepping into the blow disabled the unlucky human punching dummy. Millicent broke Ali's nose and knocked him out cold.

Seconds later, Jace ran up to find the terrorist on his back and blood pouring from his face. "You're late," Octavia deadpanned.

Panting from the chase, and his eyes round in surprise, "I knew you had it under control," he said as nonchalantly as he could.

***

Angie Shackleford was fresh out of the Basic Field Training Course at Quantico. Her supervisor was uncomfortable placing her in the pressurized and dangerous environment of a riot and terror threat with no field experience, so he assigned her to assist the group from Norfolk.

After she dropped off Special Agent Madson and her team, she had to stay close and ready to help when Grace called. She parked her cruiser at the fringe of the protest on Connecticut Avenue, facing Lafayette Park. The action was on the opposite side of the square, so she wouldn't get tangled in the confusion and could be where Grace needed her in a minute or two.

Angie watched fireworks through the windshield of the car. The radio network told her mortars hit the White House, and those calls mixed with urgent announcements of shots fired. She squirmed in her seat, listening to the constant crackle of her fellow agents providing situation reports and calling for medical teams. And then November 1 radioed that she was shot. *That's Grace!* Her stomach turned, and her mind raced with indecision. *Did they forget about me? What should I do?*

A weird, black wave swallowing Lafayette Park and flowing through the streets, including up Connecticut Ave in her direction, interrupted her worries. Soon, she would be in a tactical scenario and would have to react in a calm, professional way. Her training took over. A single man sprinting ahead of the wave, but on the opposite side of the avenue from her, drew her attention. She observed him duck behind a large concrete column. He hid from the view of anyone following him or directly in front of him, but Special Agent Shackleford had an unobstructed sightline from across the street. She watched as he ripped off his rioter's clothing to expose blue jeans and a red t-shirt. It was strange that he undressed and threw his expensive gear — helmet, gas mask, goggles, and backpack — into a pile, but when he bent over and removed a handgun from his pack and placed it in his belt, she knew he was out of place. All guns in DC are illegal unless you have an extremely difficult-to-get permit, and he didn't look like someone who rated that.

Angie swung her unmarked cruiser into a U-turn, stopped 30 feet ahead of the suspect, exited her car and approached him, gripping her service weapon. The wave to his rear had slowed to a walk as the fleeing protesters calmed themselves and looked behind them for signs of what happened. As she neared the man, she held up her hand, motioning him to stop, and then she drew her Glock from its holster.

The special agent surprised Tomas. Mohammad's plan didn't tell him what to do if he got caught, but he gave him a gun. He grew up on the streets of Jersey City and his crew always ran from the police, but they all swore if the cops ever cornered them, they'd shoot it out.

Emboldened by his street credo and the body armor under his shirt, Tomas pulled his handgun from his belt. Angie was new. She barely had enough time in the DC field office to learn everyone's name. But FBI agents are the best-trained police officers on the planet. Special Agent Shackleford reacted according to her training and shot the young man twice in the chest before he could level his gun at her. He fell to the concrete sidewalk, stricken but not incapacitated. It hurt, and he couldn't breathe, but the bullets didn't penetrate his vest. If he had accepted his fate and dropped his weapon, he would have escaped with bruised ribs and a prison sentence. In fact, there was probably no way to prove he was one of the terrorist shooters. But sitting up, he raised his pistol to shoot the cop, giving Angie no choice but to end his 17-year-old life.

***

"Is he dead?" After calling in her report and receiving medical care from undercover agents,

Grace's attention turned back to Mohammad.

"I think so," Charlotte answered. She was too concerned for Grace to care about him. She rushed to her side, and there was no time to check his pulse and verify he was dead.

"Check."

"Alright." Charlotte looked over her shoulder and got to her feet. Injured people lay splayed in a 360-degree arc, many getting medical attention from whoever was there to help. But at the center of the carnage, where she and Grace shot Mohammad, there was no body. Her heart pounded as she ran from one person to the next searching for the tall middle eastern-looking man. "Where's the guy who was laying there?" she asked everyone within earshot. "Where is he? Did anyone see?"

"That tall dude? I did," a pretty, young woman said. She had taken off her protective gear to reveal her strawberry blond hair, more blond than red, and deep ocean blue eyes. "He got up and staggered away. He went that way." She pointed north toward Lafayette Square. Charlotte looked to find mobs of people dressed alike, clearing the park. She thought about running after them, looking for the tall man, but he was lost in the inky night.

Chapter 78

"**U**nnamed sources told National News Network that President Hargraves ordered the Attorney General not to share details of the events last night in Washington, DC. However, those sources tell us a direct connection between the assassination attempt on Speaker Andrea O'Shea's life and the domestic terror attack in front of the White House has been established.

"The mostly peaceful demonstration by thousands of Americans turned to pandemonium Friday when, sources say, the President ordered the Secret Service to clear away the demonstrators because they were disturbing his gathering of supporters on the South Lawn. The Metropolitan Police Department and federal officers responded by firing tear gas and rubber bullets into the gathering, causing people to panic and run.

"Simultaneously, three domestic terrorists believed to be members of the far-right, white supremacist group called The Proud Order, began shooting AR-15 assault rifles into the crowd of peaceful demonstrators. Those men killed 11 protesters and injured 51 with the very gun championed by conservative Second Amendment advocates in this planned terror attack.

"According to a statement by the Director of the FBI, agents shot all three terrorists while in the act of shooting. A special agent who recently graduated from the academy at Quantico, and only a few weeks into her first field assignment, shot dead one of those terrorists. A second terrorist suffered only bruises to his torso because he wore a bullet-proof vest. That shooter fled but agents apprehended him, and he is in custody. A third terrorist was shot multiple times, but he escaped. Authorities say body armor protected him from debilitating injuries, and he was able to recover enough to stagger away while the agent at the scene lay wounded from the shootout.

"We bring in reporter Bess Williams who was covering the demonstration last night when the shooting occurred. Bess?"

"Thanks Megan. Yes, I was here at the fringe of the protest at H Street and 16th, on BLM Plaza where I stand now. Thousands of peaceful demonstrators packed Pennsylvania Avenue and Lafayette Square. As they celebrated with fireworks, the police moved in from both sides of Pennsylvania Ave with pepper spray, tear gas, and non-lethal bullets, pushing the throng north on 16th Street. At that instant, gunshots rang out, perhaps hundreds, coming from several locations in and around the protest. The crowd in front of me panicked and ran up BLM Plaza away from the gunfire. A woman I talked to said she saw a man dressed in black shooting in all directions with an assault rifle. She told me she ran as hard as she could to escape the bloodshed. Another person said he witnessed a woman gun-down a young white man wearing jeans and a t-shirt on Connecticut Avenue, one street over from here. We think that is the alleged terrorist killed by the FBI, but we are unsure how he got to Connecticut Ave. That's all the way across Lafayette Park plus a city block from where the shootings occurred. And he was wearing normal clothes, not the black clothing reportedly worn by the shooters. Disturbingly, the witness insisted that the woman executed the man by shooting him in the head. A lot of questions remain, Megan. Back to you."

"Bess Williams at BLM Plaza. Thank you. We now go to Sam Perry reporting from 15th Street outside the White House. Sam?"

"Thanks, Megan. I'm standing next to the southeast gate of the White House where the protest last night spilled into 15th Street. The guests of the President were leaving the grounds from this gate after police dispersed the protesters. To set the scene, there were thousands of people to the north of the White House and thousands to the south. When police moved in on both groups, mayhem ensued, and large numbers of protesters converged on this one spot. Conflicts broke out between demonstrators and Hargraves supporters, then someone yelled 'gun' and everyone scattered. Beside me is Tamryn who witnessed it all. What did you see, Tamryn?"

"I was standing over there across the street, watching. The people all dressed up coming out of the White House were hitting and pushing protesters. Then I heard a scream, 'Gun. He's got a gun. He was shooting at us,' and everyone started running. Then I saw a white guy in the middle of the road, and he had a machine gun. Then some tough black chick in a red dress knocked his ass out. Punched him smack in the face. And right after that, a dude showed up and he was calling for assistance like he had a radio. He must have been a cop. And then police came from everywhere and beat us back out of the way."

"There you have it, Megan. Apparently, there were undercover agents among the Hargraves supporters. One of them assisted with the takedown and capture of the white supremacist at the southeast gate on 15th Street. Another witness told me the gun the terrorist had looked like an AR-15, the gun favored by ring-wingers."

"Sam Perry reporting from the visitors' gate of the White House. Thank you. Stay tuned to NNN and we'll tell you more on this developing story after this break."

"That is wrong, Mom," Millicent said to Octavia as they watched the news from their hotel room. They gave their statements the night before and were getting ready to head home. "That guy wasn't white. How would she know? He was completely covered up, and she wasn't anywhere near us."

"She saw what she wanted to see and told them what they wanted to hear."

"We didn't even see what he looked like until Jace took off the guy's goggles and helmet. He was definitely middle eastern."

"That wouldn't fit their narrative, Hon. At least you're a tough chick in the red dress. She got that right."

"Welcome back to the news. I'm Megan Marche. In his statement today, FBI Director Raymond said there is no connection between the assassination attempt on Speaker O'Shea and the domestic terror attack on protesters outside the White House, but sources told NNN the same extremist organization is responsible for both. The two attacks, one at The Lincoln hotel and the other five blocks away on Pennsylvania Avenue, were timed to occur at precisely the same moment. Our sources said white supremacists carried out the well-planned assaults intending to kill the leader of the Democrat Party, Speaker O'Shea, and to strike at antifascists who they say organized the protest. The white supremacist group called The Proud Order claimed responsibility for both attacks on social media and declared a victory in their fight against democratic socialism.

"Reaction around Capitol Hill is one of sadness mixed with anger. Speaker O'Shea said this earlier today."

"We are deeply sorry for the loss of Representative Youngblood. She was a fresh face with important new ideas. I condemn President Hargraves for his divisive rhetoric that fosters this dangerous and seditious thinking in his party. The blood of Congresswoman Youngblood is on his hands. He is to blame for The Proud Order and others like them that spew nothing but hate and are an imminent threat to the United States of America."

Chapter 79

THE WEEK AFTER

Once again, the Special Investigations Unit from Norfolk proved their worthiness. They said there would be an assassination attempt, and there was. They warned of a riot to distract law enforcement from the hit, and it happened. And despite its success, they uncovered and disrupted a terror plot in the middle of it all.

Fortunately, the FBI responded to the threats swiftly and thwarted the attacks to limit the loss of life. Their SWAT response saved Andrea O'Shea from certain death. She and three others sustained minor flesh wounds, and the freshman congresswoman from California was an incidental casualty, but they prevented the assassination of the Speaker of the House — at least that's how they played it. They couldn't explain the disappearance of the perpetrators, but the Bureau was confident they would hunt them down.

They knew better. Everyone from the Director to Angie Shackleford realized it was a professional hit. The first two rounds into the heart of the victim from a semiautomatic MP5 were obviously a double tap on the target. Even the lack of the finishing round to the brain told them the shooter was a consummate pro, sparing them the unnecessary gore. Clearly, from interviews of the victims and forensic analysis, the shooters placed their shots carefully. And the attackers took pains not to injure law enforcement. The kill team knew exactly what they were doing and executed it precisely. Authorities didn't disclose they suspected a former U.S. special forces operator and they let him slip away before the assassination.

The FBI reported their agents on the ground prevented further loss of life by shooting the three terrorists, which was true — sort of. Twenty-six rounds in Mohammad's rifle hit a victim. Luckily for them, most took only one round each and only five people died. The protesters wore ballistic vests as protection against non-lethal projectiles. That's standard for the black bloc, but the light Kevlar didn't stop the high-velocity bullets of the AR-15 at close range. Both Grace and Charlotte shot Mohammad, and he went down. That kept him from reloading and claiming more victims, the feds touted. He must have been wearing body armor because in the riot's pandemonium he regained consciousness and escaped.

Another 'agent' shot a second attacker, preventing more injuries. That shooter also fled but was chased and apprehended before he could continue his attack. Only two of his victims died. An alert and unflinching rookie special agent killed a third shooter responsible for four deaths. Authorities did not release the terrorists' names pending the completion of the investigation.

The FBI stated they had no evidence of a connection between the terror attack and the assassination. But no one believed it was a coincidence, especially since a right-wing group calling themselves The Proud Order claimed responsibility for both.

The Secret Service said arrests in the assault on the White House were imminent. But they had no way to identify who broke the law and who were just exercising their constitutional rights to free speech and assembly. The rioters and protesters dressed alike and covered their faces specifically for that reason. Some of the injured would be arrested, but their charges wouldn't stick.

Gin's plot resulted in one purposeful death, as she intended, and nine injured — Andrea, two billionaire donors, and the USCP officers. Congresswoman Youngblood was not just a left-wing extremist advocating for more taxes to fund social and climate change programs. Gin could live with that. But she led a small, communist-leaning faction in the House that endangered the massive fortunes of the nation's billionaire class. Her elimination by 'right-wingers' was divine. It cut off the head of the poisonous snake, and at the same time, swayed public opinion against the politicians of the dangerous right. Gin would have her liberal President, and Congress too.

She had no knowledge of Chen's terror attack.

Perpetrated by 'white supremacists,' it resulted in 11 protester deaths and 51 injured. He didn't admit to Gin that it was his doing, and she didn't ask. It was best that way. But she was not naïve and made a note to be careful with Chen in the future.

Chapter 80

SAN FRANCISCO — TWO WEEKS LATER, GIN'S OFFICE

"The President has no chance. He's being crushed in the polls and there's no time to recover from this."

"Fate twists in extraordinary ways, doesn't it? Two weeks ago, they tried to kill you, but what they did was hand you the Presidency, the House, and the Senate — their worst nightmare. Of course, you've hammered Hargraves relentlessly on The Proud Order. That's what did it, Andrea."

"Yes. It was quite fortuitous," the Speaker laughed at her campaign against the President. "It was too easy after that. Although I like to think we would win anyway, their moronic attempt to take me out really swayed public opinion our way."

"I'm just sorry we lost Congresswoman Youngblood. I'm the one who insisted you bring her along, and I feel responsible." Gin did her best to feign remorse.

"Yes, too bad." Speaker O'Shea also tried to show genuine regret over the phone but couldn't help the grin that snuck to the corners of her mouth.

"Although, she was a thorn in my side, I don't mind saying. She fought me tooth and nail and had turned many of the freshman representatives against me."

"Besides the optics of party unity, I hoped we might use the dinner to persuade her to tone down her rhetoric. I thought inviting her to a power engagement would give us that opportunity."

"Well, we'll never know, Gin."

"No, I suppose that problem solved itself. Oh, what a terrible thing to say."

"Never mind. We were both thinking it." The Speaker dismissed the idea, but it haunted her since the night of the killing. She remembered everything so clearly, as though it were in slow motion. She saw the gunman enter the room. He studied the faces, searching for someone, and her eyes locked with his. Then he moved on, found Youngblood, and killed her. Two bullets to the heart, the FBI briefed her later. They didn't say it, but they were impressed with the accuracy. Then she watched as he looked back at her. His eyes weren't looking into hers or at her chest. He focused on her arm. That's where he aimed, and that's where he shot her. *I told the investigators that, but…*

"Andrea?" Gin interrupted her thoughts. "I'm just glad you're all right."

"Thank you, my friend. I do need to get going, though. I have heads poking into my office."

"How's the Speaker?" Chen asked.

"Fine — sounds like the same old Andrea. Those

flesh wounds were unexpected but added a convincing flair, I must say. Your operators were masterful.

"Yes, ma'am. They are the best. May I say the same about you?"

"How so?"

"The media immediately jumped on the white supremacist, domestic terrorism narrative and linked it to the assassination 'attempt.'" Chen curled his fingers in air quotes. "That was impressive."

"It literally took no effort. I knew the press would slant that way, but they did it before we even planted the claim by The Proud Order that they were responsible. It was far too easy — frighteningly so. And the FBI is so predictable, so helpful. They're burying the facts under the guise of an ongoing investigation, playing right into our hands. They're too smart not to realize Youngblood was the true target. And the pretty girl in the red dress, the one that knocked out that 'white supremacist?'" It was Gin's turn to use air quotes. "She told the reporter the terrorist was middle eastern, not white. The news didn't air that part of the interview. I saw it on the internet. A middle eastern man in a terror attack in DC? How is that not the story? It doesn't matter, though. Everything will come out eventually, long after the election. And by that time, no one will care. It was so easy, Chen." Gin mused in wonderment. She knew it would work, but it was just so perfect.

"Yes ma'am. Much too easy." Chen smiled.

Chapter 81

The election went Gin's way, as she expected it would. Her candidate ousted the sitting President, and her best friend won another term as Speaker of the House. Voters had enough of the civil unrest, the looting and rioting, and the party branded as the racists who caused it all, and removed them from power in the Senate, too. The legislation and policies that would inevitably come — higher taxes, more regulations, more debt — would widen the gap between the haves and have nots, not narrow it. Those things burden only those who are producers trying to grab their share of the pie, not the billionaire appropriators who already own most of it.

With the help of the government, Gin's wealth would grow to levels only she could imagine. She could buy whatever she wanted and do whatever she pleased. Only a few ultra-elites shared the rarified air she breathed. But far too many plums begged to be plucked for her to stop having her fun.

Chen used Gin's ambition and influence to remove an unfriendly American president from office and he became a living legend in the Ministry of State Security. His country was free once again to dominate the South China Sea and control the Strait of Malacca through which 5.3 trillion U.S. dollars in maritime trade passed every year. Economic and geopolitical sanctions against China would disappear, Chinese government-propped industry would thrive at the expense of American companies, and America's intellectual property would be easy prey. With the acquiescence of the United States, China's economic and military power could manipulate global economies. And the door would soon be open to taking Taiwan for its own.

Chen wanted to stay right where he was, and his handlers did too.

The Justice Department did not divulge the assassination was a precise hit perpetrated by special operators, and the Speaker was not the target. They didn't want the public to know they uncovered the conspiracy days before it happened, and they might have prevented it but let one of the suspects elude them. It was better nobody knew the terrorists, at least a couple of them, anyway, were Muslim and their leader was the same person who plotted the attack in Norfolk a year earlier. An Islamic jihadist cell loose in America already responsible for two deadly attacks was not something they wanted to disclose. The feds were even aware the protest that night would turn purposefully violent, but there was no convincing the media that it was something other than a peaceful demonstration.

The FBI found Ice's real identity easily. Old teammates and military records saw to that. But he disappeared. Zo told them he would.

The dead kid, Tomas, and Ali, the other 'white supremacist' knocked cold by Mil, provided clues that led investigators to Jersey City, but Mohammad was gone.

They milked their confidential informant, Zo, for all he could tell them, but it wasn't much. They got a list of names of antifascists who supposedly rioted at the White House, but that's it. After the night of October 1st, the meth deal between Kel and him seemed like old news from long ago. The Norfolk team never mentioned it, and neither did he. There was no evidence that could be used in court that it ever happened. Zo left DC as soon as he could and never looked back.

Christian's employer continued to funnel cash to Jaana, and others like her. And she persevered with street actions as the leader of Antifa Direct Action. After the election, nothing changed, and she had to keep up the fight. He was still a journalist for The Main, but he made Portland his base so he and she could be together.

Kelena, Noah, and Missy left the illegal drug trade behind them. They recognized the opportunity to get out, and they took it, relieved to have their lives back. Noah moved into the beachfront home with Kel, and they both started college. He entered the Criminal Justice program and Kel, of course, was a business major. Missy took off for the isles but didn't say which ones.

The FBI closed the investigation into the Corporation due to a lack of evidence and witnesses.

Millicent was always known for her effervescent smile and cheerful, almost bubbly air. That changed with the terror attack in Norfolk. But she was still the same person everyone loved to be with. Her disposition was the same but tempered with the reality that evil people exist. And like her mother, she was someone who would not be pushed around. She watched the press mischaracterize, even lie about the events of October 1st, and the politicians used the tragedy for partisan advantage. That would end. She wasn't sure how, but she was going to stop it. She started with her video on social media, exposing the truth about Ali, the 'white supremacist.'

Charlotte joked with Grace about developing the habit of catching bullets from deadly weapons. Her vest slowed the bullet fired from Mohammad's AR-15 and it lodged in her shoulder. This time damaging only flesh, and not life-threatening. Her recovery was quick, both physically and mentally. She had dealt with emotion and doubt and indecision a year ago and was over that. Her superiors insisted she take two weeks off for her wound to heal, but she had other ideas. Mohammad's trail was hot, and there was no way she and her team would wait to join the hunt.

Grace teased Charlotte about losing her touch. She had the habit of gunning down terrorists, but she let the last one get away. She was a hard-nosed prosecutor. Opponents in court preferred to plea deal than face her in a courtroom trial. She didn't like bad guys and felt an obligation to take them off the streets. So, even though her partner joked about Mohammad escaping, it was personal to her, and it was to Grace too. Twice, now, they allowed him to slip their grip, and he left a trail of death both times.

He was an engineer. His adult life, up to a year and a half ago, consisted of facts, data, and design. Psychology, parapsychology, and ESP were not things he was comfortable with or believed in. But Jace knew his clairvoyance was real. His mentor, Ike, said it was stronger than in anyone he'd ever seen. That's why Jace turned over his company to his leadership team and is doing what he's doing. He felt obligated to help.

But most people are skeptical, and when they make it obvious, Jace's practical side lets his self-doubt creep into his psyche. When that happens, his perception seems to dim. He didn't do enough this time. He saw the terror attack and the assassination, but it was too late, and he left his team no chance to react. That can't happen again. He had unfinished business.

The time had come to hunt the bastard down.

THANK YOU FOR READING

ANARCHY

If you liked it, please take a minute to write a short review and post it on Amazon. Amazon uses complicated algorithms to determine what books are recommended to readers. Sales are a big factor, but so are the quantities of reviews my books get. Only a few words are needed, and by taking a few seconds to leave a review, you help me out and help new readers learn about my work.

If you are interested in seeing more from me, you can sign up for my email list to learn about upcoming books and engage with me about my stories and characters.

Sign up at my website: www.davewallwrites.com

BOOKS BY THIS AUTHOR

On American Soil: Jihad

Book 1 of the Preserve, Protect and Defend Series

FBI Special Agent Grace Madson and Assistant U.S. Attorney Charlotte West discovered terrorists slipped into the U.S. from Mexico and headed to Norfolk, Virginia. Theirs was a race against time to uncover the jihadists' plot and face them down. But they needed help, and it came from an unlikely source — Charlotte's husband, Jace.

Anarchy

Book 2 of the Preserve, Protect and Defend Series

FBI Special Agent Grace Madson, Assistant U.S. Attorney Charlotte West, and consultant Jace West uncovered a plot to assassinate an influential U.S. politician. Their unique Special Investigations Unit had only nine days to determine who's the target and prevent the killing. But that's not all that was at stake. Powerful forces conspired to manipulate the upcoming presidential election with anarchy, propaganda, and terrorism.

The Hunt

Book 3 of the Preserve, Protect and Defend Series

TO BE PUBLISHED IN THE SPRING OF 2022

Immediately following a mass shooting in front of the White House, FBI Special Agent Grace Madson, Assistant U.S. Attorney Charlotte West, and investigative consultant Jace West, set out in hot pursuit of the terrorist responsible. But little did they know, someone else wanted him as much as they did.

ABOUT THE AUTHOR

D. S. Wall

I'm a recovering Nuclear Engineer
and MBA with 38 years' experience
writing technical and professional
documents of all kinds. I retired
from the U. S. Navy as a civil ser-
vant in January 2020, expecting to
become a gig-writer providing
technical content to clients. I de-
cided to sacrifice that boring life to write novels in
my favorite genre — action-adventure-thrillers.

I use real-life current events and places to bring real-
ism and suspense to my stories and strive for technical accuracy in the details of my writing. Having
lived and worked near the world's largest navy base
my entire career, I've wondered why it hasn't been
the target of terror attacks — or maybe it has been
and the public never knew.

That thought was the basis for my debut novel, and
I added a twist embodied in my Jace West character
that most action-thrillers don't have. Jace develops
an ability to sense things that others cannot and his
wife and her partner on the FBI's Joint Terrorism
Task Force use him to hunt down terrorists. My first

novel with Jace, his Assistant U. S. Attorney wife, Charlotte, and Special Agent Grace Madson is called On American Soil: Jihad. It is Book 1 of my Preserve, Protect, and Defend series. Anarchy, a political thriller with a heavy dose of domestic terrorism is Book 2. Book 3, titled The Hunt, chronicles a cross-country chase of a notorious terrorist and should be published in the spring of 2022.

ACKNOWLEDGEMENT

Thanks to Kelsey, my beta reader, who improved the flow of my story.

Thanks to Lexi, my proofreader, who fixed my mistakes and improved the story's readability.

Thanks to Lori for her logistical and marketing support.

Made in the USA
Coppell, TX
06 September 2021